Carlie B

Introductio

Home for the Holidays by Mildred Colvin
Overshadowed by her "perfect" sister, Anna Wilkin craves acceptance. To please her papa, she agrees to go east to finishing school although she'd rather walk through her beloved woods. . .and learn more about a logger named Jeremiah. After a fire takes his parents, Jeremiah Tucker is afraid to love. Yet more than anything, he wants a home of his own. Falling in love with a tomboy like Anna takes him by surprise. Her sister would make a better wife and be less of a risk to his heart. Wouldn't she?

One Evergreen Night by Debby Lee
Emma Pearson is an orphan whose last living relative is her older brother. When he takes on the dangerous occupation of lumberjack, she hopes to find some way for them to move into the safety of the city. Frederick Corrigan is a reckless man who blames himself for a terrible logging accident. Both Frederick and Emma long for security and love, but will they find it in the dangers of the woods? Or will circumstances derail their hopes and dreams?

All Ye Faithful by Gina Welborn
Every week for the last two years, E. V. Renier has petitioned the local brewery magnate for permission to marry his daughter. Despite receiving a sound rejection each time, E.V. continues in hopes of proving the faithfulness of his character. Heiress Larkin Whitworth has no idea of the quiet yet charming sawmiller's devotion. Not until awful rumors about her rip through the town. As the annual Christmas soiree approaches, Larkin fears E.V.'s love might not be as strong as the shameful truth she's trying to hide.

A Carpenter Christmas by Mary Davis
Natalie Bollen has been anxiously awaiting her eighteenth birthday so she can start courting. With five men to every woman, she expects a few suitors, but truthfully, there is only one man she hopes comes courting. Willum Tate has been burned once by a woman he loved, and he's not sure he's ready to risk his heart again. Are Natalie's feelings as strong for him? Or does she just think of him as another big brother?

A CASCADES CHRISTMAS

FOUR-IN-ONE COLLECTION

MILDRED COLVIN, DEBBY LEE,
GINA WELBORN AND MARY DAVIS

Print ISBN 978-1-61626-845-9

eBook Editions:
Adobe Digital Edition (.epub) 978-1-62029-070-5
Kindle and MobiPocket Edition (.prc) 978-1-62029-071-2

All scripture quotations are taken from the King James Version of the Bible.

Cover design: Kirk DouPonce, DogEared Design

Published by Barbour Publishing, Inc., P.O. Box 719, Uhrichsville, Ohio 44683, www.barbourbooks.com

Our mission is to publish and distribute inspirational products offering exceptional value and biblical encouragement to the masses.

Printed in the United States of America.

Home for the Holidays

Mildred Colvin

Dedication

To Jim and Jon for letting me bounce ideas off them.

For we are his workmanship, created
in Christ Jesus unto good works,
which God hath before ordained that
we should walk in them.
Ephesians 2:10

October 1888

Anna Wilkin missed her trousers. Not that she wore them all the time, but they were a lot more comfortable than the new party dress she'd made for her best friend, Larkin's, birthday party. The lace around her neck scratched, and the bustle Larkin talked her into adding felt like a cage attached to her backside. She ran her finger around her neck for the tenth time.

"Stop that," Anna's older sister hissed in her ear. Kathleen could be so bossy. "You're scratching like a hound dog, and you're liable to tear that nice dress."

Anna ran her finger under her chin again just to annoy her sister. "I shouldn't have listened to you and Larkin in the first place. The only reason to wear something this fancy is if you're trying to snag a man, and I'm not."

She didn't wait for Kathleen's next comment but moved to stand by Larkin near the refreshment table. Looked like she needed rescuing from Abigail Leonard anyway. Although a friend of Anna's, Abigail didn't like Larkin for some reason.

"What are you two talking about?"

Abigail turned and looked right past Anna. Her eyes widened

and a smile curved her lips.

Anna swung around. All she saw were four men standing in the doorway looking uncomfortable. Maybe she'd missed something. She looked back at Abigail. Oh, but of course. Abigail always took note of new men. But even Larkin seemed focused on them.

Why? Anna narrowed her eyes and studied the men. The tall, dark-haired one might be all right. Another one was maybe an inch shorter with lighter hair. He had a square jaw with a cleft in his chin. Another, some might consider the most handsome, stood between those two. He glanced their way with bright blue eyes but didn't seem to take notice of any of the girls. An unfriendly sort maybe. Anna didn't bother with the fourth man.

Larkin's father greeted the four newcomers, welcoming them as if he'd always known them.

Kathleen moved beside Anna. She leaned forward to look at Larkin. "Didn't I see you talking to those men last Sunday after church?"

When Larkin didn't respond, Anna turned to look at her friend.

Larkin's hazel eyes had a glazed look, the kind she got when she was deep in thought, something she often credited to her mama's Chinook blood.

Anna frowned. Larkin couldn't be interested in those men, could she? Of course, she was nineteen years old now—plenty old enough to marry. In another three months, Anna would be eighteen. Little more than a year younger, but she was in no hurry to grow up.

Anna sighed. If Larkin was smitten, she wouldn't give away her secret. In fact, a change of subject might be a good idea. She swiveled around to face the table. "Hey, what happened to all the cookies? They're almost gone."

From a group of girls gathered at the other end of the table, Abigail's younger sister Elizabeth stepped closer. She giggled and held up a half-eaten cookie. "Maybe I should offer some to our new guests."

Abigail frowned. "Hush, Lizzie, you're too young to even be thinking about such things."

Elizabeth's eyes opened wide. "What? Eating?"

"No. Men." Abigail lifted the tray off the table. "Someone may as well eat what's left of these. I'll take them around." She smirked at Larkin. "Maybe you should have let your cook make the refreshments."

Larkin didn't flinch at the jab, but the words had to have hurt her. Anna glared at Abigail. She might be her friend, but she could be so cruel sometimes, and she never had a good thing to say to or about Larkin. Everyone else loved Larkin.

"She didn't make them, Abigail." Anna stepped between her two friends. "I did. There's more in the kitchen. I'll go get them while you ladies drool over the new men."

Anna spoke over her shoulder as she left. "You can carry cookies to them if you must, but you'll never catch me falling all over myself just to get attention."

What made girls act so silly when it came to men? Maybe someday marriage to the right man would be all right, but not yet. Being free to be herself meant so much more. Working with Papa in the woods, helping him the way he'd expect a son to, that's what she liked. A husband would be a hindrance for sure. Maybe that's why she and Larkin had become so close. Larkin liked fishing, climbing trees, and swimming, same as she did. Larkin was sweet and kind, too. She and her family often delivered food to the needy, which was something to respect.

Anna admired Larkin's home as she crossed the room. Tonight, the formal parlor had become a festive faux ballroom to celebrate Larkin's birthday. The elegant room had been emptied of furniture, so there'd likely be dancing later. Anna snickered. If her parents gave her or Kathleen a birthday party, it'd probably be held in their barn. They mostly stayed at the logging camp, but they owned a big two-story house in town where they spent their weekends. They didn't have a room as large as this one, or as nice. Considering where Larkin lived, most people might expect her to be a snob, but she wasn't. And the fifteen months separating them didn't stop her from being Anna's friend.

A small orchestra in the music room played one of Anna's favorite songs. She could hear it in the kitchen as she worked. She arranged the tray of cookies while she hummed with the music then sang the chorus to the catchy new tune called "Clementine." "Thou art lost and gone forever. Dreadful sorry, Clementine."

Her feet itched to dance when the band switched to a lively polka. She headed back down the wide hall, carefully holding the tray of cookies. A quadrille had started. Oh my, Larkin and Kathleen were dancing with two of the newcomers. Abigail and her brother, Garrick, along with the reverend's son and daughter, Matthew and Natalie Bollen, made up the other set. She shook her head. Couldn't they have mixed it up so Abigail and Natalie didn't have to dance with their brothers?

She held the cookies high to navigate past the swinging dancers. She'd almost made it to the refreshment table when Garrick stepped back against her shoulder, knocking her off balance.

"Oh." She stumbled, and her tray tilted. Garrick grabbed for it and hit her instead, knocking her into a hard wall of warm flannel.

"Oomph!" A male voice huffed in her ear.

The aroma of bay rum aftershave surrounded her. His arms closed around her, and she landed in a very undignified heap on the floor, or more precisely, on his chest while he sprawled on the floor.

Again he *oomph*ed in her ear.

Anna scrambled away and turned to stare into the most beautiful light blue eyes she'd ever seen. The man shook his head as if to clear it and rolled to a sitting position, holding his stomach. Cool air rushing up past Anna's ankles brought her to her senses, and she jerked her dress back into place. She should have worn her trousers. The uncontrollable urge to burst out laughing took over, and she buried her face in her arms before she gave in. Everyone's stares and the poor fellow trying to get his breath filled her awareness, yet the music played on. Her shoulders shook from the laughter she held in. Didn't the musicians know she'd taken their job of entertaining? A very unladylike snort escaped her nose.

"Miss, are you all right?" a deep voice asked while a warm hand cupped her shoulder. "Are you hurt? I'm sorry. I got my feet tangled in your skirt when you hit me."

That remark, and the effort to keep from laughing, brought tears to her eyes. Her shoulders shook again.

"Anna, are you all right?" Larkin knelt beside her.

Garrick joined Larkin. "I'm sorry, Anna. I didn't see you."

One peek at the worried expressions on their faces broke Anna's control, and her laughter pealed forth. A moment later, Garrick laughed, too.

With a crooked smile, Larkin stood and waved at the others who'd pressed close. "All's well. Papa, would you have the orchestra play something new so we can begin another dance?"

When he nodded, she turned to Anna and the poor man struggling to get off the floor. "This seems the appropriate moment for introductions. Anna, this is Jeremiah Tucker from Seattle. Mr. Tucker, I'd like for you to meet my dearest friend, Anna Wilkin."

On her feet again, Anna smiled at the tall, dark-haired man who watched her as if she might break. "I'm glad to meet you, Mr. Tucker. I'm sorry I bumped into you. Garrick hit me in one of the turns. Did my. . .did I hurt you?"

Her face burned. She'd almost mentioned her bustle. She still felt bruised where she'd landed on the thing. Why she'd agreed to wear it, she had no idea.

He chuckled. "No, I'm fine, except I believe you owe me a dance, Miss Wilkin."

Anna motioned to the scattered cookies. "I can't. The mess—"

"Go ahead." Larkin touched her shoulder as if to guide her away. "I'll—"

"We'll clean it up." The blond man with the cleft chin drew Larkin closer to him and out of Anna's way. "Go dance."

"Thanks, E.V." Mr. Tucker motioned to where the other dancers were lining up. "I became quite concerned when I thought you were crying."

"Crying? Me?" Resigned to dance with the poor man, Anna shook her head. "I assure you, I would not be crying over a silly spill such as that."

Jeremiah Tucker kept a close eye on his dance partner. She was a petite young woman. He'd hate it if she were injured. Thankfully, she didn't seem to be. A pleasant smile brightened her pretty face while her quick, sure steps kept time to the polka. Something about her struck a chord in his memory. Rebekah would be about the same age if she'd lived. She'd always been as plucky as this girl, too.

They locked arms and twirled in a circle. He grinned at her. "Tell me, Miss Wilkin, what's a fun activity you enjoy even more than dancing?"

"Fishing." She giggled and moved away.

She was teasing, and he was intrigued. They came together, and he took her small, gloved hand to lead her through the steps. He could tease, too.

"So you sink worms and like it?"

"Of course, every chance I get. Mama thinks it's unladylike, but she cooks all the fish I catch." Her dark brown eyes sparkled with humor.

How refreshing to talk to a girl who didn't bat her eyelashes. "Go fishing with me Sunday afternoon. Maybe you can show me how."

A light flickered in the depths of her eyes before the dance carried her away from him. She'd caught on to his skepticism. The girl was fun, cute, and smart.

When she returned, she accepted his hand, twirled, curtsied, and stepped into place beside him, graceful and light on her feet.

"I will, with my friend. Right after lunch. Meet us at the lake."

"I'll be there, Miss Wilkin." He hadn't expected her to accept. His grin remained as the set came to a close. He bowed, and she offered a little curtsy.

"Mr. Tucker, there you are." A beautiful young woman resembling Anna, her sister perhaps, hurried toward him. "The orchestra has agreed to play some popular songs for us to sing. Please say you'll join our group."

"I'd be delighted." Jeremiah turned toward Anna in time to see her long blue skirt flare out as she pivoted away. She stopped beside Garrick Leonard, one of the workers at the logging camp. They exchanged words then walked to the refreshment table where E.V. and Miss Whitworth were talking. About time his friend found a female who could woo a conversation out of him.

Movement at his side brought his attention back to Kathleen. "Your sister and Garrick Leonard seem to be good friends."

A frown touched her brow. "Yes, they are."

Jeremiah chuckled.

"Is something funny?"

"Sorry, your kid sister just doubled up her fist and punched Leonard."

Kathleen shrugged. "Anna is a child. Garrick—Garrick is—" She turned away with her fingers pressed to her eyes. "Will you excuse me? Something's in my eye."

As she hurried away, Jeremiah wondered if he should follow, but Anna's laughter rang out, capturing his attention. Rebekah would have loved her, but his little sister was gone, taken in the same fire that killed his parents. He watched Anna, captivated in a way he'd never been before. A fishing companion? He chuckled again. He couldn't wait to watch her touch a worm. If she even showed up.

Chapter 2

Anna sat beside Abigail and tried to listen to Reverend Bollen's sermon. If Mama knew how Anna's insides skittered in anticipation for this afternoon's fishing excursion, she would withdraw the privilege of leaving the family pew to sit with the Leonards.

Would Reverend Bollen ever finish preaching? If nothing else, she'd have a fun outing with Larkin. Competing with Jeremiah would add to the fun. Her lips twitched upward. She really shouldn't think of him by his given name. Mama wouldn't like that any more than she would the squirming, but she couldn't call a fishing buddy Mr. Tucker, could she?

"Please stand for the benediction."

Anna rose with the others and bowed her head. As soon as the amen sounded, she darted into the aisle.

Garrick stopped her. "Where are you headed in such a hurry?"

The light of curiosity in Abigail's eyes cautioned Anna. If she told them about the fishing contest, Garrick would want to come. Then Abigail might tag along. She didn't want anyone but Larkin there, and Abigail could never get along with Larkin. "Home for dinner of course."

"You must be hungry." Garrick moved closer.

Her stomach growled on cue, and she grinned. "I am."

She turned toward the back. Already a line of folks had formed at the door to speak to the minister and his wife. Mama and Papa had just reached them. Kathleen stepped out the door—with Jeremiah.

A fist of dread slammed into Anna's midsection. Kathleen had taken over Jeremiah last night at the party, and she was doing the same today. It wasn't fair. Just because Kathleen had Mama's dark auburn hair and porcelain skin and everyone said she was beautiful didn't give her the right to take Anna's friends away.

She couldn't take Jeremiah if he didn't want to go.

Anna ignored the voice of reason in her mind. Men always liked Kathleen best.

She turned back to her friends. "I really do need to go. The preacher's family is coming for dinner today, and Mama will need my help."

Abigail fanned herself with her lacy white glove. "That means the Bollen sons will be there. If your mother needs extra help, let me know."

Anna laughed. "All right, but it isn't likely."

She hurried past several people waiting to talk to Reverend Bollen. She couldn't honestly say she knew what he'd preached about today, so she slipped past.

Jeremiah stood in the churchyard, grinning at Kathleen as if he'd been smitten just like every other fellow in Tumwater. Oh! If Anna wasn't such a lady, she'd stomp her foot—right on top of Jeremiah's toes. Obviously, Kathleen hadn't dragged him out of the church and held him hostage. She wasn't even touching him.

Anna ran to catch her parents. "Papa, I'm going to walk home today."

He nodded. "All right. Be careful."

"I will." She turned on her heel and set a brisk pace through an unusually sunny day. Too bad Kathleen had to put a damper on it. She'd probably talk Jeremiah into doing something else this afternoon and the fishing competition would be cancelled. As if she cared. She'd have won anyway. She'd turned on Division Road when footsteps pounded behind her.

"Hey Miss Wilkin, wait." Jeremiah skidded to a stop.

Anna looked past him, but didn't see Kathleen.

"So are we still going fishing?" His lopsided grin held her attention. "Or did you chicken out? Decide you don't want to touch a worm after all?"

"Ha! I'm not the chicken here. I've probably baited more hooks than you have." Anna glared at him, one fist landing on her hip.

He threw his head back and laughed. "Not likely, little one. I'm going to eat with my friends, but I'll see you after that—if you show up."

"I'll be there." Little one? She'd show him little when she caught more fish than he did. He was halfway to the church when she called after him. "My name's Anna."

She didn't wait for him to respond, but set her mind to getting away from the house. If she was lucky, she'd be able to slip out after dinner. Of all days for the Bollens to come, why did it have to be today?

Anna rushed about, setting out the pies Mama baked the night before. She started the dishwater and had the pots scrubbed clean before Mama called her into the dining room. The fact no one seemed to notice the work she'd done should have bothered her, but today she didn't care. She only wanted to have dinner over with so she could be on her way to the river.

Reverend Bollen ate the last of his potatoes then leaned back in his chair "Mrs. Wilkin, you've outdone yourself today. Everything was delicious."

Mama's cheeks grew pink, and she smiled. "Thank you. My girls are a big help."

Anna began clearing the table. Maybe if she washed the dishes, Mama wouldn't say anything about her leaving in a few minutes.

Kathleen stood and motioned for Natalie. "Come upstairs, and I'll show you the pattern I was talking about."

In *Godey's Lady's Book*, no doubt. Anna carried the first load of dishes to the kitchen while the others left the table.

Mama hurried after her. "Anna, we don't need to clean up right now. We'll let it rest and visit. I've already told Mrs. Bollen we don't need help."

Anna set the stack of plates on the counter beside the sink. "I don't mind, Mama. You and Mrs. Bollen go visit. I've already done the pots. The rest will be easy if I do them now before they stick."

Mama took a couple of tea towels from the drawer. "If you're sure you don't mind. I'll cover the table in case anyone wants something later."

"Mama, I promised Larkin I'd be over this afternoon." Anna held her breath.

"Are you coming?" Papa stuck his head in the kitchen.

Mama ignored him. "Anna, you need to stay here while the

reverend is visiting. How would that look if you up and run off?"

Papa gave Anna a wink. "Anna's done her duty. This is Sunday. The day of rest. The reverend will understand her need to get out of the house on such a pretty day. See that sunshine out the window? Days like this are few and far between. Makes me dream of a fishing pole on the riverbank."

"But—"

"But nothing." Papa touched Mama's shoulder. "Come. Your company's waiting."

"Thank you, Papa." Anna's held breath rushed out.

He gave her another wink and ushered Mama from the kitchen.

Anna washed dishes faster than ever then carried the water to the back door and threw it out. Would Jeremiah still be at the lake? She'd taken far too much time, but what else could she do? If she hadn't offered to clean up, Mama would never let her go. And if Papa hadn't intervened, it wouldn't have mattered how much cleaning she'd done.

In the garden shed, Anna changed from her dress slippers to the work boots she wore at the logging camp. She grabbed her fishing pole and held it so her body shielded it from the house. If Kathleen looked out an upstairs window and saw it, she'd be sure to tell Mama. Anna didn't relax until she turned the corner and the house was no longer in sight. Then she set long strides to Larkin's house and found her ready to go.

They walked to the edge of town, stopping not far from the lake. "Next to go is this skirt," Anna said. She stepped behind a tree to shed her skirt and petticoat, revealing the trousers hidden beneath. After rolling them together, she propped them in the fork of a tree.

Larkin smiled and shook her head. "If your mother saw you now, what would she do?"

Anna shrugged. "I imagine she'd faint dead away. But Mama doesn't understand how important fishing is. She doesn't love the forest, the trees, and the river the way I do. If not for Papa, I'd have to act just like Kathleen." She spotted Jeremiah by the lake and grinned. "Can you imagine anything more dreadful?"

Jeremiah found a likely spot on the riverbank and baited his hook. A quick flick of his wrist, and he sent the worm into the water. He leaned back against a tree, letting his muscles relax. So Miss Wilkin didn't show after all. She'd looked so cute boasting about being the best fisherman. He chuckled. Sure would've been fun to show her up. Like he used to do to Rebekah. Of course, no one could take Rebekah's place, but it might be fun to have a substitute sister.

By saving every penny he could from his job, he'd soon have enough to start building a new house on his land. He sighed. A home of his own without the bad memories.

A tug on his line alerted him to a bite. He grinned. The only thing missing was a certain female to listen to him gloat.

He reeled in his first fish and dropped it in a pail of water beside him. A quick glance down the trail toward town revealed nothing. She wasn't coming. He might as well give up. He sank another worm and leaned back to do some serious fishing.

Kersplash! Jeremiah jumped a foot off the ground. Water arched from the lake and soaked his feet and legs. His heart took off running without him. Something had hit the water right in front of him, and it wasn't a fish. He swung around at the sound of giggles—out-of-control giggles.

Miss Wilkin and the Whitworth girl stood behind him, clasping hands and laughing at him.

He deliberately placed his pole to the side and anchored it with a rock. Keeping his quarry in sight, he rose, speaking in a low tone. "Did you throw something at me?"

Anna's eyes grew to twice their normal size, and the other girl stepped back. A squeal such as he hadn't heard in a long time almost shattered his eardrums. Anna took off running with him right behind. He caught her waist and swung her around as a loose pebble threw him off balance. He fell, taking her with him. This time when she slammed against him there was no bustle to knock the breath from his lungs.

She hadn't stopped giggling. Her laughter was just as contagious as Rebekah's had been. He could never stay angry with his sister. Looked like his substitute sister would be the same in that respect. His laughter joined hers. He released her, letting her scurry away.

"You little scamp. What'd you throw at me?" He sat up and rested his arms on his bent knees.

She shook her head, still laughing. "Nothing. Not at you. I threw a big rock in the water."

"You could've hit me." He took a second look at her. "What is this? Does your father know you're wearing trousers?"

She stuck her pert nose up. "Maybe. Mama doesn't know I went fishing though, and she wouldn't understand if I came home with dirt and grass stains on my skirt." She grinned and tugged at her pant legs. "She'll never see these, so it's okay to get them dirty. Come on, I want to fish. Larkin has already started."

Jeremiah watched Anna and her friend bait their own hooks, and his eyebrows rose. Within minutes Anna pulled a fish as big as his from the river. He shook his head. Rebekah would have loved going fishing with Anna. Larkin was a nice enough girl, but Anna seemed to bubble with fun. "You know what?" he asked.

She turned her pretty dark brown eyes on him, and her lips curved the least bit. "Not unless you tell me."

He grinned. "I think I'll call you Little Bit. Yep, that'll be my special name for you. Miss Wilkin sure doesn't fit." He laughed for no special reason, but he'd done a lot of that this afternoon. "Little Bit fits you just fine."

A wide smile lit her face. "Okay, then I get to call you Tuck like I heard your friends doing."

He chuckled. "Sure, but you'd better be careful around your mother."

She rolled her eyes, and he laughed long and loud.

Chapter 3

Here, Papa." Anna handed the hatchet she'd been using to her father. A misty rain hung in the air, but she didn't mind. She'd rather work in the rain with Papa any day than be cooped up inside cooking. "I need to go. Mama will have a fit if I'm late again. She sure didn't like it when I was late on Tuesday."

He set the hatchet aside and grinned. "She runs a tight ship, does she?"

"Oh, you can't imagine." He was teasing, but Anna shuddered as if she took him seriously. "Between her and Kathleen."

"Maybe I work you too hard. This isn't a job for a girl."

Now this was no joking matter. "I like working with you, Papa. I love the woods and the fresh air."

"Next time I need some help, I'll see if I can get you another hour of freedom." He chuckled as she started away. "You got a skirt stashed around here somewhere?"

"Oh, I almost forgot." Anna turned and ran back to the stump where her skirt lay. She quickly pulled it on over her trousers. Mama would have more than a fit if she showed up looking like one of the lumberjacks. At least Papa let her be herself. On impulse, she gave him a hug. "Thanks, Papa."

She ran toward the logging camp, her father's love as warm and secure as his arms had been around her. At the large mess hall, she walked in the back door. Kathleen didn't bother to greet her—she just handed her a potholder. "Take one end of this pot and help me carry it to the serving table."

Anna hung her jacket and ignored her sister's glares. She carried her end of the large pot of pinto beans through the kitchen door to set it inside the dining area. What was the matter with Kathleen? Anna had permission to help Papa.

"You're late." Kathleen whispered the words.

"I am not." Anna took her place behind the serving table as the outside door opened.

Men poured into the crude building, forming a line where the tin plates and utensils sat. They grabbed what they needed, and the first man held his plate out toward Kathleen just in time to keep her from scorching Anna's ears. Anna grinned at Garrick for saving her, but he was looking at Kathleen, reaching for the slice of bread she held. Their fingers touched, and Kathleen blushed. Good, she should be embarrassed for almost yelling in front of the men. She could be a real prude.

That group of men had no sooner cleared out than another came in on their heels. Anna dipped a ladle of beans and plopped them on Jeremiah's plate. "Hey Tuck, how ya doin'?"

She almost giggled at Kathleen's lifted eyebrows.

He grinned. "Good. How about you, Little Bit? Been fishin' lately?"

This time Anna did giggle at the soft gasp from her sister. "Not for a few days."

"Then how about Sunday afternoon? I plan to be at the lake

then if the weather holds. Maybe I could give you some fishing tips." He took the corn bread she handed him.

She hesitated, but couldn't think of anything she'd like better. Why not go? Papa would let her even if Mama didn't like it. She flashed a quick grin at him. "All right, but you'd better plan to learn a few things from me."

Jeremiah's laughter brightened her day until movement to the side let her know Mama had returned. The scowl on Mama's face told of her disapproval more than her rebuke might have. Nothing unusual about that. When did Mama ever approve of her? It wasn't that Anna disliked ladies' activities. She enjoyed making her own clothes, and she loved to embroider. Cooking and cleaning were okay. But what she absolutely loved the most was being outdoors and running through the woods or sitting on the riverbank with a fishing pole. She felt useful when she helped Papa with his chores.

Anna turned to the next man in line. She'd find some way to go fishing Sunday. Tuck was fun. Even more fun than being with her best friend, but she wouldn't tell Larkin that or she might not go with her.

Jeremiah ate his lunch and watched Anna bustle about helping her sister and mother. Little Bit. He chuckled under his breath. That name fit her perfectly. Little and as pretty as a china doll, she looked just as feminine.

He walked out of the warm mess hall and back toward work with the other buckers. Yep, Anna was a little thing, but he had a suspicion she was also a bit of trouble just waiting to happen. The question was what kind of trouble.

"Hey Tuck!"

Jeremiah turned toward the sound and realized he was walking beside the railroad track leading into the woods. His mind had been so locked on Anna, he hadn't seen Frederick or the Shay locomotive he drove to haul logs to the sawmills around Tumwater.

"I've been yelling at you. Anything wrong?" Concern covered Frederick's face.

"Naw, just getting back to work after a good meal." He couldn't tell his friend he'd been thinking about a little slip of a girl. He'd never understand. "You getting a load ready to take down?"

Frederick nodded. "I'm heading into the woods here in a minute. Want a ride? Beats walking in the cold."

"I would, except you're going the wrong direction for me." Jeremiah waved and started walking again. "I'll catch you Saturday. I'm staying in town with Willum so I can go to church."

"Okay, see you then." Frederick turned back to his locomotive, and Jeremiah went on.

Nope, Frederick wouldn't understand his fascination with Little Bit. She continually popped into his head. Had since they'd gone fishing. He needed to get her out of his mind and start looking for a suitable wife. Saturday he'd talk to Willum about building a house. The other men would pitch in to help, too, when they had time. The desire for home and family filled Jeremiah's heart. He had neither anymore. Only memories that impressed on him the longing to replace what he'd lost.

Although Anna stayed fresh on his mind, he shoved her image aside and replaced it with one after another of the girls he'd met since moving to the area. He thought of the birthday party he had attended in that big, fancy house. Larkin. She was attractive and seemed nice. Then there was Abigail Leonard, Garrick's sister. Anna sat with her at church Sunday. He shook his head, pushing both Abigail and Anna from his mind. What about her sister, Kathleen? While the other girls were pretty, Kathleen was beautiful. Yet he felt drawn toward Anna.

Jeremiah picked up his ax. He'd be helping cut a log into sixteen-foot lengths for boards this afternoon. If he didn't keep his mind on his job, he might cut something besides a tree. He didn't need Anna intruding in his mind so much. Yep, the little bit of trouble he sensed about her could be something more than a physical injury. She had the potential to cause pain in his heart. He needed someone who wouldn't tear his heart out if she left the way everyone else he'd loved had done.

Chapter 4

Anna pushed from the table and, like the Sunday before, began stacking plates.

Kathleen stood. "Mama, we can put the food away. You go relax with Papa."

Mama smiled. "You girls are spoiling me, but I'll take advantage of it this time. I don't think we'll want anything until later. Thank you."

"You're welcome, Mama." Anna tossed the words over her shoulder as she carried her load to the kitchen. Last week she'd done everything alone. Maybe with Kathleen's help the work would go quickly, and she could get to the lake before Tuck gave up on her. Anna had the dishwater prepared in the sink before Kathleen pushed through the door with a dish of food in each hand.

Kathleen put the pie in the safe and the bowl of potatoes on the counter. "We'll eat this tonight, so I'm leaving it here. Maybe make potato patties. What are you doing this afternoon?" Her question was tossed out too casually.

Anna looked up at her sister, who didn't even glance her way. "I thought I'd go see Larkin for a while."

That wasn't a lie. She did plan to go by Larkin's to see if she wanted to go fishing, too. Maybe Tuck would invite one of his friends the next time. Then Larkin would have her own fellow. Heat rose in her face at the direction her thoughts were taking. Tuck was not courting her. She needed to remember that.

Kathleen continued putting away food while Anna washed dishes. After a while, Kathleen picked up a dish towel. "I'll dry the dishes. You go see Larkin."

"Thank you." Anna didn't waste time untying her apron. She hung it on a hook by the back door, grabbed a coat hanging there, and slipped outside into a damp cloudy day. Why couldn't the sun be shining like last week? Anna shrugged. At least it wasn't pouring down rain. She spoke back into the kitchen. "If Papa or Mama ask, you can tell them where I am."

"Sure."

Anna ran across the backyard to the garden shed. She changed into her boots and grabbed her pole. If only she could stash her skirt here. No, she had to wear it in town. Someone would see for sure and tell Mama.

As she turned to leave, the door opened and Kathleen stepped in. "I didn't think you were going to Larkin's."

"I am, too." Anna flushed under her sister's steady gaze.

Kathleen shook her head, her smile knowing. "No, you're going fishing. You're running off to meet Jeremiah Tucker, aren't you? I heard you make plans with him the other day, so don't deny it."

"With Larkin. What's wrong with that? Papa doesn't mind if I go fishing with friends."

Kathleen's eyebrows lifted. "Mama does."

Anna wanted to stomp her foot, but Kathleen would love that

show of frustration. "You're going to tell, aren't you?"

"No." Kathleen folded her arms. "I don't care. Go meet your beau if you want." She laughed. "How long do you think he'll stay interested if you keep acting like a hooligan? You're almost eighteen. Don't you think it's time you grew up and became a lady? I know Mama and Papa are getting tired of your tomboy ways."

"Not Papa." Anna's protest sounded weak even to her. Hadn't he said she shouldn't work in the woods?

"I wouldn't be so sure." Kathleen shrugged. "I heard them talking about a school back East. A finishing school. Mama says it's the only way now to turn you into a lady."

An angry flush rose in Anna's face. "Papa won't let her send me away."

Kathleen's laughter rang out in the shed. "Papa agreed with her. I'm sorry, Anna, but everyone's getting tired of your behavior. It's past time for you to grow up. I think it'll be good for you. Look at this as an opportunity, not a punishment. I wish I could go."

Kathleen left, and a tremble worked its way through Anna's body. She leaned against a table. Kathleen had to be wrong. Papa wouldn't do this to her. Emotions raced through her until her mind whirled without direction. She shoved her pole back into place with the others and pushed out of the building, slamming the door behind her.

She ran toward Larkin's through wisps of fog that hung in the air and added to her dismal emotions. She had to tell someone who would understand. At the Whitworth house, Larkin let her in. "Anna, what's wrong?"

"Mama and Papa are sending me away." Anna knew she didn't

make sense, but Larkin led her upstairs to her room. There, with tears pouring down her cheeks, Anna told what she'd just learned.

"Oh Anna, how terrible." Larkin's tears of sympathy blended with Anna's.

Anna dried her eyes with the back of her hand and straightened her spine. "I'll show Papa and Mama I can be a lady. I'll act like Kathleen. They'd never send her away."

"There's nothing wrong with you the way you are," Larkin sympathized. "You aren't like Kathleen. They shouldn't expect you to be."

"But they do." Anna forced a smile for her friend. "It's all right. I can do it. I have to because I would simply wilt away without my forest."

Jeremiah set a rhythm Monday morning with another bucker on the two-man saw. The scent of cedar filled the air and sawdust flew over him while they sliced a six-foot-diameter log into shingle bolts. He hadn't seen Anna at breakfast. Where'd she been yesterday? He'd caught enough fish for Frederick to fry for him, Willum, and E.V. for supper, but they didn't make up for Little Bit's company he'd missed earlier. Something must have happened.

When the noon whistle blew, he strode toward camp and the mess hall, eager to talk to Anna. His eyes adjusted to the dim light inside as he moved through the serving line. "Hello, Mrs. Wilkin. Mmm, boiled potatoes and gravy. Looks good."

She smiled. "I imagine anything would look good after working all morning the way you boys do."

"That may be true." He grinned, but let his gaze roam down

the table. Kathleen handed out bread and dished up heaping ladles of green beans near the far end. Where was Anna? He moved down the line.

Kathleen glanced up with a smile. "How are you today?"

"I'm fine." He held his plate under her ladle. "I haven't seen your sister lately."

"She's working in the kitchen today." Kathleen set the ladle in the pot.

"She wouldn't be avoiding me for some reason, would she?" Why had he asked that? He sure didn't need Anna's sister thinking he cared.

"Not that I know of." Kathleen slanted him a glance. "Why would she do such a thing unless you've done something you shouldn't? Like enticing her to go off alone with you for the last two Sunday afternoons."

Heat crept up his neck. Had Kathleen twisted a few hours of fishing into a romantic interlude?

Before he could defend Anna, Kathleen handed him a couple of slices of bread and smiled. "If you want to see Anna, why don't you come by our cabin tonight? You know where our family stays here at camp, don't you?"

He nodded.

She glanced down the line and back at him with a bright smile. "Please do come to the cabin tonight, Jeremiah," she said in a strong voice. "We'd love to have you visit."

Someone cleared his throat. Jeremiah turned to see Garrick waiting behind him with a frown on his face. "Oh, sorry." He gave Kathleen a nod. "I'll stop by later tonight."

Kathleen's invitation didn't sound sincere. Maybe she'd only asked to get him to move on so she could serve Garrick and the rest of the men. Jeremiah let her words play through his mind until late afternoon, but he couldn't find the answer. Whatever her reasoning, he appreciated the chance to see Little Bit.

Long strides took Jeremiah through the cold November air to the log cabin set back several yards from the mess hall. Anna hadn't served supper either. She must be avoiding someone. If not him, who?

Kathleen opened the door at his knock. "Oh, Jeremiah."

"You said for me to come by tonight. To see Anna." He shifted his weight. Maybe he shouldn't be here. He looked past her. "Is she home?"

"No, she's out somewhere with Papa." Kathleen stepped back. "Please, come in. They should be back soon, and Mama's here."

Jeremiah accepted a cup of coffee and slice of cake from Mrs. Wilkin. "Thank you, ma'am."

She and Kathleen sat across from him sipping coffee. Mrs. Wilkin lowered her cup and gazed at him. "How do you like working in the woods, Mr. Tucker?"

He allowed a smile. "I imagine it could be worse."

"I'd guess logging isn't your calling?" Her smile answered his. "What would you rather do?"

That was an easy question. "Farming."

Mrs. Wilkin's eyebrows lifted. "Doesn't a farm require land, animals, equipment?"

"Yes ma'am. I hope to have all that within a year's time." Truthfully, he had most everything except a house to live in. After the fire that took Rebekah and his folks, he sold the farm and all of Pa's animals except his best team. When the next-door neighbor offered to board them and store Pa's plow, wagon, and other tools, Jeremiah accepted.

"I see." Mrs. Wilkin stood. "I'll take your plate if you're finished. Would you like more coffee?"

"No ma'am. Thank you." Jeremiah stood until she left the room. He turned to Kathleen. "I should be going."

Kathleen walked him to the door. "I'm sorry you didn't get to see Anna. She's probably wandering around in the woods like always. She's angry right now because Mama and Papa are sending her to school next spring or early summer. By then she'll have had plenty of time to get over it and see this is best for her."

Jeremiah narrowed his eyes. "What do you mean, sending her to school?"

"Back East. Chicago, I think. Where Mama went. She should be glad to go. I would be, but Anna is such a tomboy, she's the one who needs polishing."

"Finishing school?" Jeremiah frowned. Little Bit didn't belong in finishing school any more than he did. She'd smother there. No wonder she'd been avoiding him.

"Yes." Kathleen smiled. "She has to grow up someday."

Jeremiah's mind whirled with images of the two sisters after he left. Beautiful, graceful Kathleen and fun-loving, cute Anna. So different. Why'd Kathleen invite him tonight? For Anna or for herself? Why wasn't Kathleen married? She'd make a wife any man would be proud of.

Chapter 5

A leaf, dried on the tree and only now letting go, drifted toward the ground in front of Anna. She bent, picked it up, and twirled it between her fingers. The days were slipping past and she still had no solution to her problem. How long had she walked? An hour? Two? She'd been so upset when she left the kitchen, she hadn't even changed into her trousers. A short laugh escaped her lips. Mama would be proud of her.

She lifted her gaze toward heaven and the top of the stately old pine beside her. *Lord, where is the answer? Must I go to school? Is that Your will for me?*

So many questions, but no answers. She couldn't leave her woods. She just couldn't. And what about Tuck? Their friendship was new but precious. A tear escaped, and she brushed at it. Why would Papa do this to her? Her insides churned when she thought about confronting him. Maybe Kathleen was wrong, and they wouldn't send her away. It was just talk at this point anyway, wasn't it? She should ask Papa tonight after supper and find out the truth. Or maybe even now. He'd gone to the shed to sharpen axes. She could help him before she had to help with the evening meal.

Again, her stomach rolled. She couldn't talk to Papa if she got sick just thinking about it. She shuffled her toe through old, soggy leaves and soft pine needles on the forest floor then turned toward camp. Maybe if she offered to help, he'd tell her Kathleen made up the story about school just to be mean, or maybe she'd mention it to Papa first, and he'd tell her she could decide if she wanted to go. That sounded more like Papa.

Anna set off with long strides toward camp. How hard could it be to tell Papa she didn't want to go away? He always understood.

At the tool shed, she stopped and took a deep breath before opening the door and slipping inside. Papa sat on a stool with an ax across his knee. He ran a long file along the edge of the blade then stopped and looked up at her. "Anna. Did you come to help?"

She nodded. "Yes. What can I do?"

He grinned. "Take your pick."

Anna straightened the tools on Papa's worktable. The steady rasp of his file on the blades scraped her nerves in a way it never had before. How could he sit there acting as if nothing was wrong? How could he send her away?

"Papa?" She turned to meet his questioning gaze. "Does it bother you for me to wear pants when we're in the woods?"

A soft smile lightened his expression. "I wouldn't let you if it did."

"Oh." She looked down. "Mama doesn't like it, and Kathleen's always the perfect lady."

He chuckled. "Your mama doesn't know, does she?"

She grinned. "She knows, but not how often I wear them. I don't think Kathleen knows either."

"Kathleen's a good girl." Papa smiled and turned back to his work. "Just like her mother. She'll make a fine wife someday."

Air huffed from Anna. "Like I said, always perfect."

Papa shook his head. "Not perfect, but she knows what's important." He looked up. "Don't worry, little one. You'll learn, and one day you'll be ready for marriage, too."

Anna wrinkled her nose and turned back to stack wedges, alternating them so they were even. She sighed. Papa wanted her to learn—to get ready for marriage. He'd confirmed what Kathleen said. Papa wanted her to go to finishing school. Maybe if she started acting like a lady all the time, they'd let her stay home. She could do that. Surely she could. Only she wouldn't give up wearing her trousers when she went into the woods alone. Or with Papa. Or Tuck.

Tears burned her eyes, and she blinked them away. "Papa, I'd better go. Mama will want me in the kitchen before long."

"Okay, that's fine. Thanks for your help." He didn't even look up.

Outside, Anna saw no one. Today, Kathleen helped Mama prepare the food. Tomorrow would be Anna's turn. She had at least an hour before she was needed to serve. Her heart weighed a ton. How could Papa be so unfeeling? To send her away was cruel. A cool November breeze brushed past as her feet carried her toward her beloved woods and the tall pines that gave her solace. Their scent was like balm to her soul. Tears blurred her eyes because of the unfairness of her situation. She loved her parents, yet they found her lacking. Under cover of her trees, she ran while the forest passed in a blur of movement and tears. Finally, she collapsed at the foot of a fir tree in a soft bed of damp moss, her body shaking with sobs.

Jeremiah headed back to camp early. He'd cracked his ax handle, and the foreman told him to go see if Mr. Wilkin had another.

A flash of red to the side caught his eye. Anna's long, dark braid flew out and bounced against her red plaid jacket. Her dad's, no doubt. He chuckled. Only Anna would wear a man's jacket with boots and a skirt. His smile faded when she fell to the ground and curled into a tight ball with her face against her knees. Had she hurt herself?

Jeremiah's strides lengthened as he altered his course toward Anna. He leaned the ax on the opposite side of the tree and knelt in front of her. She sniffed and sobs shook her shoulders.

"Anna?" He murmured her name, not wanting to startle her. "Little Bit, what's wrong?"

Her head lifted. Tears trailed down her cheeks. He brushed a damp tendril from her cheek and tucked it behind her ear. "Tell me what it is."

She swiped her sleeve across her eyes. A hiccup brought a curve to his lips. No other girl could be so adorable in the midst of a crying spell.

"Is this about you going away to school?"

Her eyes widened.

"Kathleen told me."

"Oh." She turned away from him so he couldn't see her face. "She would. She wants me to go. So do Mama and Papa."

"But do you want to go?" He touched her chin and brought her back toward him. "You're the one who needs to decide, right?"

She shook her head and blinked as her eyes filled. Two big tears ran down her cheeks.

He caught them with his thumbs and brushed them away.

"Oh Tuck." Her voice caught. "I don't want to. I have to. I just talked to Papa. He wants me to go."

If he could, he'd wipe the worry from her face. She should always smile and be happy. Her hurt brought heaviness to his heart. "I thought Kathleen said you'd leave in late spring or early summer. That's months away. Your parents could change their minds by then. I wouldn't worry about it now."

Anna's eyes brightened for a moment. Then, as a cloud covered her countenance, she shook her head, and another tear eased from her eye. "No, Mama will never change her mind. Papa said I should learn to be a good wife. He wants me to be like Kathleen. He wants me to go away."

Another tear fell and yet another. Jeremiah's heart broke. Without thought of the consequences, he reached for her, and she fell into his arms. He patted her back. "Hey Little Bit, don't cry. It's cold out here. You'll freeze your face."

Her only answer was a sniffle. A tremble moved through her body. His arms tightened, and he tucked her head more securely under his chin. He'd do the same if she were truly his sister. Only his heart had never acted up like this when he consoled his sister. Emotions, having nothing to do with brotherly love, surged through his awareness.

His muscles tensed, and she looked up. Tears glistened in her lashes. Her full lips pulled down into a pout. His heart pounded as if he'd run a mile. He stared into her wide, chocolate eyes until they blurred, and his nose touched hers.

He jerked back and fell to the ground as if he'd been hit. What just happened? He'd almost kissed the pout from her lips. He'd wanted to kiss Little Bit. His nose still tingled from the brief contact. What on earth had he been thinking?

Chapter 6

He was crazy. That's all there was to it. Taking advantage of Anna's innocence that way. He felt sorry for her. Nothing else. No reason to start kissing her.

He scrambled to his feet. "I'm sorry, Little Bit. I need to get this ax to your father. The handle broke."

She sat on the ground looking up at him with wide, luminous eyes. No doubt calling him a few choice names for his behavior.

He grabbed the ax. "Well, I better go. You take care now."

She never spoke, and he didn't look back. Better if he didn't. Seventeen years old. Same age Rebekah would have been. Little Bit. Little sister. He thumped his forehead with the heel of his hand.

Sure, he cared about Anna. She was fun to go fishing with. Her chatter would keep anyone entertained. But to court? To kiss? Not likely. Her father would have his job if he knew what had almost happened. Better if he took a second look at Kathleen. At least she was closer to his age.

Jeremiah strode through the forest's carpet of leaves and broken sticks, stretching the distance between Anna and him. What appeal drew him to Anna? He searched his heart and had to admit he cared. Far too much. Girls like her were the ones who could tear a man's heart out. She was family, pure and simple. Only more. Could be a lot more. Enough to get hurt again, because family didn't always stay.

He dodged a tree branch and took a deep breath of the pine-scented air then let it out in a rush. His plans didn't include waiting around for a little girl to grow up. Sure, he needed a wife, because come spring, he planned to be living on his own farm. He'd carry on the tradition of farming his grandfather and dad had left him. He needed a woman suited for marriage. Someone who didn't turn his emotions inside out and set his heart pounding like a drum. Maybe Kathleen would be the best choice. Her mother seemed to like him, and Kathleen did invite him to their cabin. Wouldn't hurt to think about it, pray about it, and maybe ask her father for permission to court her.

Camp came into view, and he quickened his stride. His heart had returned to normal. He shoved both sisters far from his mind. Willum had promised to build a house for him. He'd even joked about it, saying it would be one less man taking up space in his tiny cabin on weekends, so he'd be glad to do it.

Clouds blanketed the sky, releasing a gentle rain when Anna tugged the horse to a stop in front of Tumwater's grocer and set the brake. She hopped from the wagon, her skirt flaring out before settling back down to cover her ankles.

"Anna, be careful." Kathleen climbed down, scarcely exposing the toe of her shoe. "You could fall and get hurt jumping like that. What if your foot got caught on something or you slipped in the mud?"

"It won't." Anna twirled toward the mercantile three doors up the street. "Oh Kathleen, there's Larkin. She's wearing the new dress she got for her birthday. You won't need me for a few minutes, will you? I'll be back in time to help load the wagon."

Kathleen sighed. "Go ahead. At least you drove."

"Thanks." Anna ran up the boardwalk steps, her boots clomping on the wood. Her green calico looked shabby next to Larkin's fancy blue dress, but Anna didn't care.

Larkin turned, a dimpled smile brightening her face. "Anna, I didn't see you."

"Kathleen's in the grocery. Mama didn't feel well and asked us to shop for her. I'll have to help, so I don't have a lot of time. I wonder if they have any new embroidery floss."

"I don't know, but I'd love to see, too." Larkin held the door open. "Are you feeling better? You've been in my thoughts and prayers all week."

Anna stepped into the mercantile. She'd like to forget this past week, except for one special part. Every time she thought about Tuck's nose brushing hers, her stomach jumped just before her heart took off like a horse in a race.

"I'm fine." She tossed the answer over her shoulder, her boots beating a hollow staccato against the wood floor. What would Larkin say if she knew? They had shared a lot of secrets in the past, but maybe not this one. It was too new. Too unsure. Tuck sure had acted funny after it happened.

Larkin caught up with her at the thread counter. "Have your parents said any more to you about finishing school?"

Anna fingered the embroidery floss. "Mama hasn't, but Papa says he wants me to learn to be a lady, so that's what I'm doing."

She sighed. "Sure do hate to give up fishing."

Larkin's eyes widened. "You're giving up fishing? You can't. You love to fish."

Anna glanced around the store and grinned as she leaned closer to Larkin. "Maybe ladies can still fish."

"Of course they can." Larkin picked up a violet hank of floss and grimaced. "This is Mama's new favorite color for next year."

"It's pretty."

"Try wearing it all year."

"So is this green one. Kind of reminds me of the woods." Anna couldn't stop the catch in her voice.

The warmth of her friend's hand on her arm almost brought tears to Anna's eyes. Larkin patted her arm. "I'm so sorry. Why don't we plan a fishing party to prove to your mother you can fish and still be just as much a lady as your sister? Once she sees that, you can stay right here in Tumwater. My Chinook grandfather always said a fish fry makes everything better, and the *Farmer's Almanac* predicts this dry spell will continue through the next month at least."

At Larkin's mention of the almanac, Anna smiled, her tears banished. "You and your weather talk. And tempting me with fishing. When can we have the party? How many shall we invite?"

"As many as you want. Would next Sunday afternoon work?"

Tension seeped from Anna as excitement took its place. "Yes, we can bring food and cook the fish we catch."

"Now, how about this embroidery floss? Do you want any?" Larkin began picking out several hanks of brown and gold shades.

Anna took the green one she'd admired earlier. She'd make something she could take to school that would remind her of her woods. Maybe ivy on a pillowcase. "I'm getting this one, then I've got to get back to the grocery before Kathleen tells Mama I ran off."

Larkin gave her a quick hug. "I need to look at some other things, but I'll see you tomorrow at church."

"All right." Anna paid for the floss and hurried out the door, almost bumping into Abigail coming in. "Oh, I'm sorry."

"That's fine." Abigail looked into the store with a frown marring her face. "I see Larkin is here."

"Yes, we were just talking." Anna stepped onto the boardwalk.

Abigail followed, letting the mercantile door close. She fell into step with Anna. "I don't know why you hang around with her. Just because her father's the richest man in town doesn't lessen the fact she's a mixed breed."

"Most people around here are. I'm a mixture of Dutch and Scots."

Abigail patted Anna's shoulder as if she were a foolish child. "Sometimes you say the strangest things. What were you and Larkin talking about?"

Why don't you like Larkin? If it'd do any good, she'd ask. "We've decided to have a fishing party out at the lake. Everyone's invited. Why don't you and Elizabeth come? And Garrick. It's for the fellows and girls, both. We'll bring potluck and fry the fish. It'll be lots of fun."

Abigail nodded. "I'm sure it will. I haven't been fishing in ages."

"Then it's time you did." Anna's heart lifted at the thought of everyone gathered around the lake. Larkin always knew how to make her feel better. Now to convince Kathleen their idea was a good one.

"Anna, the order's ready. Are you?" Kathleen stood in front of the grocer, her hands on her hips.

"Yes, I said I'd be right back." Anna frowned. What was wrong with Kathleen?

Kathleen headed toward the wagon. "You could have stayed and helped instead of running off."

"I didn't. . ." Oh, what was the use? She could argue all day that Kathleen gave permission, and still her words would get turned around somehow. "Larkin wants us all to meet next Sunday afternoon for a fishing party at the lake."

"I don't like fishing." Kathleen wrinkled her nose and shifted toward Abigail. "Are you going?"

Abigail nodded. "Yes. I'm sure Elizabeth and Garrick will, too."

Kathleen's eyebrows lifted. "Well, I suppose I could." She looked back at Anna. "Mama should approve of your fishing with a large group rather than going off by yourself or alone with—"

"I know, Kathleen." Anna climbed to the high wagon seat. "You don't need to complain. I've decided I'll be a lady from now on."

"Ha." Kathleen laughed. "I can't wait to see this come to pass. If you can act like a lady at a fishing party, it'll be a miracle. Abigail, it was nice seeing you. We've got to get home. Most of what we bought is for the camp."

"I understand." Abigail walked on down the street.

Anna shook her head at her friend's behavior. She'd been going into the mercantile until she saw Larkin. What could she possibly have against Larkin? Anna picked up the reins and flicked them above the horse with a click of her tongue. There was no understanding some people. But one thing she knew. Mama would have nothing bad to say about this fishing trip. Not with Kathleen going. Now all she needed to do was spread the word. Would Tuck and his friends come? Her tummy did its familiar little jump, and she smiled. He'd better come. If she didn't have a chance to ask him at church tomorrow, she'd make sure to during the week. Maybe they could bump noses again.

Chapter 7

Jeremiah squinted at the overcast sky above the church. "Looks like a good day for fishing. At least it's not raining."

"Good thing." Frederick grinned. "I've got a craving for fried fish and good company."

E.V. nodded. "So the plan is to head to the lake this afternoon and fish for our lunch, right?"

"Right." Jeremiah's gaze shifted to the Wilkins' buggy pulling to a stop beside the church.

Anna climbed out and turned toward him. His rebellious heart raced without his permission. His eyes refused to look elsewhere. What was wrong with him? He'd kept his distance ever since he'd almost kissed her. She wouldn't have stopped him either. Would she have known to? She'd probably never been kissed, and he almost took advantage of her. She'd been crying. Upset, vulnerable. Disgust for his actions landed on his heart, bringing it under control.

"There's the Wilkin family." E.V. nodded toward the girls. "Didn't I see you talking to the little one, Tuck?"

Little one. Jeremiah almost laughed. Even his friends thought she was too young. "Yes, she gave me the invitation for this afternoon. Said to invite all of you, though I can't imagine why."

Frederick gave him a playful shove. "Watch it, buddy."

Jeremiah laughed. His gaze shifted to Kathleen. A chestnut ringlet brushed her smooth cheek. Her eyes, dark and wide, looked across the yard. He looked, too. Garrick and his sisters walked toward them from the opposite way. Jeremiah looked back at Kathleen. A soft smile brought out the loveliness of her face. She was a real beauty. A woman any man would be proud to claim for his wife.

Anna twirled and ran back to the wagon, taking his attention from her sister. He shook his head. Kathleen's beauty paled next to her rambunctious sister.

Kathleen walked past and smiled. Every man lifted his hat and acknowledged her presence. What better time to set his plan in motion? He stepped forward but felt a hand on his arm.

"Tuck?" Anna smiled at him. "Are you going to the lake this afternoon?"

His heart melted at the sparkle in her dark eyes, the endearing tendril of hair blowing across her face. He resisted the urge to catch it and tuck it behind her ear. Instead, he grinned. "Miss a chance to go fishing? Now, what do you think?"

"You'll be there." She laughed. "I will, too. I plan to catch more fish than you do, you know."

"Ha, as if that's possible." His heart pounded. "Hey, I need to catch someone. I'll see you later."

"Okay." A crease between her eyes told him she didn't want him to go.

He resisted the urge to stay with her and ran up the steps just before Kathleen disappeared through the door. "Miss Wilkin?"

"Yes?" Kathleen turned with her eyebrows lifted.

Jeremiah ignored the buzz of male voices behind him. He'd probably shocked his friends, but he had a goal to fulfill. More than anything, he wanted a family. Kathleen could give him that without danger of losing his heart. He'd already suffered more loss and pain in his life than he wanted. He could learn to care for Kathleen, but not too much.

He pulled his hat from his head. "Would you mind if I sat with you this morning?"

Kathleen hesitated only a moment before a smile crossed her face. "I would be honored by your company, Mr. Tucker."

She slipped her hand through his arm, and he felt no more than her gentle presence. Perfect. He nodded with his best smile. "Please, call me Jeremiah."

"Of course." She seemed pleased by his invitation. "I'll expect you to call me Kathleen from now on."

Anna's foot hit the ground and her arms crossed. How could Jeremiah do such a thing? *I need to catch someone.* Who might that be? None other than Kathleen! To walk away in the middle of their conversation just so he could smile and offer his arm to her sister. Oh! Again, her foot stomped.

"Anna, is something wrong?" Larkin stopped beside her.

"I'm sorry, I didn't see you." Anna turned from the scene at the door to force a smile for her friend.

Abigail and Elizabeth joined them. "Hi, Anna. Are you sitting with us this morning?"

Garrick waved then walked toward the church with Jeremiah's friends.

Anna sighed. "I suppose I might as well."

"Are you all right?" Larkin persisted. "You seem so sad this morning. Aren't you excited about the fishing party?"

"Oh yes, of course. I'm fine. Maybe we'd better go in and find a place to sit. Church will be starting soon." At least Larkin didn't press for a more honest answer. What could she say? *Oh, I'm just jealous of my sister because she's so beautiful every man in the territory falls at her feet. Even Tuck, who almost kissed me, is at this very moment sitting beside her. Mama will be thrilled of course. Papa, too. Kathleen is so perfect, she'll be the perfect wife.*

The perfect wife for Jeremiah. A sob caught in her throat. She would not cry. No matter how angry or hurt she was, she would not let anyone know she cared.

She latched on to Larkin's arm when they reached the door. "I haven't done very well being a lady. I need to try harder."

Larkin patted Anna's hand. "Oh Anna, you're exactly the way God made you. You don't need to change a thing."

Spoken like a true friend. Anna smiled. "Thank you. When I need lifting up, I know who to come to. You're my best friend, Larkin."

Larkin nodded. "Always."

Anna didn't want to look when she walked past the pew where Jeremiah and Kathleen sat. She tried not to—and lost. One glance told her everything she needed to know. Jeremiah held his Bible in his lap, a satisfied smile on his face. So he thought he'd caught the best fish in the sea, did he? If he only knew Kathleen, he wouldn't think that. Anna loved her older sister, but there were times when they didn't get along. *Humph.* Like now.

Anna sat beside Abigail and tried to pay attention. She sang the right words to the songs. She closed her eyes during prayer, and she sat quietly while Reverend Bollen preached. She even caught a few words before her mind wandered again. Maybe she should try harder to be a lady. Mama said ladies should walk, not run. She could do that. What else did a lady do? She should know. She'd heard the rules all her life, but at the moment every one of them fled her mind. She sighed. How would she ever change if she couldn't even remember what to do?

"Let us stand." Reverend Bollen's voice and the rustling across the church brought Anna's mind to the present. She stood and bowed her head for the closing prayer.

An hour later, Anna slung her fishing pole over her shoulder and turned to her sister. "Aren't you taking a pole?"

Kathleen stood just outside the open door of the shed with her umbrella. She rolled her eyes. "No, Anna. Just because we're going to a fishing party doesn't mean I have to act like you." She wrinkled her nose. "I'm going to visit, not fish."

Anna shrugged. "Suit yourself. I plan to fish. And don't tell me ladies don't fish, because the other girls will. You'll more than likely be the only one who doesn't."

Kathleen's laughter trilled behind her as she headed toward the street, picnic basket in one hand and umbrella in the other. "I seriously doubt it."

Anna let her bonnet hang down her back, and she didn't carry an umbrella. Larkin said it wouldn't rain, and she usually knew. Of course, Kathleen had to have both bonnet and umbrella. A little rain might muss her hair. Then who would sit with her at church?

No, she would not think about Jeremiah sitting with Kathleen. Why had he done such a thing, anyway? It didn't make sense. Anna clutched her smaller basket that held a bowl of potato salad and another of baked beans and willed her mind away from Jeremiah. The food should keep well now the weather had turned cooler. After all, November would soon be past.

"I told Jeremiah I'd catch a bigger fish than he does."

Kathleen looked toward Anna's fishing pole. "I don't know why you'd want to even try. It certainly isn't ladylike. How do you ever expect to catch a husband if you're continually trying to outdo men? Besides, impaling a worm and throwing it in the lake is so barbaric."

Anna laughed. "Papa says the worm doesn't feel a thing. God made them for bait."

"Oh really?" Kathleen's eyebrows lifted. "Mama told me God made worms to loosen the soil in our garden. That's still a lowly job, but at least he doesn't have to die doing it. And no one has to force him to."

"Maybe." Anna shrugged. "Could be God made worms to do both jobs. Besides, fishing's a lot more fun than gardening."

"Not for the worm." Kathleen met Anna's eyes with a twinkle in hers.

When she laughed, Anna joined in. Sometimes, Kathleen could be fun.

They turned onto the path leading to the lake and Anna quickened her stride. Larkin and Abigail would be there. Would Jeremiah? He promised before he sat with Kathleen at church. He'd be there. Why not? He probably made plans with Kathleen.

Voices rang out. And laughter. Anna ran ahead around the

gentle curve where she saw her friends. There must be twenty people. She laughed and turned. "Come on, Kathleen. We're late. I think everyone's already here. The Bollens and the Leonards. There's Larkin and Tuck, and some of the other fellows and girls, too. This should be lots of fun."

"Anna, wait."

What for? Anna stopped until her sister caught up.

"Maybe this would be a good time for you to behave like a lady."

Anna stared at her sister. Was she trying to help or hinder? "I know, Kathleen. I intend to."

"Good." Kathleen smiled. "Mama said I should help you. She's counting on it."

Which meant Kathleen would tattle if she did anything unladylike. Anna turned away and walked as fast as she could toward the others. Larkin had a pole in her hand. Good. She intended to fish.

Someone had brought a wagon. Probably the Bollen brothers. They had the tailgate down with a tablecloth spread on it. Anna ran over and left her basket with the rest.

"Anna, come on." Larkin waved.

Anna trotted across the ground toward her friend. "Hey, I see you have a pole, too."

"Of course, that's what you do at a fishing party."

A group of young men sat on the bank, talking and casting out their lines. Tuck laughed at something Frederick, the engineer who carried logs on the Shay engine, said. They seemed to be awfully good friends. As close as she and Larkin.

Larkin nudged Anna. "Want to join them?" Her dark eyes sparkled.

A slow grin spread across Anna's face. "Sure."

"Anna." Kathleen's call stopped her in her tracks.

What now? Anna turned toward the wagon where Kathleen and some of the other girls stood.

"You need to come and help. Did you see this fish?" Kathleen pointed to the makeshift table and a bucket sitting on it.

Anna sighed. Fishing with the men wasn't the most ladylike thing she could do. If she didn't help, Kathleen would tell, and Mama might send her away before Christmas. She turned to Larkin. "I want to fish, but Kathleen's going to tell Mama if I don't act like a lady."

"I'll help." Larkin's gentle smile sympathized. "It'll be fun. You'll see."

"I know. I just wanted to fish." Anna flashed a quick grin. "Maybe later."

Anna took over the job of cooking the fish the men had cleaned. Tuck seemed to be having a good time with his friend. He pulled a fish in while Anna watched. She ached to run across the grass to sit beside him. They'd laughed and talked that first time when they scarcely knew each other. Now look at them. One almost-kiss and they scarcely spoke.

Larkin helped set out food while Anna arranged the pieces of fish in a cast-iron frying pan. She crouched beside the fire pit someone had fixed and set her pan across the hot rocks at the base of the fire. While the fish heated, she glanced toward the lake. Tuck's place was empty. Her pan sizzled and spit hot grease, making her jump. She grabbed the spatula to turn the fish.

She sensed his presence just as his hand covered hers. Tuck. She turned toward him.

"Hey Little Bit, be careful there. Why don't you back up and let me do this?"

She met his gaze. "I can do it. This is woman's work."

He chuckled. "Not outside on the ground over an open fire. Besides, you're too close. Your skirt might catch fire. You back up now just a little."

Anna slid her hand from under his and missed the contact. Her heart spoke with a mind of its own. She scooted back while he deftly scooped the fish and turned each piece. She loved him. No, she didn't. How could she? Papa wanted her to go to school. She didn't have time to fall in love. But she did love him, with all her heart. She'd never forget Tuck as long as she lived. She'd love him forever.

"There you go." He looked at her with a wide grin and stood, holding out his hand.

She slipped hers into the warmth of his and allowed him to help her stand. Her heart fluttered dangerously and broke in two when he looked away—toward Kathleen.

"Be careful." He glanced back at her, concern in his eyes. "Tuck your skirt out of the way if you're going to cook, okay? I don't want you hurt."

"I should have worn my trousers." She clamped her hand over her mouth. Tuck didn't want a tomboy. He wanted a woman like Kathleen. One who knew how to act like a lady instead of run around in men's clothing, fishing, and helping Papa in the woods all the time.

His laughter rang out, and he cuffed her jaw. "That's my Little Bit. You remind me of my sister, you know? I like that."

Anna stared after him. *His sister!* How could he make such

a remark then turn and walk away? Her foot hit the ground and her arms crossed. He walked straight toward Kathleen and stopped with a smile on his face. Tears burned Anna's eyes and her shoulders slumped. Why wouldn't he prefer her sister's company? Kathleen was beautiful, and she always acted like a lady.

Chapter 8

Anna ran up the stairs to her bedroom in their house in town. Although the cabin in the woods should seem more like home since they spent more time there, it didn't. This house was where they spent every weekend and where she kept most of her belongings. Here, she didn't have to share a bedroom with Kathleen. Since Tuck had started paying so much attention to Kathleen, sometimes just looking at her sister was a chore.

It had been two weeks since the fishing party. Maybe today she could stop thinking about Tuck and Kathleen. Larkin always made shopping fun, and they'd be looking for Christmas gifts, which would be even more fun. Her soft green dress lay on the bed where she'd placed it before lunch. She dressed and started to smooth her errant hair back into place when a deep voice drifted up the stairs and through her open doorway. Tuck. Her heart thudded. Here? At their house? He must have only now arrived in town from the logging camp.

Anna knelt beside the floor vent in her room and bent low to hear.

"Certainly. We'll go into the parlor where it's private."

At Papa's words, Anna straightened. What would Tuck have to

say to Papa in private? A problem at camp? She stood and peeked out her door. Assured no one else was upstairs, she crossed the hall to her parents' room, which was above the parlor. She slipped inside and closed the door without a sound then knelt beside the heating vent on Mama's side of the bed.

"I've secured the land I'll need for my farm, and Willum has started building a small house for me. If I need more room later, I can add on."

Tuck had land and a house of his own? Weight pressed against Anna's heart. But how could she have known? They'd spent so little time together, and when they did, their conversation had been fun, lighthearted. There was so much she didn't know about him, but she wanted to know everything. If only he wanted to court—oh my!

She clamped a hand across her mouth, her eyes opened wide. Could he be asking Papa's permission to court her? Then why had he been acting so friendly with Kathleen? Her stomach leaped and her heart pounded.

". . .to court your daughter."

Anna almost fell on the vent. What had she missed?

"Let me get this straight." Papa's voice rose through the vent. "You want to court Kathleen, not Anna?"

After a pause, Tuck repeated the one name. "Anna?"

Anna pressed against the vent. *Don't pick Kathleen, please don't.*

Silence filled the room before he spoke. "Isn't she a little young? I understood she'd be going away to school in a few months."

"Yes, that's true." Papa's deep sigh sounded, then a rustle below as if the men stood. "All right, you have my permission to court Kathleen if she agrees."

"Thank you, sir. I think she will."

Anna didn't wait for Tuck to leave. She ran to her room, grabbed her coat, hat, and mittens then rushed down the back stairway to the kitchen and out the door. For a moment, she stood in the backyard, lost. Where was she going? What should she do? He didn't love her.

A sob caught in her throat. She'd fallen in love with Tuck. How long ago? Since October and it was December now. Two months since she'd knocked him to the floor at Larkin's party. Time didn't matter. She loved him as she'd never loved before, and she could never tell him now.

Larkin. They were going shopping. She'd be waiting at her house, wondering what had happened. Anna held her skirt just high enough to run without hindrance. So what if ladies didn't run? She'd never be a lady now. Not ever. Her vision blurred before she realized she was crying. Of their own accord, her feet slowed to a walk, and she brushed the tears from her cheeks with her woolen mittens. More took their place, so by the time she reached Larkin's house, sobs shook her shoulders.

Larkin let her in. She tossed her own coat aside and led the way upstairs. In Larkin's room, Anna fell into her friend's arms and cried even harder. "How could Tuck do this to me?"

Larkin rubbed soft circles on her back. "Oh Anna, I'm so sorry. First school and now this. But maybe you won't go away, and maybe Kathleen will tell Mr. Tucker no."

Anna took a shuddering breath as she pulled back. "He chose my sister. That's what matters. I want to go to school now. Maybe I'll marry someone back East and stay there."

"But your family?"

"Papa might miss me, but Mama and Kathleen won't. I'll go, and I'll never come back."

Tears glistened in Larkin's eyes. "Oh Anna, where is your faith?" She picked up her Bible from the bedside table and flipped pages toward the back. "Here it is in Romans. It says, 'All things work together for good to them that love God.' Don't you believe that means you?"

Anna stared at the scripture verse while conflicting emotions ran through her soul. Anger, fear, jealousy, remorse, and love were a few she recognized. Finally, she nodded. "I know you're right. I've been acting like a spoiled brat. But if Kathleen and Tuck fall in love and get married, I'll have to stay away. I couldn't bear to watch them together." She lifted a moist gaze to her friend. "A person can't help who they love, can they? Not Tuck, but not me either."

With a soft smile, Larkin shook her head. "No, they can't. But this verse also tells me God has the perfect man picked out to be your husband. 'All things work together for good.' That means if Kathleen and Mr. Tucker marry, it's for your good as well as theirs. Isn't that right?"

A sigh escaped Anna's lips. "Yes, you're right, as usual. Maybe someday my heart will stop hurting so much and then I can accept this. Come on, let's go to town."

Anna walked beside Larkin, but her mind wouldn't shut out the sound of Tuck's voice asking to court Kathleen. Her heart still felt as if a log had fallen and crushed it. Would she ever get over Tuck? Any other man would have to be very special to take his place in her heart.

Garrick stepped out of the feed store as they neared it. "Hey, what are you two up to?"

Larkin stopped, so Anna did, too. "Just Christmas shopping."

"Really?" Garrick looked at Anna. "You look like you're going to a funeral. Where's the happy girl we're used to seeing?"

Anna shrugged. "I guess she grew up."

"What's wrong, Anna?"

"Nothing." She turned from his questioning gaze. Garrick was the big brother she'd never had. He'd protected her more than once, even took blame when the rock she threw at a bird broke a neighbor's window. She didn't want to burden him with this, too.

"Did Kathleen do something to you?"

Tears filled Anna's eyes just when she thought she'd used them all. She shook her head, then nodded. "If you must know, Jeremiah Tucker came to the house before I left and asked Papa's permission to court Kathleen."

Garrick's eyebrows shot up. "You heard him?"

Anna nodded. "Yes, and Papa said yes." Tears rolled down her cheeks, and she covered them with her mittens. "Kathleen doesn't love Tuck. I do, but he wants her. Oh, it doesn't matter anyway. Papa's sending me away. Kathleen's perfect, and she's staying here."

Jeremiah stepped off the Wilkins' front porch. He should be walking on air, but he felt as if his feet were dragging through six-inch-deep mud. He had permission to court Kathleen if she agreed. She hadn't been home, but he'd talk to her tomorrow at church. That didn't concern him, but Anna did. How could he spend time with Kathleen without running into Anna? He couldn't. When had she become more to him than a substitute sister?

He turned and walked toward the lake, his mind and emotions roiling. He should be happy. He'd just been given the opportunity to win the hand of the prettiest girl in Tumwater. Or so everyone else seemed to think. Why had her father asked if he'd meant Anna? A man should want his oldest daughter to marry first.

Jeremiah shook his head and stood at the lake, taking little note of his surroundings. He might as well go to town and pick up a few things from the mercantile. Retracing his steps, he broke into a run. Maybe the exercise and the cold wind would clear his mind. A few minutes later, he slowed to a fast walk and concentrated on Kathleen. Beyond her outward appearance, she seemed attractive inside. Her manner was gentle. She worked hard at camp just as she had at their fishing party. She was—

Jeremiah slowed to a stop, his gaze locked on Anna. She stood across the street by the feed store with Garrick and her friend, Miss Whitworth. His heart ran faster than he had. What was wrong with him? A glimpse of Anna turned him into a smitten schoolboy.

Garrick held his arms out to Anna, and she fell against him for a tight embrace.

Jeremiah's stomach twisted. His heart constricted. Anna always sat with Garrick and his sisters in church. He'd seen them together talking before. A harsh, short laugh tore from his throat. He'd fallen in love with a girl who belonged to another. Good thing he'd asked for her older sister instead.

Disgusted with himself, Jeremiah turned away from the cozy scene and almost bumped into E.V., who was stepping off the boardwalk. "Oh, sorry, I didn't see you there."

E.V. grinned. "That's pretty obvious. What's got your dander up?"

"Nothing." He heard the growl in his voice even before E.V.'s eyebrows rose.

E.V. looked toward the feed store. "Ah, I see. I thought you were spending more time with Miss Wilkin than mere friendship. What was she doing hugging Leonard?"

"How should I know? It's none of my business." Jeremiah took off at a fast walk down the street. So what if they hugged? Pain squeezed his heart.

E.V. fell into step with him. "None of your business? If you have feelings for Miss Wilkin, why don't you let her know?"

"Because I plan to court her sister."

"What?"

"I just got permission from her father." Jeremiah couldn't resist a quick glance over his shoulder. He breathed better when he saw Anna heading one direction and Garrick the other. He forced a laugh. "Besides, Anna's only a kid. I'm looking for a wife. I just need to convince Kathleen she wants the job."

"Job? How romantic." E.V. stopped and turned as if to walk away.

Jeremiah looked at him. "Where are you going?"

"Somewhere away from this foolhardy path you're trodding." E.V. waved over his shoulder. "Good luck, my friend. You'll need all you can get."

Chapter 9

Jeremiah sat with Kathleen the third Sunday in a row. Even after two weeks of courting her, his gut instinct was to run. Fine. That's exactly what he wanted. A woman who wouldn't tear him up inside if anything happened to her. He glared across the church where Anna sat beside Garrick. Ever since he saw them hugging in public, they'd sat side by side.

"And 'the just shall live by faith.' " Pastor Bollen's voice brought Jeremiah's attention to the front where it belonged. He forced himself to listen. Better to focus there than across the aisle. A lot better than what he wanted to do. Especially since asking a friend to step out of church for a round of fisticuffs would shock more than a few in the congregation.

He'd lost Anna, and he might as well accept it. No, he'd never had her. Marriage with Anna would never work anyway. She was too young, and crazy as it sounded, he cared too much for her. He'd never been in love before Anna, but he'd get over her.

"Let's talk about faith now." Again the reverend's voice intruded. "The Bible says faith comes by hearing and hearing by the word of God."

Another glance revealed Garrick leaning toward Anna while

she whispered something to him. Jeremiah looked away and squirmed, bringing a sharp look from Kathleen.

"Sorry," he whispered.

She smiled.

He couldn't ask for a sweeter girl than Kathleen. She'd make a perfect wife. Must run in her family. Anna was sweet, too. She was fun, smart, beautiful—and lost to him. He slanted a glance toward Kathleen. His choice was best. Anna had his heart in a twist now, and she wasn't even his. Kathleen would never do that to him. Maybe he should ask Kathleen to marry him right away. Why wait? Get it settled. Then he wouldn't be pestered with thoughts of Anna all the time. He gave a decisive nod and settled back with his arms crossed to listen to what was left of the sermon. Before he had time to make sense of the reverend's words, they were standing, and it was time to go.

He turned to Kathleen. "Would you go for a walk with me this afternoon? I'll pick you up around two if that's all right."

She nodded. "Yes, that would be nice."

"Fine. I hate to go off and leave you now, but I need to catch up with the other men. We're all eating together. Since we don't work in the same area, we try to get together at least once on the weekend."

"I understand. I don't mind at all." Kathleen smiled and touched his arm. "You go ahead. I have a way home with my parents."

"All right." Jeremiah returned her smile and headed outside where the others waited.

Anna breezed past him as if he were standing still. "Anna," he called out when he should have kept his mouth shut.

She froze for a second before turning with the fakest smile

he'd ever seen. What was wrong with her?

"Hello, Mr. Tucker. What are you doing?"

He frowned. "What happened to Tuck?"

She waved a gloved hand in front of her face. "Oh, I think Kathleen wouldn't like me calling her beau that."

"Why would she care? She seems agreeable." A lot more than her little sister. A lot more boring, too.

Anna laughed. "Yes, she's agreeable most of the time. Well, nice talking to you. I need to get home."

She crossed the street before Jeremiah got his breath. He might have watched her until she was out of sight, but Frederick called to him. "Hey Tuck, we're heading out. You comin'?"

"Yes." Jeremiah turned on his heel and followed the men.

E.V. dropped back beside him. "Sure you know what you're doing, buddy?"

Jeremiah glanced toward Anna hurrying down the road. The muscle in his jaw ticked, but he nodded. "I'm positive."

"I hope so. Your girl is pretty, but her sister is, too, don't you think?"

"Yes." Jeremiah nodded. "Pretty young."

E.V. gave a sad shake of his head. "Is that what you think?"

Jeremiah drew his brows together and lengthened his stride. Maybe he didn't really think that, but it made a good excuse. He'd been hurt enough for one lifetime.

He followed the others in the diner where his stomach rebelled against the tasteless food they complimented. Their conversation turned from friendly banter to deeper issues as the food disappeared.

"The talk about statehood's been getting serious lately."

Willum leaned back after cleaning his plate. "Won't be long until it's signed, sealed, and delivered."

What difference did it make? Jeremiah pushed his plate away. At the moment, he didn't care one way or the other what became of Washington. Territory or state, it was all the same to him. If he was going to talk Kathleen into accepting his proposal, he needed to go. No wonder he'd been unable to eat. He was nervous. Perfectly normal reaction. He just wished the unease stirring his insides would stop. Maybe when she agreed to marry him, it would.

He stood. "Sorry, but I promised Kathleen we'd go on a walk this afternoon. I'm due to pick her up pretty soon."

Frederick lifted his eyebrows. "Sounds like things are getting serious."

Jeremiah shrugged.

E.V. met his gaze, looked as if he might speak, but didn't.

A quick nod and Jeremiah headed toward the Wilkins' house.

After greeting Anna's—or rather Kathleen's parents, he walked beside her down the street. Anna hadn't been at the house. Or hadn't made herself known. After church, when he stopped her, he recognized the hurt in her eyes, as if he'd disappointed her. But he couldn't think about Anna now. Not when he intended to ask for Kathleen's hand. "I thought you might like to go out to the falls. It's always nice there. You're warm enough, aren't you?"

She gave him a sweet smile and clutched her coat lapels with both hands. "Yes, I'm fine, and I'd love to see the falls."

"Good." He lapsed into silence to match hers.

As the falls came into sight, he slowed and Kathleen did, too. He turned to face her, only then taking her hand in his. "Are you all right?"

She nodded, watching him with wary eyes. Wary? Why? Surely, she wasn't afraid of him. He attempted a smile. "I have a farm not far from town. My friend, Willum Tate, has been working on a small house out there. It isn't finished. He can only work between jobs that pay better, but progress is being made. Do you like the country?"

Her gaze skittered away for a moment before returning with her nod. "Yes, but not as well as Anna does. She'd live in the woods if she could."

"Yes, that's probably true." Why did she say that? Didn't he have enough trouble keeping Anna from his mind? He shook his head. "But I'm talking about you. You and me. I want to know if you'd consider marrying me."

Kathleen sucked in her breath as if he'd surprised her. Surely, she'd had some suspicion of his intentions. Of course, he was rushing things.

"I know we haven't had a lot of time together. We've known each other only a few months, but I'm serious about this. If you need to see the house first, I understand. I just thought maybe we could be engaged right now. There's no rush to marry." He gave a quick laugh. "I mean the house isn't even built yet. It will be soon, though. Definitely by spring."

When she only stared at him, he tried again. "Kathleen, will you marry me?"

She nodded, her eyes wide and solemn. The word whispered through her lips. "Yes."

That one word slammed into his midsection then wrapped around his heart as if he'd been chained. His voice sounded rough when he spoke. "That's good."

Her eyes puddled with unshed tears until one and then another rolled from her lower lashes to slide down her cheeks. She covered her face with her gloves. "I'm sorry, Jeremiah. I thought I could do this, but I can't. I just can't."

Sobs shook her shoulders. He pulled her into his arms and let her cry against his chest. He'd never asked a girl to marry him before, but surely this wasn't a normal reaction. He hated when women cried. He patted her back then pulled a handkerchief from his pocket and tucked it into her hands. "What's wrong? Did I do something?"

"I can't marry you. I love s–s–someone else. I love G–Garrick. He s–scarcely looks at me. If I try to talk to him, he stammers and leaves."

Garrick? Did Garrick feel the same for Kathleen? Images filtered through Jeremiah's head as he remembered Garrick standing nearby more than once when he'd been with Kathleen. Garrick scowling at him, and he hadn't known why. But what about Anna? Didn't Garrick want Anna? Why else would he have been holding her that way in front of the feed store? Poor Kathleen. He knew what it was like to love someone you couldn't have.

Anna sat on the Leonard's front porch in the cold December air, her back propped against a corner post, her coat wrapped around her bent legs. If they were lucky, it would snow.

Garrick leaned against the opposite post. "Life isn't always fair, Anna. The both of us might as well face it."

She blinked the burning from her eyes. Abigail had been her

excuse for this visit, but she'd been glad when Garrick told her the girls weren't home. He was the one she wanted to see. He understood. She knew why when he admitted he loved Kathleen.

Anna shrugged. "I guess, but if that's true, how does anyone ever find happiness?"

"Not by the abundance of the things you possess, but by every word that proceeds from the mouth of God." Garrick met Anna's gaze. "I guess that means you don't need everything or everyone you want. All you need is God."

Anna giggled. "You're wonderful, Garrick. I'd love for you to be my brother-in-law, but you need to study your Bible a little more. You got the verses mixed up."

"I did?" Garrick frowned. "So my meaning isn't right either?"

"No. I mean yes." Anna giggled again. "The meaning is right, especially if you consider both verses. The first was from the Gospel of Luke. It really says, 'A man's life consisteth not in the abundance of the things which he possesseth.' The other is in the New Testament, too. I don't remember where, but it's where Jesus was being tempted by the devil. 'Man shall not live by bread alone, but by every word that proceedeth out of the mouth of God.' You memorized verses when you were little. I know you did."

"Sure, how else would I have known those two?" Garrick lifted his chin as if offended.

"And thought they were one." Anna grinned at him then dropped her chin to her knees. "But you're right. It doesn't matter how much we love someone. The important thing is our love for God. I guess what we need to do is forget them."

"How?" Garrick looked as glum as she felt. "I've loved Kathleen since I was a kid. She's beautiful and kind. Sweet, gentle, and smart. She never looked my way, and I was afraid to tell her how I felt. Good thing I didn't. She'd have broken my heart. 'Course, she did anyway. At least, I've had most of my life to prepare for this."

Anna searched his face and saw sincerity. "I never knew you loved my sister."

"No one knew but me."

A long sigh escaped Anna's lips. "I'm in love with Jeremiah, and I haven't had any time to prepare. I wish I could go to school now. What are we supposed to do while they keep company right in front of us?"

Garrick's mouth curved. "I guess we could get married. We're good friends, we get along, and who else are we going to marry? How about it, Anna? Think that's a good idea?"

Anna's heart skipped a beat. She looked into Garrick's eyes and the little patient smile that begged for acceptance. What would it be like being married to Garrick? Pleasant for sure. He was right. They liked each other, even loved each other. As friends. But maybe they could learn to love as husband and wife. Not everyone married for love. Why not?

A smile tugged the corners of Anna's mouth upward. "You have a point. If you think you can put up with me—"

At the sound of a familiar voice, Anna stiffened and turned to look out toward the street beside Garrick's house. Jeremiah and Kathleen. They walked past as if lost in their own world. She couldn't hear more than an occasional rumble from Jeremiah then Kathleen's soft tone answering. Neither looked toward the house. Kathleen clung to Jeremiah's arm as if she belonged there.

The sharp pain shooting through Anna's heart brought tears to her eyes. She brushed them away to see the stricken look on

Garrick's face. "Garrick." She called his attention back to her. "If your offer still stands, and I can get out of going to school, I think I'd like to accept."

Chapter 10

Jeremiah woke far too early and stared into the darkness above his cot, wrestling with the same tormenting thoughts that had kept him awake the night before. Snores from the men sleeping around him vibrated the bunkhouse, but they hadn't awakened him. Visions of Kathleen's tears and Anna's pain-filled eyes danced through his head. What sort of mess had he gotten them all into? He should have stayed in Seattle. Maybe after Christmas he'd pack up and go back.

He huffed a laugh. Go back to what? There was nothing in Seattle for him anymore. That's why he'd jumped at the chance to go south when Willum suggested it. In one night and a raging fire, his entire family had been taken from him. The house was gone and most of their belongings. Only the stock, barn, and farm equipment had survived. And the land he'd sold for a new start.

Anna.

His heart yearned for the young woman with the heart-shaped face, the pert nose, and ready grin. How had he fallen in love with her? A girl in love with another man. The memory of her sitting on the Leonard's front porch with Garrick taunted him. He'd tried to ignore them, but he'd seen just the same, and his heart had twisted at the sight.

So Anna loved Garrick, and Kathleen confessed her love for Garrick, too. Unless he was mistaken, Garrick loved Kathleen. Poor Anna. Maybe sending her away to school was the best thing her father could do for her. Maybe then Garrick and Kathleen would tell each other their true feelings.

Jeremiah watched dark shapes of the night take form and color as dawn crept into the sky. He sat up and buried his face in his hands. *Lord, I've made a mess of things. You are sufficient to meet our every need. I pray for Your will to be done. Seems the only two who might find happiness here are Kathleen and Garrick. They're good people and need Your blessing. Jesus, help them find each other and happiness in serving You together. Amen.*

At breakfast, everyone seemed to be ignoring everyone else. When Jeremiah went through the line, he recognized Kathleen's red-rimmed eyes for what they were. She was grieving over Garrick. All Jeremiah had done was open an old wound for her.

Anna didn't meet Jeremiah's gaze. Garrick followed him into the mess hall, but sat across the room from him. The only time their eyes met, hostility glared from Garrick's. Jeremiah ate eggs, sausage, biscuits, and gravy, but scarcely noticed the taste. If he wasn't the villain here, he didn't know the meaning of the word. Someone needed a happy ending and since it wouldn't be him, he'd better see what he could do to help Kathleen and Garrick.

When Garrick got up to leave, Jeremiah stuffed the last bite of biscuit into his mouth and followed.

"Garrick." Jeremiah ran to catch the departing form of a man he still considered a friend. "Wait. I've got something to tell you. Something you'll want to hear."

Garrick looked over his shoulder but didn't slow his pace. "Not interested, Tucker. Keep your news if it makes you happy." He stopped then and turned around. "Oh, speaking of news. I've got some, too. Yesterday, Anna Wilkin and I decided to get married as soon as we get her father's blessing."

Jeremiah stopped as if he'd taken a hit to his gut. Garrick laughed and strode away.

"Tucker, come on." One of the guys from his crew called, and Jeremiah turned toward the sound. Pain twisted his heart. Anna couldn't marry a man who loved her sister. Her life would be miserable. A rock settled into the cavity where his heart should be. He needed to talk to Garrick, but he probably wouldn't see him until evening.

Jeremiah joined the other men heading to the work site. While he manned one end of the bucksaw to cut slices from a log, Garrick's face stood before him. Garrick hadn't understood Jeremiah's news. He thought he was going to announce his engagement to Kathleen.

Had Garrick been serious about marrying Anna? No, he'd only been trying to get even. What a mess. Jeremiah's grip on the saw slipped, jerking him back to his job.

"Hey, watch it!" Henry, his partner on the saw, yelled. "This is the second time you've done that."

"Sorry. My hand slipped. I'll pay better attention." If he didn't, he could get himself or someone else hurt. He'd seen injuries happen when men were careless. He'd have to deal with Garrick later.

The sound of something crashing through the forest brought the men's work to a halt. Jeremiah turned to watch a horse and cart hurry past. In the back of the cart, calking boots below a blanket-covered form told the story. A man had been hurt. How bad was hard to tell. Who it was remained a mystery. Jeremiah sent a prayer for the man toward heaven as he went back to work until the lunch whistle blew.

On the short walk back to camp, Jeremiah listened to the buzz of speculation about the injury. He followed the others into the mess hall and met Anna's gaze. She stood behind the serving table, her eyes luminescent and red rimmed.

When he stood in front of her, he searched her face. She'd been crying. "Anna, what's wrong?"

"Oh Tuck, it's Garrick." Two big tears hovered on the edges of her eyelids before rolling down. "He's hurt. His leg—" She sucked in a breath.

Her tears tore at his heart. He ached for her, but he also ached for himself. She loved Garrick, not him. "Little Bit, don't cry. He'll be okay. How bad was it?"

"I don't know. Papa and Kathleen went with him to the hospital. Oh Tuck, they said he wasn't paying attention and a limb hit him. He fell, and his ax cut his leg. What if he dies?"

"We'll pray and he'll be fine. They'll take good care of him." Jeremiah longed to take Anna in his arms and wipe the tears from her eyes. He wanted to make her forget Garrick and love him instead. Each silent tear trailing down her face burned his heart, but he was powerless to stop them. She belonged to Garrick now. He let her fill his plate then moved to a far corner to eat.

Jeremiah ignored the conversation around him and dug into food that held no appeal. Anna finished serving and moved into the kitchen. Her mother covered the bowls and pots on the table.

Where was Kathleen? When he didn't see her, Anna's words came to the surface of his mind. Kathleen went with Garrick to the hospital. Kathleen? Why not Anna? Just this morning Garrick said he and Anna were getting married. Something didn't add up.

Still puzzling over his discovery, Jeremiah left his unfinished plate and walked into the woods to be alone. He wanted to pray for Garrick, but soon the cleansing power of repentance poured from his soul. He'd been out of God's will in pursuing Kathleen. While he admired her, he didn't love her. She might like him, but she didn't love him, and was smart enough to realize it. But that wasn't where he'd failed God. No, he was like Abraham, who'd moved ahead of God's will for his life when he took Hagar as his concubine. Jeremiah's reason was different, but the lack of trust was the same. His fear of losing another loved one seemed foolish under the ray of God's loving conviction. Why hadn't he trusted God to take care of Anna? To take care of his hurt. Now he'd lost her without her ever being his.

He fell to his knees. "Lord, I'm sorry for not trusting You. I ask Your forgiveness. Maybe someday I'd have lost Anna, but at least she'd have been mine for a while. Now I've lost her anyway. I'm sorry."

Jeremiah lifted his head and rose. The hurt was still there, but God forgave him, and he'd do his best to trust Him from now on, even if he never married.

Garrick might die. Hot tears ran from Anna's eyes and dripped into the dishwater. She turned her face first one way and then the other to blot them on her shoulders. Her heart ached for Garrick.

And for Kathleen. She'd never seen her sister so worked up over anyone as she was Garrick. Mama was shocked but adjusted well when Kathleen confessed her love for Garrick. She said it was better to find out now than later. Anna agreed.

Lord, please spare Garrick's life. Let him know how much Kathleen really cares. He loves her, and she loves him. If she doesn't know her own heart, help her see it now. And please, Lord, forgive Garrick and me for talking about marrying each other. I see now we were wrong. My love for him is of a good friend, not a wife. Please don't let him die. Touch him and give him healing. Amen.

Anna pushed her worries aside and worked hard throughout the afternoon. She knew that praying then continuing to worry showed a lack of faith, but she was afraid that even if he lived, Garrick might lose his leg. She dropped the broom.

"Anna, are you all right?" Mama looked up, her hands stilled on the bread dough she'd been kneading.

"What if they cut off Garrick's leg?" Anna fought more tears.

A crease formed between Mama's eyes. "I don't think that will happen. Garrick will be fine. Your worrying will do him no good."

"I know." Anna picked up the broom. "But Kathleen is in love with him. He loves her, too. He told me so yesterday. I've always thought of Garrick as a sort of brother. Now he could be, and this had to happen."

Mama smiled. "Yes, but don't worry, I believe Garrick will be fine. Kathleen isn't one to let a missing limb stand in the way of her love. I thought from the start Jeremiah was wrong for her. They'll come through this."

Anna turned back to sweeping. Maybe Kathleen and Garrick would be all right, but would she? She loved Jeremiah. He'd be hurt

Kathleen loved someone else. Why couldn't he love her? Mama was glad Kathleen loved Garrick. She wanted her daughters to be wives and mothers in their own homes. Anna wanted the same thing. But she wanted to be true to the way God made her, too.

She should have stood up for herself long ago. Now, just before Christmas, might be the best time to talk to Papa and tell him she didn't want to go away. Maybe tonight she'd get a chance.

She kept watch for Papa and Kathleen while she worked, but Papa's wagon wheels didn't crunch against the ground outside. It seemed they were taking an awfully long time. After supper, she and Mama closed the mess hall and went to their cabin.

"It isn't a good sign for them to be so late, is it, Mama?" Anna hugged her arms close to ward off a chill more from unease than from the cool December air.

"I wouldn't worry, Anna." Mama's smile looked tired. "Kathleen may have wanted to stay with Garrick as long as she could. You'll understand someday when you fall in love with a young man."

Her mother's words cut deep into Anna's heart. She'd already fallen in love, and she did understand, but there was no point in saying anything. Jeremiah didn't love her. She followed her mother into the cabin. "I'm tired. If you don't mind, I think I'll go to my room."

She climbed the ladder to the loft room she shared with Kathleen and lay across the bed. Her eyes drifted shut while exhaustion lulled her to sleep. A sound in the quiet darkness of night woke her, and she sat up.

With only moonlight filtering into the room, Kathleen sat on the edge of the double bed. "I'm sorry, I didn't mean to disturb you."

"Is Garrick—"

"He's going to be okay." Tears mingled with relief in Kathleen's voice. "He plans to be at the Whitworth's Christmas party."

Anna's breath rushed out. "I'm so glad."

"Papa let me stay until he woke." Kathleen turned to face Anna. "I thought I'd lost him. Did you know he was afraid of me?"

"No, why would he be?"

"I don't know, but he said I was too good for him. Too pretty. Too perfect." Kathleen caught Anna's hand. "He's loved me for years, and I thought he didn't care."

Anna laughed. "Poor Garrick. Did he propose?"

Kathleen's head bowed. "Not yet. I think he will though, when he's better."

Anna changed into her nightgown and crawled into bed beside her sister. She'd talk to Papa later. As soon as possible. She lay in the dark, no longer sleepy as Tuck filled her thoughts. Kathleen hadn't mentioned him. His heart would be broken when he found out Kathleen didn't love him.

Long into the night she lay awake imagining how life as Jeremiah's bride might be until sleep and dreams took over, renewing her determination to win his love if it took the rest of her life.

Thursday after Anna finished her work, she found Papa in the tool shed where he often spent his evenings. He turned with file in hand when she stepped in and closed the door. "Anna. What are you doing out here?"

She grinned. "Tagging along after you like always."

He chuckled. "That's my tagalong Tootsie."

Even as she laughed with him, a lump caught in her throat. He hadn't called her that in years. Now she felt seven years old, and like a child, she blurted out her complaints. "Papa, I don't want to go away."

His eyebrows shot up. "To school?"

"Yes." Tears threatened her eyes. "I love our life here. I want to stay home. God made me just the way I am, and I don't see why everyone wants me to change. Why do you want me to go away?"

"Anna." Papa's voice was calm in the midst of her storm. "You know I love when you help me. I'd like to keep you with me, but if you don't go to school, you'll miss a chance to better yourself. It's a good opportunity, don't you think?"

An invisible cord tightened around her insides as she looked into the pleading in his eyes. He really did want her to go. She blinked against the burning tears that threatened. "All right. If you really want me to, I will. I'll go for you, Papa, not me."

Papa's chuckle returned. He held his arms out, and Anna stepped into his warm embrace. His chest rumbled when he spoke. "It won't be for me, Anna. Your mama came up with this idea and convinced me it's for the best. If you're sure you don't want to go, I'll talk to Mama and set things straight. I'd rather you stay here. I'm happy with the girl you are. I'm pretty sure God is, too."

The tears Anna had tried so hard to keep under control rolled down her cheeks. She didn't have to go away, but what had she gained? Jeremiah didn't love her, and now she'd be here to watch him find someone to take Kathleen's place.

Chapter 11

Anna studied her reflection in the mirror. Where had the sparkle in her eyes gone? Her family was staying in town through Tuesday for Christmas, so she hadn't seen Jeremiah all weekend, and she missed him. Today she should be looking forward to the Whitworth's Christmas Eve soiree, but all she could think about was Jeremiah.

"Aren't you ready yet?" Kathleen stepped around the edge of the doorway. As usual, she looked beautiful.

Anna sighed. "Yes, I'm ready."

What difference did her appearance make? Jeremiah might not even be there. Just because he had an invitation didn't mean he would come. Anna listened to Kathleen chatter with Mama on the short buggy ride across town and shook her head. At least her sister had found love with Garrick.

At the gaily decorated Whitworth mansion, Anna followed Kathleen in and stepped aside to allow her parents room. The house buzzed with activity as townspeople spilled from the formal parlor through wide double doors into the entrance hall.

Anna looked for Larkin, but Kathleen grabbed her arm and pulled her toward the parlor. "There's Garrick."

"Let go, Kathleen. I'm coming." Anna jerked her arm free and hurried after her sister. They stopped beside Garrick's chair. His leg stretched out, resting on a footstool. "What's your rush? It isn't as if he's going to run away."

"Anna, what a horrible thing to say." Kathleen scowled.

Garrick laughed. "She's right. I won't be dancing tonight either." He looked up at Kathleen. "If I could, I'd fill your card."

Pink tinged Kathleen's cheeks, and Anna turned away. She didn't hear her sister's response because there by the front door stood Jeremiah. The waltz, played by the small orchestra in the music room, faded to background music for the dance steps of her heart. Hers and Jeremiah's, only his heart wouldn't be dancing with hers now that it was broken by Kathleen's rejection.

Her breath caught in her throat as his eyes held hers, and he stepped forward. A shadow moved between them, blocking him from her view.

"Anna, you're here." Larkin clasped her hand and stepped back. "You look so much older with your hair fixed that way."

Jeremiah stepped past Larkin. After giving Anna a quick glance, he shook hands with Garrick. "Glad to see you're able to be here. I want you to know I wish you the best."

Anna didn't hear more as she allowed Larkin to lead her away. Jeremiah lost Kathleen and was stepping graciously aside. She turned for one last look and saw the sadness in his eyes. Why couldn't he have loved her instead?

She smiled for Larkin's benefit. "Your family always has the best parties."

"Thank you. Mama and Papa both enjoy entertaining."

As Anna went with Larkin from one person to another,

visiting for a few minutes before moving on, she kept her smile in place. She danced with one of the Bollen brothers and then forgot which one when she saw Jeremiah scowling at her. He looked so unhappy. Tears burned her eyes, but she refused to let them fall. Why did Jeremiah keep watching her? She slipped out of the parlor into the hall. If she could get away from him, maybe she could catch her breath. She stood against the wall, smiling at no one in particular. If only she could forget Jeremiah. She leaned her head against the flocked wallpaper and closed her eyes. Still Jeremiah took form in her memory. So near, yet so out of reach.

"Anna."

His deep voice sounded in her head, and she smiled.

"Little Bit, are you all right?" He sounded concerned.

She jerked, her eyes popping open. "Tuck."

He stood before her, a frown darkening his eyes. He touched her wrist. His fingers burned through her gloves as his hand surrounded hers. "Come with me, Anna. Away, where we can talk."

She tugged against his hold, but he didn't let go.

"Please?" His brows drew together. "It's important."

As if a magnet drew her to him, she nodded and stepped forward. How could she resist? Even if he wanted to talk about Kathleen, she would listen. She loved him.

Jeremiah nodded toward a closed door. "Where does that go?"

"The library, but we can't go in there."

"Why not? We'll leave the door open." He guided Anna inside. A soft light glowed in the corner near a desk, but he didn't move away from the door. No need to risk Anna's reputation.

He kept her hand in his and looked into her questioning eyes. "I love you, Anna."

Only the slight widening of her eyes gave indication she heard.

He took a deep breath. "I didn't intend to fall in love. You're too young. Then there's school. I was afraid of you, so I courted your sister."

"Afraid?" Anna shook her head. "I don't understand."

"When you love someone and lose them, it hurts—more than you can imagine. That's what happened with my family. I didn't know if I could go through that again. What if I lost you? Then I realized my error when I saw you with Garrick. I'd already lost you. I tried to tell Garrick Kathleen loved him, but he wouldn't listen. Then he got hurt."

Anna rubbed her forehead. "Aren't you in love with Kathleen?"

He shook his head. "No, Anna. I fell in love with a little tomboy. My love is for all time, whether you are mine for one day or for the next sixty years."

He released her hand and stepped back. "I wanted you to know how I feel about you. I know you can't marry me now. I'm willing to wait, but there's no other girl who can ever take your place in my heart. When you finish school, if you haven't found someone else, I'd like the chance to court you. I understand if you don't love me."

Jeremiah swallowed the lump in his throat. He'd laid everything out before her and had nothing more to say. He walked out the open door.

"Tuck." Anna's sweet voice followed him.

He stopped but didn't look back.

"I'll be eighteen in two weeks. I'm not a child."

Jeremiah took a ragged breath. Still he didn't turn. "What about school?"

"I'm not leaving."

At her touch on his arm, he turned and searched her face.

"I've talked to Papa. He never really wanted me to go. It was Mama's idea."

Jeremiah grabbed her hand, and with his heart pounding the rhythm of his love, he knelt before her in front of anyone who wanted to see. "I love you, Anna. Can you find it in your heart to care even a little for me? Will you marry me?"

On the fringes of her vision, Anna saw people standing in the hallway, making a semicircle around them, but she couldn't tear her gaze from the insecurity in Jeremiah's eyes. He truly loved her. Not Kathleen, but her. She laughed, and her feet bounced as she tugged at him to stand.

"Yes!" As quickly as he rose, she threw her arms around his neck. "Yes of course, I love you. I'll marry you, and don't you dare back down."

"Never." His voice choked on the one word. His cheek touched hers as applause filled the hall where they stood.

Anna released her hold and turned with Jeremiah to see Larkin standing in front of a group of their friends, her lips curved in a smile. Garrick sat behind them with Kathleen by his side. All smiled and clapped their approval then surrounded them, offering congratulations.

Jeremiah took Anna's hand. "This isn't official without your father's blessing."

"Then I suggest you ask now." Papa pushed through and shook Jeremiah's hand. "You know, I don't think this is right. A father shouldn't lose both his girls in the same night."

"Garrick and Kathleen?" Anna bounced inside.

Papa nodded. "Yes, and now you." He turned to Mama. "What do you think about this?"

Anna held her breath when Mama looked from her to Jeremiah. Finally, she shrugged. "Just one question. Are you sure you want this tomboy?"

Jeremiah threw back his head and laughed. He pulled Anna close and looked into her eyes. "Oh yes. I'm positive."

Mama smiled. "Then you have my blessing as well. When do you plan to marry?"

Jeremiah raised his eyebrows in a question. "Before spring planting?"

Anna looked toward her sister. "Maybe we could have a double wedding."

Kathleen stepped close and hugged Anna. "Garrick says he plans to walk before we marry, so we are thinking about March."

Anna laughed. "That's perfect. We'll be married in March and everyone's invited. We'll have the biggest wedding Tumwater has ever seen."

She turned to Jeremiah as he lowered his head to cover her lips in the first of what she hoped would be many kisses.

Mildred Colvin is a native Missourian with three children, one son-in-law, and three grandchildren. She and her husband spent most of their married life providing a home for foster children but now enjoy babysitting the grandchildren. Mildred writes inspirational romance novels because in them the truth of God's presence, even in the midst of trouble, can be portrayed. Her desire is to continue writing stories that uplift and encourage.

One Evergreen Night

Debby Lee

Dedication

This is dedicated to my mom, who has helped me along the way; to my dad, who helped me with the technical stuff in the story; to my husband, Steve, and my five children for putting up with me; to my four classmates and friends, Jeff Pratt, Nick Sorensen, Steven Stover, and Del Ray "Buzzy" Hughes, for giving me this idea; to Mr. Hoglund, my high school English teacher, who was the first one who thought I could write a book; to my friends at Crossroads Church who prayed for me and helped me discover God's calling on my life; and last but not least, to my Savior, Jesus Christ, for not giving up on me.

Except the LORD build the house,
they labour in vain that build it.
PSALM 127:1

Chapter 1

Washington Territory, September 1889

Frederick Corrigan piled firewood into the furnace of the locomotive. The rattletrap he'd given the pet name Inferno swayed violently from side to side as it careened down the hill. Frederick braced his hands against the walls and struggled to remain in a standing position. At the speed the train was going, he would have no time to jump if it derailed.

Steam poured from the engine. Frederick's chest ached as he sucked the sweltering air into his lungs. The furnace door burned red hot and could potentially explode from the pressure at any moment, but getting the load of logs to the mill on time was crucial. His job depended on his ability to deliver the timber as quickly as possible.

When he reached the bottom of the steep slope, Frederick pulled hard on the brake lever in order to round Widow's Bend looming ahead. The brakes protested with a grinding shriek. The screech of the wheels pierced his eardrums with a painful force. Sparks flew from the wheels that gripped the flimsy rails. *Lord, let the tracks be stable.* The corner approached with frightening speed. He was going too fast. . .again.

As the landscape alongside the tracks flew past with a blur, Frederick held his breath. He stood frozen for what felt like eternity.

"Turn. . .turn," he whispered, prayed. He leaned opposite of the turn. His two hundred pounds wouldn't make a difference in a true emergency, but the action made him feel better. For a brief moment, he thought he felt the wheels lift from the tracks. He white-knuckled the sides of the car as if sheer force of will could push Inferno back onto the rails.

The rickety wheels somehow stayed on course. With the corner behind him Frederick relaxed his grip and breathed a little easier, especially since the path ahead was clear of animals. Such wasn't always the case. Derailing would surely curtail his chances of getting the promotion with Kenicky Logging, the company he worked for, and then where would he be?

The rolling hills of Tumwater came into view. Small farms where cattle grazed in green fields skirted the town. Farther down the line, he spotted several wooden structures clustered along Main Street. Few people were milling about the lively town he called home when he wasn't stuck up in the logging camp.

Clutching the throttle, Frederick checked the pressure gauges as a short wooden bridge approached. He gave a cursory glance behind him to check on the logs and make sure they were still on the flatcars. It was a wonder they were considering the way he drove, but he hadn't lost a load yet, and he didn't intend to.

The wheels rolled onto the bridge with a shaky bump and again Frederick held his breath. Pieces of twisted metal and broken railroad cars lay on both sides of the tracks in the creek below. Remnants of a recent crash that killed one of his coworkers, one of his friends. Frederick shuddered. *But for the grace of God. . .*

As Inferno rolled over the tracks, the wheels made an eerie *thumpity-thump*, drowning out the sound of rushing water in the creek. Slowly the locomotive passed over the bridge. Frederick relaxed when it was on solid ground on the other side.

He blew out a sigh of relief and mopped the sweat from his face with a red bandana. He was going to make it in one piece. The last guy who rode these rails wasn't as lucky, as evidenced by the wreckage behind him.

As the small businesses that dotted the landscape began to whip past his line of vision, Frederick applied the brake again. More sweat caused his hair to stick to his forehead. The noise made him want to cover his ears, but he had to keep his hands on the levers and his eyes on the gauges. Renier Lumber Company lay just ahead, and the team of men waited to take this load of logs and turn them into lumber.

Frederick pressed hard on the brake lever and steam poured from the locomotive. The heat caused his muscles to grow weak as he came to a stop at the loading dock of the mill. "Thank You, Lord," he whispered under his breath.

He climbed down the rough metal ladder. "Morning, E.V."

E.V. strode up and gave Frederick a slap on the back. "Looks like you had a good run there." He raked his fingers over what had to be at least three days' stubble on his chin. E.V. only shaved on Wednesdays and Sundays.

"Sure did." Frederick stood back and took a breather as E.V. pulled on a pair of worn leather work gloves and joined a team of men nearby.

Frederick couldn't help but feel pride in his accomplishment of getting the train safely to Tumwater. If all continued to go well, he just might get that promotion. If only the boss could overlook the recent loss of the previous engineer. The accident hadn't been Frederick's fault, but he felt somewhat responsible anyway. He should have been there that day.

"You all right?" E.V. asked with concern buzzing through his tone.

"Yeah, I'm fine. Let's get this thing unloaded so I can get back up to the landing and get another load." Frederick moved with precision, although his thoughts vacillated between a gnawing hunger to impress his boss; Albert, his coworker's widow with two fatherless children; and anxiety at his own father's home teetering toward the auction block.

"Shoo, shoo!" Emma Pearson charged after a rat, knocking over a wash bucket as she chased the vermin out of the bunkhouse. Once the rat darted into the woods, she halted her chase and paused to catch her breath. She looked over her shoulder into the open bunkhouse door. "Oh no," she groaned at the mess she'd created.

Getting the sheets off the beds, washed, and dried was proving to be much more work than she had originally anticipated. Nonetheless, the job had to be done before the men came back in from the woods, or she would be in a heap of trouble that night.

Muttering under her breath, she traipsed back inside. She picked up the water bucket and winced as the dirty soapy water sloshed on a recent burn she received while taking dinner rolls from the cookstove.

Emma hated living in the rough and dirty logging camp. The work was so hard and the conditions were so. . .primitive.

Mr. and Mrs. Wilkin were kind enough to offer her a loft in their cabin. The tiny room offered little privacy, but it held her most prized possession, her mother's dark green ball gown. The garment had frayed around the collar and sleeves over the years, but to Emma it was a dress fit for a fairy tale.

"Lord, I know Your Word says to be content in all circumstances, but this?" With no place to go and nobody to turn to for help, she gritted her teeth against the pain in her burned fingers and resigned herself to finishing the sheets. First she had to get a bucket of fresh water to replace the one she'd spilled.

"Stupid rat." Emma stomped down to the creek, her thoughts drifting in the direction of town and all the excitement going on there. Many of her friends were attending fancy parties at the Whitworth mansion, plays at the local theater, and a real church on Sunday mornings. If only she wasn't stuck in this isolated and dirty place. Immersed in her dreams of all the activity in town, the pain she felt in her burned fingers subsided.

About the time she unpinned the last sheet from the makeshift clothesline, the sound of the men arriving in camp brought her back to the present. Emma's older brother, Jake, sidled up to her, gave her a pat on the head, and then began gathering the clothespins. "You look like you've had a hard day," he said with a lopsided grin.

"Every day is a hard day," she replied, grimacing as the grin fell from his face like a giant oak crashing to the ground.

"I'm doing my best, sis, to support us."

With dark hair and dark eyes mirroring hers, he was the only living relative she had left in the world. She was glad he was home safe, at least for the night. "I know," she answered, "and I'm sorry for complaining."

"I start training for driving the loads into town tomorrow." Jake eyed her as if to gauge her reaction. "Frederick Corrigan has been kind enough to put in a good word for me and is willing to show me the ropes."

Emma tried to smile but couldn't, not any more than she could count on her burned fingers how many times a day she prayed for her brother's safety. From what she heard of Frederick Corrigan's driving, they could use the prayers tomorrow, and the days after to boot!

"Don't be angry, Emma. Compared to the job I'm doing now, it's twice the pay—"

"And five times the danger!" How could she make him understand that, after losing their parents, she couldn't bear to lose him, too?

"Fred is a good man. He's a skilled driver and will teach me well." Jake rambled on about Frederick Corrigan's proficiency, but few words soaked through the dry and brittle exterior of her heart. The company's driver took daring chances on the rails—chances she didn't want her brother taking.

"Emma, I need you to come and help me take up the potatoes, please." The voice of the camp's cook, Mrs. Wilkin, floated to Emma, drawing her from her thoughts.

"Go on, sis, I need to wash up." Jake strode to the creek. "I'll see you at dinner."

Emma quickly picked up the basket full of clean sheets. "Be right there," she called toward the kitchen. She hadn't taken more than two steps before she bumped into someone and nearly dropped the laundry basket. Clothespins fell to the ground and rolled every which way. Exasperation bubbled within her.

"Of all the—" Emma bit her lip to stifle the exclamations swirling in her head.

When she looked up, Frederick Corrigan stood blocking her path.

Chapter 2

"Afternoon, Miss Pearson." He tipped his hat and nodded.

Emma noted the twinkle in his sky blue eyes as he smiled down at her. What, pray tell, he had to smile about was beyond her. From what she heard, his father's house was in foreclosure and one of his lumberjack friends had just died in a horrible accident.

"Afternoon, Mr. Corrigan," Emma said, noting all too well the cold flatness in her voice. She had once thought him to be handsome and daring, but now that he had agreed to teach her brother—her only living kin—his reckless ways, she could only see him as a means to her brother's death.

"May I help you with that basket?" Mr. Corrigan reached for the load she carried, and she shied away from his touch.

"No, thank you, I can manage just fine on my own." Emma's curt words dripped with disdain.

"Since your brother will be riding with me, I would think we could at least be friends." He cracked a bright grin.

"I'm really very busy." Emma adjusted the basket on her hip and turned toward the bunkhouses. Since when would she like to be friends with the likes of this rough scoundrel?

"You don't approve of me, do you?" He stood in her path like a towering pine, with his hands on his hips. His eyes reminded Emma of the sky on a cloudless summer day, much as she hated to admit it.

"It isn't that I dislike you. I just don't care to see my brother taking the same reckless chances on the rails that you do."

He glared at her with stormy intensity. The eyes that were a lovely shade of blue only a moment ago now took on a thunderous darkening. "I'm the best engineer this company has, and I'll teach your brother well."

"I've no doubt you'll teach him to properly deliver the timber, but will you teach him to be safe? Speedy delivery didn't fare well for the last driver, now did it?" Emma didn't wish to be confrontational or tell Mr. Corrigan how to do his job, but the last thing she wanted was her brother becoming the next casualty in the logging camp.

He aimed an icy glare straight at her.

"Do you think I'd intentionally endanger another man's life?" Rage and hurt pride were evident on his tanned face. His nostrils flared and his jaw was set in hardened lines.

Emma sucked in her breath. Something in her gut coiled as the hair on the nape of her neck prickled. She had seen men angry like this before. If she lived to be a thousand years old, the sight would always trigger fear.

He sneered through clenched teeth. "I'll see to it your brother's kept safe." Without another word, he turned on his boot heel and stomped away, leaving a gasping Emma to cope with his blunt words.

"Emma Pearson is sure angry with me." Frederick spoke with E.V. the next morning at the sawmill. He could almost feel his blood heating in his veins. "She doesn't want me showing her brother the ropes of train engineering."

"Can you blame her?"

E.V.'s words gave Frederick pause, and he thought about Emma's situation. Having lost both her parents, she probably lived in daily fear of losing her brother, too. And with an engineer's recent death, her fears had to be multiplied.

Frederick shook his head. "No, it's dangerous work, much as I hate to admit it. I just wish she'd understand I'm not the daredevil she thinks I am."

Even though E.V. owned the sawmill and had his employees to do the grunt work, he pulled on a pair of leather gloves and began to help Frederick with the current load of logs. "Why don't you do something nice for her?"

"I don't want Miss Pearson thinking I'm sweet on her."

E.V.'s gaze shifted to the street where Larkin Whitworth exited the mercantile, holding boxes precariously balanced. "Doing something nice doesn't mean you have to start courting. See a need and then meet it." He dropped a log onto the pile then patted Frederick's back. "I'll catch up with you when you bring the next load in."

Frederick watched as E.V. ran across the street to the mercantile and helped Miss Whitworth with her packages. *See a need and then meet it.*

With that thought in mind, Frederick tromped back to Inferno and climbed aboard.

The afternoon went by with a blur, quite literally, as he sped back to the woods, refilled his string of flatcars with timber, and returned to Tumwater. This didn't allow for any time to check on Miss Pearson at camp, but it did allow for time to pray for compassion and insight as to what made Miss Pearson tick. She had to have some type of need.

Yet the only answer he heard from the Lord was *"Seek, and ye shall find."*

As Inferno's engine cooled from the day's frantic pace, Frederick pulled his red bandana from his trouser pocket and wiped his face. He climbed down, helped unload the logs, then headed down the street looking for a nice peace offering.

An hour later, with his nerves frayed at the edges, Frederick stomped down the wooden-planked boardwalk. Everything he "sought" had too high a price.

"I could use a little help here, Lord," he grumbled.

"Seek, and ye shall find."

Not sure where he was supposed to seek, Frederick stopped walking and looked around. Karl's Feed and Seed was the only business he hadn't visited. "All right, Lord, I'll keep seeking."

He hurried across the street. After entering Karl's, Frederick walked around, examining every shelf before roaming to the pens in the corner. Baby pigs rooted around and climbed over each other in an effort to get to the food plate. Two of the scrawnier ones looked up at him with big dark eyes.

"Just came in this morning," Karl called from the side counter where he scooped grain from a large bin into bags.

"Twelve, that's a good-sized litter."

"Thirteen, actually. I heard the runt in the litter had to be disposed of."

"That's too bad." Frederick studied the wiggling creatures.

Karl reached for some twine to tie off a full bag. "You heading back to camp tonight?"

"Yup—do you need me to do something?"

Karl walked to him, carrying a gunnysack. "Johnny isn't back from the last delivery, and I have all these customers. Could you take this watering can to Mrs. Wilkin? She ordered it awhile back for her chickens and it just arrived."

"Sure thing." Frederick took the sack, slung it over his shoulder, and headed out the door. Within minutes, he and Inferno were on the rails again. His father's house was still in foreclosure, Miss Pearson still hated him, and the guilt he felt every time he saw the bridge continued to grow. As the bridge approached, Frederick slowed the locomotive in an effort to be extra cautious.

"Lord, I pray You'll take Albert's family by the hand and walk with them through the valley of the shadow of death. Give them a comfort that only You can bring."

When God's peace washed over him, he glanced over the bridge. *What in creation?*

He leaned far out the locomotive's window to get a better view. A tiny pink piglet clung to the wreckage. Probably the runt piglet Karl had mentioned. The water was plenty cold for late September.

Frederick jerked Inferno to a stop. He climbed down and slowly made his way to the riverbank. With great care, he maneuvered across the wreckage and managed to grab the creature by the head and pull it from the icy water.

The piglet protested at this treatment with a series of ear-piercing squeals and wiggled with more force than what Frederick thought possible.

Climbing back up the ravine to the train, Frederick bundled

the piglet inside his wool coat. He whistled a lullaby all the way back to where Inferno was parked on the tracks in hopes the tune would help calm the squirming animal. Once they were back inside the train, Frederick pulled the watering can out of the gunnysack.

"Not sure why I saved you. All you're good for is a few strips of bacon," he said, wrapping the squirming piglet in the gunnysack. He placed it in the kindling bucket. "Can't have you falling out on the way home."

The piglet lay down, content.

Frederick grinned as he fired up the locomotive and headed off in the direction of camp. Large, fat raindrops descended from the gray sky. He needed to hightail it home. The rails were a temperamental part of logging equipment, as moody and unpredictable as a woman scorned. He shuddered, thinking of Widow's Bend. The curve of slippery metal lay only a few miles ahead.

Chapter 3

Weary of life in the primitive logging camp, a determined Emma would use any excuse she could to go into town. Now if only such an excuse would present itself.

She sat a few feet from the kitchen door and plucked another feather off the chicken. Cooking was a dirty job and not in her normal duties, but when Mrs. Wilkin ran behind schedule, she needed Emma's help. It was difficult, to say the least, keeping up with the appetites of the hordes of hardworking lumberjacks.

Ridding the deceased poultry of their feathers was a job she especially disliked, but a job she had to do for dinner. The dead birds stunk to high heaven, causing her to gag. She considered lighting a match to get rid of the smell, but the wet feathers stuck to her fingers with frustrating tenacity and would make lighting matches difficult at best.

Finished with the second bird, she grabbed the next one in line, submerged it in scalding water, and yanked at feathers till her forearms ached. She tried not to look at the pen containing nine more waiting their turn for a neck wringing and a dunk in the boiling pot.

Emma longed for her quiet time after dinner when the washed

dishes were put away for the night. Then she could crawl into a hot tub of water. If only she had some dried rose petals to take away the stench of dead chicken. Resigned to her duty, she focused on the only thing she could make a difference in—praying for her brother's safety.

"Lord, please protect Jake from danger—and Mr. Corrigan, too," she added for good measure, hoping God would hear her prayers. A decent and worthy way to pass the time even though, in her opinion, prayers hadn't done much good for her mother, who had been left to support two children after their father had died. Warm clothing had been scarce in cold winter months, not that they had any finer clothing in the summer. She remembered frequent hunger, but Mama had always prayed before every meal, no matter how meager it might be.

"Oh Mama." With tears pooling in her eyes, Emma pulled in a ragged breath of air. "I wish you were here."

"Emma, could you come in here, please?" Mrs. Wilkin called out the kitchen door.

"Be right there." Emma dropped the half-plucked bird and strode toward the small but sufficient kitchen.

"Mr. Corrigan would like to speak to you." Mrs. Wilkin jerked her thumb at Frederick Corrigan, standing in the corner with his arms folded across his barrel chest. "I'll attend to the chickens." She walked outside carrying what looked like a shiny new watering can.

Mr. Corrigan pointed to a little wiener pig rooting through the rancid garbage pail in the corner. As small as the creature was, it had no difficulty in tipping over the bucket and spilling the contents onto the floor. Another mess for her to have to clean.

"Would you accept my peace offering?" Mr. Corrigan had a cheesy grin plastered on his face, as if he expected praise for the "offering." "I thought you could raise him for a while and then we'd butcher him when the time was right. Or you could sell him."

Emma stood speechless.

The piglet lifted its nose and looked her way. Brown smelly gunk covered its tiny snout. It eyed her with what had to be curiosity and sniffed.

"Um, thank you." Emma raised her eyebrows and hoped it was enough of a response. What else could she say? No one had given her a gift in years. While it wasn't rose petals, she supposed it was still sweet of him.

"Go say hello, Bacon," Mr. Corrigan chided. He gave the piglet a tap on his two-strips-of-bacon belly. Much to Emma's horror, the animal let out an ear-piercing squeal and limped straight toward her.

The locomotive's wheels rolled along to the tune of a well-oiled machine. Frederick stood next to Jake Pearson, ready to take control of Inferno in case an emergency arose. He hoped things would continue to run with smooth efficiency. After a week of intense training, Jake had done quite well. He hadn't even been intimidated rounding Widow's Bend. Fear could be as dangerous as rain on the rails. But then, so could cockiness.

As the landscape passed during a straightaway, Frederick asked Jake how his sister and Bacon were getting on.

"She was busy with dishes last time I seen her and didn't say much about it." When Jake didn't say more, Frederick decided to let the matter go.

But he couldn't forget about it, about Miss Pearson. There was something about her that kept invading his thoughts. He wanted to know more about her. He wanted to convince her he'd keep her brother safe. He wanted to see her smile.

The locomotive rolled over the bridge leading into town. Just a few more miles to go and then another few dollars would be added to the precious hoard in the bank. Dollars meant for saving his father's house in town.

Much to Frederick's chagrin, Jake piled more wood into the furnace. An uneasy feeling did a slow roll in Frederick's gut. In almost no time, the train picked up speed.

"I know you're getting good at managing the engine," Frederick warned the greenhorn, "but its best not to get too cocky with the rails."

"I've got control over this thing!" Jake shouted above the racket of the locomotive. He seemed quite confident in his abilities.

Frederick wished he could say the same. Anxiety and a rising anger twisted around his heart.

"We're going fast enough!" he yelled back. He braced himself against the wall of the car as it rocked and swayed. He knew how to handle Inferno at that speed, but Jake didn't have enough experience yet.

Images of Miss Pearson flooded Frederick's thoughts. If her brother died on the rails, she'd never forgive him, and Frederick doubted he'd ever forgive himself either. And he wasn't about to have another accident like the one that killed his good friend. No. Not on his watch. Miss Pearson would survive if he died, but she'd never recover from the loss if anything happened to her brother.

He pushed himself off the wall and grabbed Jake's arm. "Jake, put the brakes on," he ordered. They were approaching the mill with unsettling speed. Sweat beaded on Frederick's forehead, and not just from the heat. "Do it, or this thing will jump the tracks when we get to the end of the line at the sawmill."

"I've got it. Back off, will ya?" Jake hollered at Frederick and gave him a rough shove to the side. "I need to learn how to do this so I can take care of my sister."

"You can't take care of her if you're dead," Frederick bellowed.

Jake pushed him again. "I'm going to make more money at this than you do and give her all the pretty things she deserves."

Frederick would have loved to debate the issue, but time was of the essence. He wrestled the controls from Jake and shoved him up against the wall of the locomotive. "Until you've proven yourself, this is *my* train. Now step aside or you'll be back logging trees." He released Jake and focused on the tracks in front of him.

The mill up ahead loomed closer still. If he didn't slow Inferno down, they'd crash into it. He didn't want to think of the number of possible deaths.

"Think of your sister, for pity's sake!" Frederick reproved.

For what seemed like an eternity in slow motion, Frederick pulled hard on the brake lever. Jake slumped against the wall and sneered at Frederick with a red face and fists clenched at his sides. Frederick didn't care. He wasn't about to have another casualty on the roster of Kenicky Logging.

Bacon squealed with the force of a lumberjack yelling "timber" as Emma bathed the gunk from his body in the creek. Careful inspection of his back legs explained why he had been rejected by his owner. The left leg was stunted and twisted at an odd angle, making it difficult for him to move easily.

Emma ran her hands over the disfigured part of Bacon's body. If anyone understood the pain of being small in a big world without a mother, it was she. No wonder the poor thing squealed all the time. Tenderly, she wrapped a towel around him then held him close so he could get warm.

An hour later, while sitting outside the cookhouse shucking corn for the evening meal, Emma eyed her new wiener pig. Wariness and caution sat on one end of her heart's seesaw while pity and protectiveness balanced on the other. He was a cute little creature, even if he was from Frederick Corrigan.

A pig as a peace offering. A new hat or a bouquet of flowers or even material for a new dress would have bought her more pleasure, but the strangeness of the gift actually brought a curve to her lips.

Bacon let out a squeal, and Emma looked down in time to see a rat scurry past them. The piglet loped inside with as much speed as he could muster and hid behind the woodbox in the corner. Emma laughed so hard the shucked corn dropped to the ground. Whoever heard of a wiener pig being afraid of a rat?

When she regained her composure, she moved to comfort the poor thing.

"It's all right, Bacon. A rat's nothing to be afraid of. I'll protect you," she soothed as she squatted in front of the woodbox. She reached behind it and grabbed the squirming creature, pulling him out from his hiding spot. Not caring who might see them, she cradled him close. He let out a few grunts and rubbed his wet snout against her neck. It tickled, and she couldn't help but laugh and squirm.

"What's so funny?" Mrs. Wilkin asked as she strolled into the kitchen. "That little pig Frederick got you causing a stir?" She chuckled and set about peeling potatoes.

"I think he's starting to grow on me," Emma replied. A quick shudder went through her. What would Miss Abigail Fancy Pants say about her having a pet pig? She pulled Bacon closer and kissed the top of his soft head. The Bible said all creatures needed loving-kindness, especially the motherless ones. A determined Emma decided to give that to Bacon.

"Emma, could you please finish shucking the corn? It's getting late." Mrs. Wilkin's voice rose above the noise of a few men who were trickling in a little early, to Emma's surprise. "I'm going to stoke more wood on the fire."

While Mrs. Wilkin hustled into action, Emma set Bacon on the floor and resumed work.

She hadn't been shucking corn for more than a few minutes when one of the men came running up to her. The expression on his face spelled disaster, eerily reminiscent of when Jake told her their mother had died. Was her brother dead now, too? Why else would the men come in early?

Chapter 4

After the close call they had at Renier Lumber Company that morning, Frederick and Jake had gotten into a fistfight. Now Frederick's hands were bruised and burns covered his forearms from where he fell against the hot furnace. He sat in the bunkhouse and winced in pain while the doctor examined his wounds. Jake glared at him while waiting his turn to be seen for his apparently broken fingers.

Frederick cast his gaze at the floor. How could he make Jake understand that he cared for his sister a great deal and wished to see her at peace about their job?

Groaning with frustration as the doctor finished, Frederick stomped from the room. Perhaps a walk would do him some good. He wandered down the path that led to the creek. The water rippled over the moss-covered rocks with bubbly enthusiasm. Dipping his hands into the cool refreshing stream, Frederick splashed water over his arms and sighed at the relief. He lifted a drink to his mouth. The cold liquid felt good going down his parched throat. He never failed to appreciate how refreshing it was after a day of slaving over a blazing furnace.

When the ache in his fingers subsided to a dull throb, he stood and walked farther into the mass of towering trees. A few birds called to one another against the distant grating of the bucksaws. Before long the rest of the crew would come in for the night. It was moments like this that Frederick loved.

The buckers might need some extra help—that is, when his hands were healed properly. The pay was just as good as driving Inferno and would provide a way for him to get away from Jake Pearson and his sister. If he volunteered for the most dangerous job, he could make money that much faster.

Frederick ventured with care over fallen dead logs and through blackberry brambles, closer to the sounds of the bucksaw. No wonder the lumberjacks enjoyed their work. Here in the midst of God's handiwork, peace and tranquility permeated the air. He should fit right in, or so he thought.

A sharp, loud crack split the silence like a jagged bolt of lightning. Frederick jumped. A tree was falling. The swishing of tree limbs was followed by a long drawn-out "Tiiiimmmbbbeeerrr!"

With a rapid glance to his left and then to his right, Frederick had little time for making an assessment as to which direction was safest. Additional creaks and groans from the monumental tree reverberated throughout the forest.

"Lord God, protect me." A prayer uttered out of sheer desperation.

Looking up to the top of the hill, Frederick spotted the crew scrambling to the left. He quickly followed suit, leaping over sword ferns, clawing his way through blackberry brambles, and digging through the dirt on his hands and knees. God forbid one of those towering pines came down on him. It would squish him flatter than a pancake.

No more than a few seconds had elapsed when he heard a thundering boom followed by squawking of birds and the shattering of tree limbs. The tree had landed. Shouts filled the air as Mr. Wilkin, the crew boss, called to check on everyone's well-being.

A voice cut through the chaos. "Look out! That widow-maker's coming down, too!" The racket of creaking, crunching, and the splintering of wood grew louder and more menacing. Observing the mass of timber above him moving to the right, common sense told Frederick to run to the left. He sprinted as fast as his legs and the terrain would allow, stumbling and panting with every step. He didn't know much about falling timber, but he had enough sense to know that he had get out of the way.

Frederick could see that it was going to be a close race for his life.

Emma swept the bunkhouse for the tenth time and filled the woodbox for the old stove. The nights were getting so cold, and she pitied the men sleeping in these damp and freezing quarters. That included her brother. And it was only early October. How much colder would it get in January? Oh, if only they could leave.

An argument just outside the bunkhouse caught her attention. From what she heard, Frederick Corrigan had nearly been killed by a falling tree!

Emma clasped her hand over her mouth. What, pray tell, was he doing traipsing through the woods? He had to have known how unsafe that was. Mr. Wilkin was arguing with a man, and Emma decided to investigate.

"You need to be more careful when you're felling timber, especially widow-makers!" Mr. Wilkin's face was red. "Corrigan could have been killed."

"I'm fine." Mr. Corrigan rubbed the back of his neck.

She took a step back in surprise. He didn't look fine—he looked as if he were going to topple over any minute. Couldn't the other men see he was in no condition to stand outside arguing about whose fault it was?

"He should have never been out there anyway!"

"I hate to say it, but he's right, Corrigan. Stanley, just try to be more careful," a calmer Mr. Wilkin said.

Emma was quite surprised to see that the boss's son was the one arguing with Mr. Wilkin. Stanley Kenicky, not a day over twenty-one, lugged at least that many extra pounds around his thick middle.

"You can forget working in the woods, Corrigan." Stanley jabbed his finger in Frederick's direction. "I'll see to that."

Frederick stepped forward, but Mr. Wilkin held him back.

Emma drew back against the door and tried to keep from trembling.

"Don't worry about this, Miss Pearson," Stanley said. "You go back inside now."

The condescending tone of his voice made Emma shift from one foot to the other with mounting discomfort. He didn't seem like a pleasant person to work with. She felt sorry for the cutting crew. She turned and headed back into the bunkhouse. The sound of arguing filled her ears as she went.

Frederick lay propped up in bed and grumbled at the bandages the doctor placed on his hands all the way up to each elbow. No thanks to Stanley Kenicky, they were now scratched and bleeding besides burned and bruised. His head ached horribly, and he had lost his chance to work in the woods.

He needed to get back to work. Not only did he need the money, but Jake was placed in charge of training another new man how to drive Inferno. That was a recipe for disaster. Jake was nothing but a greenhorn himself and not in any position to be training anybody in how to get the timber to the mills.

And what about his father's house? Frederick should take some time to visit the aging man, but couldn't afford to take time off work. His body could heal just as well at the helm of Inferno as it could lying around.

Heaving himself up and off the bed, he wobbled as his head swam.

"Frederick Corrigan, shouldn't you be resting?" Miss Pearson set a tray on the table, hurried to him, and grabbed him around the waist. Even in his wounded condition, it felt good. Her touch was something he could definitely get used to.

For the past three days after Frederick Corrigan's near brush with death, Emma had wrestled against pity knotting in her stomach for him. He had been nearly crushed by a widow-maker, but insisted on doing as much for himself as possible.

"Here, Mr. Corrigan, why don't you lie down? I've brought you some food." Emma advanced toward him, carrying a tray. The aroma of the fresh meal wafted upwards and it smelled delicious. Corn and potato chowder—his favorite—along with some fresh-baked bread and a cup of coffee.

"Thank you, Miss Pearson." He grimaced as he looked at her. His stomach growled loud enough for her to hear.

She stifled a giggle. "Sounds like you're hungry." She handed him the napkin.

He took the cloth and tucked it around his neck. He reached for the bowl of steaming chowder and began to eat.

"Mind if I keep you company?" she asked.

"Not at all." A bit dribbled down his chin.

This time she couldn't help but giggle out loud. "It's not easy eating with thick bandages from fingertips to forearms. Allow me to help you, and please, Mr. Corrigan, call me Emma." She helped him hold the spoon in his hand so he wouldn't drop it. He spooned a few more bites into his mouth before he replied.

"Pleased to have your company, Emma. You can call me Frederick if you like." A genuine grin curved across his tanned features and caused Emma's heart to jerk and skip a beat.

"Thank you, Frederick." Heat rose to her face as if she were standing in front of a blazing hot stove. "I'm glad you weren't hurt too terribly bad, and I'm glad you're on the mend."

She sounded like a giddy schoolgirl. She ducked her head with embarrassment. Several quiet moments elapsed as Frederick polished off his bowl of chowder.

"That was delicious."

"It's my mother's recipe. She made it often when Jake and I were small." Emma shifted in her seat with nervous energy. She was sorry they had gotten off on the wrong foot and wished she hadn't said such horrible things to him.

"I'm sorry for the terrible things I said to you, Frederick. I know they wounded you deeply. Please forgive me."

Frederick gazed at her with uncertainty written in his expression. His eyes were so incredibly blue, and she gazed into them, into his very soul. Could he see the longing in her eyes? Momentarily startled, she wondered where that longing had come from.

"It's all forgiven, Miss Pear—um, Emma. Don't you worry your pretty little head about a thing." Frederick cleared his throat once and then again a second time. He reached for his coffee and took a long slow drink. "And would you please forgive me for the things I said to you?"

Emma's cheeks grew even warmer. She fanned her face with the hem of her apron and gasped to catch her breath. She desperately wanted to believe him.

Time and again she had seen her stepfather say he was sorry only to imbibe again and again. And in the dark of night he slunk home to take his rage out on her mother while Emma cowered under her blanket. She'd rather be boiled in hot laundry water than make the same mistakes as Mama. It was best if she just left and didn't get attached.

"All is forgiven, Frederick. I'll take those dishes to the kitchen now if you don't mind. I've work to do before the men come from the woods." She grabbed the tray and hurried from the room. Experience had taught her well the dangers of trusting daring men who said they were sorry for their heedlessness.

Chapter 5

Several days later, with his hands and forearms mostly healed, Frederick stood on board Inferno with Jake Pearson and Stanley Kenicky. He struggled to move within the crowded space. Jake was stoking the engine with his usual arrogance, while Stanley looked ready to jump off before the train had a chance to move.

The company was in the process of acquiring a new locomotive to replace the one that had gone over the bridge and crashed. At least one more engineer was needed to run it, and Stanley's father had decided that Stanley was ready for the job.

"Nothing to worry about, kid," Jake said. "Just keep the fires burning hot and know when to use the brakes." He gave the young man a slap on the back and then threw more wood into the furnace.

Stanley looked even paler than a moment ago.

Frederick groaned. It was going to be a long day. Jake had done well learning to use the brakes and the furnace. The problem was that he hadn't learned to use them at the appropriate times. Frederick hoped to get a moment alone with Jake and ask him about his sister. He wanted to spend more time with her and become a true friend.

The furnace grew hot as the locomotive picked up speed.

"I think I'll be spending the afternoon in town running some errands for Father," Stanley stammered as he cowered against the wall. Frederick wondered about the truthfulness of his statement but wasn't about to question it. Grateful for the opportunity to have Stanley gone, he hoped to speak with Jake alone.

The locomotive rolled along the tracks at a normal speed. "We're doing real well, boys. Let's not get carried away." Frederick didn't want Stanley reporting to his father that they were reckless engineers.

"If I've said it once, I've said it a hundred times," he reiterated, wishing he could toss Jake from the engine. "You need to watch the speed and not get rolling faster than what the brakes can handle."

The temperature rose within the small quarters of the engine car and sweat blurred Frederick's vision. Widow's Bend approached.

"We're going too fast!" Stanley screamed, white-knuckling the side of the locomotive.

"We can handle this just fine!" Jake shouted.

"Just hang on. Don't worry, she always leans a little," Frederick instructed. Wheels screeched as the engine rounded the most dangerous part of the bend and lifted.

"Lean this way!" Frederick yelled.

Emma jumped up and down with excitement at the chance to go into town and do some shopping. Counting her meager savings, she prayed for money enough to purchase some lace or new buttons for her mother's green dress. Christmas was coming up, as well as a number of parties to celebrate Washington being signed into the Union. She needed time to sew something pretty to the gown.

"Let's go, Emma," Mr. Kenicky hollered above the noise of the company's new locomotive. It was good to see that the company had replaced the one that had plunged off a bridge a few weeks ago. This one had a few seats for passengers, unlike the one that crashed and left one train engineer dead. If only she could do something to help the widow and her children. Knowing the deceased man had been Frederick's friend, Emma made a mental note to add the family to her list of folks to pray for.

Hustling to the train, Emma took care while boarding to not get her best dress dirty. Mrs. Wilkin had decided to join them, so squeezing into the small space wasn't an easy feat. Emma didn't wish to rub against something that would turn her pale blue dress a horrid shade of charcoal black.

Mr. Kenicky, who also happened to be a skilled engineer, piled wood into the furnace and soon the wheels turned round and round along the tracks. Emma squirmed like a child in church the entire way. It soon grew hot in the car, but not any hotter than standing in front of a mammoth caldron of boiling wash water.

Mr. Kenicky was a cautious driver, and Emma didn't flinch in the slightest as the train rounded Widow's Bend. If anything, she enjoyed the gentle breeze that wafted into the car and cooled her flushed face.

The town's buildings soon came into view. Emma craned her neck to soak up every image she could. Three new stores and a large barn had been built on the end of one very long street. She could hardly wait to browse through each one of them.

The engine's whistle blew, startling her. She covered her ears, and the brakes screeched as if in protest. Once the train had rolled to a stop, Emma all but leapt from the locomotive.

"I'll be back in time to ride home for dinner." She waved a hand over her shoulder and rushed toward the nearest mercantile.

Strolling up and down the aisles, Emma rubbed her fingers over one bolt of fabric after another. Soft cotton, crisp taffeta, and smooth cool silks all cried out to be sewn into something beautiful, but they were out of her means. Even so, she could hardly wait to get back to camp and make use of her needle and thread.

"Oh, how are you today, Miss Pearson?" Abigail Leonard waltzed down the fabric aisle as if she clung to the arm of a prince of England. "I hear you have a pig for a pet, and a beau." Abigail's cackling echoed off the walls of the store and sank deep into Emma's heart.

"I don't have a beau."

"Oh, no? I hear you're sweet on Frederick Corrigan, and he's sweet on you." Abigail jutted her chin in the air. To Emma, the haughty girl's ruddy cheeks belied a look of pea green jealousy.

"You're wrong. Now, please just let me be," Emma snapped as she turned on her heel and stomped away. The Wilkins were such a great family, Emma couldn't figure out how their youngest daughter, Anna, could be friends with Abigail.

As she walked away from the sneering girl, a bolt of fine imported material all but leaped out at Emma. A gasp escaped her lips, followed by a soft groan of disappointment. She caressed the fabric that would never be hers, and then she jerked her fingers back as if she'd touched a rat. No sense in dreaming over something she couldn't afford. Her complaints to Jake about the drudgery of her job came back to her in a rush.

Emma wandered through the mercantile with twinges of guilt following close behind her. She shouldn't be putting so much pressure on Jake to make more money. No wonder he worked so hard. She decided to forego a dress for herself and make him a nice shirt instead. She could afford the material, and she'd pull some buttons off an old shirt to finish it.

Moving farther down the aisle, her eyes fell on a cream-colored spool of eyelet lace. It equaled in softness the finest dress she'd ever owned. She could use it to patch a few worn spots on her mother's dress and wear it to the Christmas Eve service. But she didn't have the money to buy both the lace and the shirt material.

No matter. Jake deserved a new shirt for taking such good care of her. Emma moved past the expensive dress material and the lace and proceeded to the counter.

She pulled several coins from her reticule. "I need a few yards of that new green plaid flannel, if you please."

"Yes, of course," the clerk replied, and went to retrieve her supplies. He returned a few minutes later and tallied up her purchase. Emma paid the man and was about to gather up her package when she heard an unfamiliar voice behind her.

"Why, you're Emma Pearson, aren't you? Jake's younger sister."

The hair on the back of Emma's neck bristled and her hands grew cold and clammy. She made a slow turn on her heel to gaze at a leering Stanley Kenicky.

"Good afternoon." Emma tried to keep her voice from quavering, and failed.

"Did you hear? Dad's gonna give me a job running the rails

on the new train."

"Oh." It was all Emma could think of to say. She was getting an eerie feeling deep in her stomach from the way he looked at her.

"I've seen you cleaning for the crew, helping out Mrs. Wilkin, and hanging around Frederick Corrigan."

A small gasp flew from Emma's lips. *What's he doing watching my every move?* She had to get away from this man.

"If you'll excuse me." Emma clutched her package and fled from the store.

"I'll be seeing you around, you can be sure of that, Miss Pearson." Stanley's laughter echoed behind her, but she dared not turn and give him the pleasure of knowing how much he unnerved her.

Chapter 6

The early November morning had dawned crisp and clear while Inferno rolled along the tracks. Much to Frederick's relief, Jake began to show some signs of restraint and care when it came to running the rails.

"So how is Miss Emma today?" Frederick held his hands close to the furnace to warm them against the chilly air.

"She's doing fine. She's all excited about the territory becoming a state. Been sewing on one of our mother's dresses, trying to patch it, for the occasion." Jake's hand rested on the brake lever, ready for any emergency, or so Frederick hoped.

"Er, Jake." Frederick paused and cleared his throat. "I'd like to escort your sister to the Christmas Eve service, with your blessing of course." There. He'd said it. He rubbed his hands together and then held them to his face for warmth.

"That'd be fine with me. I know you're a good man, Fred, but it's up to Emma, and she's real cautious with gentlemen."

"I see." Frederick noted the expression on Jake's face. Not used to seeing the man so serious, he raised his eyebrows and almost questioned Jake further, but then thought it best not to pry.

Perhaps a man had broken her heart in the past. But plenty of women had been spurned and went on to love again. There had to be another, more deeply rooted reason for her feelings.

The lumber mill came into view and Jake put the brakes on. When they stopped, Jake climbed down ahead of Frederick.

"I've got some business in town. I'll wait for your next trip and catch a ride home with you then," Jake called over his shoulder as he walked toward town.

"Sounds good, enjoy your lunch." Frederick waved then helped the sawmill crew unload the logs from the flatcars. He was soon on his way back to the camp, with images of Emma dancing in his head like tree branches in a gentle breeze.

"Lord, why am I thinking about her so much?" Frederick shook his head. He probably shouldn't have given her a pig for a gift. Of course he cared for her, but he was loath to admit he was falling in love, because he wasn't. At least that's what he kept telling himself.

The sound of a loud pop and then a hiss brought Frederick back to the present. Another hose had burst, and now he'd have to stop and repair it. He slapped the side of the engine then applied the brakes. Time was money on the rails, and he growled at having to stop.

An hour went by as Frederick removed the bad hose with his pocket knife and installed the new one. It wasn't a perfect fit, but with some extra twine tied and twisted here and there, he made it work. Such was life in the logging business. Men made do with what they had and learned to think on their feet.

"Thank You, Lord," Frederick murmured. At least the hose had been to something else and not the brakes. "Now back to work."

Two miles passed by uneventfully and Frederick began to

breathe peacefully again. He could go extra fast and try to make up for lost time, but after some thought he decided against it. His hand clutched at the brake lever when a doe and her fawn leapt across the tracks. He relaxed his grip as they cleared the rails with mere seconds to spare. The last thing he wanted was to stop yet again.

Frederick's eyes scanned the tracks ahead, wary of anything else that could slow his trip back to the mill.

About a mile ahead, he spied a downed tree trunk lying across the tracks. "Lord, no!" He groaned and kicked the furnace so hard his foot hurt.

Emma sewed with frantic speed on Jake's shirt. She had gotten up a little earlier to have a few precious minutes to work on it before beginning her duties for the day. Thankfully, it was nearly done. All she had left was the buttons, and he'd have something nice to wear for Christmas. Bacon interrupted her thoughts as he trotted in from outside. She pulled him close to her chest and hugged him so hard he squealed.

"I'm sorry, little friend. I didn't mean to hurt you." She stroked the top of his head and Bacon looked up at her with dark eyes and grunted as if he actually understood. He had grown in the six weeks or so since Frederick had brought him to her. In another few months he might live up to his name and be on the breakfast table as opposed to cuddled in her arms. A part of her wanted to shove him away and not allow her heart to love him, but there was something about this motherless creature that nobody but her seemed to care about. Whether she willed it or not, he was winning her love.

After setting Bacon on the floor to root around, Emma finished two buttons on her brother's shirt. She would have to wait until the next day before it was finished. She tucked it in her sewing basket then swept the bunkhouse, carted fresh water up from the stream, and tended to the many other duties of her job.

The cold afternoon drifted by as she filled the woodboxes and dried the dishes for Mrs. Wilkin. She ironed Jake's Sunday clothes and lugged water from the creek for Mrs. Wilkin to cook supper with.

"Emma, where are you?" Jake's voice carried down to her as she was fetching another bucket of water from the stream.

"Down here, Jake." Emma lugged the bucket along as fast as the awkward load allowed. Much to her relief, Jake quickly came alongside her and took the pail from her hands. It warmed her heart to know how protective her older brother was of her. She was glad she had decided to make him something nice for the holidays.

"You've been working hard, sis. Abigail told me in town that she saw you and Stanley talking at the mercantile last week. Anything I should know about?" Jake asked like it was the simplest thing in the world to answer.

"Why, I'm sure I don't know what you mean." Emma's feelings vacillated. She wanted to be honest but feared the repercussions if she told him everything. She didn't want to tell her brother about Abigail's snooty comments or Stanley's creepy remarks.

"I heard Abigail flirting with Stanley." Jake's face turned into a thunderous cloud of angry emotion. "She told me you were doing the same, with Stanley and with Frederick. Try as I might, I can't make myself believe that."

"What? That's not true, Jake. You know I'm not like that!" Emma gasped and clutched handfuls of her skirt in her fists.

"I know it isn't true, but I don't take kindly to folks referring to my sister that way. I don't want Stanley getting any funny ideas. It's bad enough I had to protect Mama from a monster of a stepfather. I don't wish to do the same for you!"

"I'll take extra care to mind my manners," Emma said.

"And stay away from Stanley," Jake ordered. "I don't trust him."

"Yes, Jake," Emma conceded. God forbid, what if Stanley watched her when nobody was around? Would he attack her or something awful like that?

Indignation rose within her. No, she would not allow herself to suffer the way her mother had. She'd defend herself if any man attacked her, and she didn't care if it meant her brother's job or not. After what had happened to their mother, she was sure Jake would feel the same way.

"Morning, E.V." Frederick climbed down from Inferno quite happy about his new raise from the boss. Soon he'd have his father's house out of foreclosure. If only he could buy Emma something girlie and nice to show her how much he cared for her.

"Morning," E.V. replied, pulling on his work gloves.

Frederick met E.V. at the end of the first flatbed. "Is that a bunch of ladies' bonnets in your office I saw the other day?"

"Yep." While his tone had E.V.'s normal good-natured optimism, the sadness that momentarily flickered in his brown eyes dampened Frederick's mood. "I need to return them to their rightful owner."

"Are they Larkin's?"

"I seem to have a knack for finding them around town."

"I take it your efforts with Miss Whitworth haven't produced any positive results?"

"Not yet." E.V. grabbed the end of a log and then paused. "Fred, if something's truly important to you, you don't give up, no matter what the obstacle is. Now let's get this timber unloaded. I've got paperwork to do."

Frederick grabbed the end of the log and lifted. The temptation to spend his raise on Emma clawed at his heart. Maybe he could find something little to let her know how he felt.

Once the train was unloaded, Frederick headed into town. The little money he had jingled in his pocket.

Inside the mercantile, he found a multitude of things any woman would fancy. Then his eyes fell on a spool of ivory-colored eyelet lace.

"Miss Pearson gazed at that same lace just the other day." The store clerk nodded toward Frederick.

"I bet this would go perfect with one of her dresses." One yard cost a fraction of what a new bonnet did. Frederick could hardly wait to give it to her.

He paid for his find. Once the lace was wrapped, he hurried back to the train.

Careful to not get the wrapping dirty, Frederick placed the package in the corner on the floor, out of the way of the furnace's soot and grime.

He stoked the furnace as full as he dared. He was in a hurry to see the look on Emma's face when he gave her the lace. In hardly any time, Inferno chugged up the hillside. Widow's Bend came and went. No trouble there, but then a mess of deer grazing on the tracks caught his eye. He pulled on the whistle, but the stubborn animals remained on the tracks and simply stared at him with their noses in the air.

"Come on, move it!" Frederick bellowed. Frustration mounting, he yanked on the whistle one last time.

Chapter 7

Emma was just finishing hanging the clean sheets on the line when a call went out for the company's doctor. Frederick Corrigan was hurt. Again.

Dropping the clothespins to the ground, she lifted her skirts and raced toward the wagon pulling into the camp. Thankfully some crew members had found him on the tracks and brought him back to camp. Jake could bring the train in later that night.

Emma stopped by the wagon. *Lord, please don't let him be seriously injured.* She was beginning to care for Frederick, and her heart couldn't take another loss.

"Is he badly hurt?" she asked.

One of the men waved a hand at her. "Nah, he'll be fine. He just went a few rounds with some bucks on the tracks."

"And lost." Stanley chuckled as the men carried Frederick to the bunkhouse.

Emma aimed her meanest scowl at Stanley but held her tongue. She could see that Frederick bled from the head and right shoulder. "I'll get some water heating and tear some bandages."

Poor Frederick babbled on about how crazy deer acted in rutting season, and something about lace for a lady's dress.

Lord, he must have taken quite a lick to the head.

Emma reached the kitchen and could see that Mrs. Wilkin was one step ahead of her. The pot of water sat on top of the cookstove. Emma piled wood under the fire to get it blazing. Next she raced back to the clothesline and snatched the most ragged sheet down. She tore several strips with lightning speed.

When she had a sufficient amount, she grabbed the bundle and hurried to the bunkhouse, gasping for breath. Frederick was semi-coherent when she stumbled inside.

"Afternoon, Miss Emma," he mumbled, his blond hair soaked red with blood.

"Hello, Frederick, I'm glad you seem well—um—as well as can be expected." Emma breathed a sigh of relief and hoped she didn't sound scatterbrained. Heat rushed to her face, and she ducked her head, lest he guess her feelings.

"I got you a more appropriate present than a pig, but it got dirty on the way home. I'm sorry." Frederick's tone lost some of its sparkle.

"Don't be sorry. I'm growing quite fond of Bacon."

"I'd be fond of him, too, on the breakfast table." Frederick grinned.

Emma bristled with mock indignation. "I can assure you, the darling little thing won't meet an untimely death and wind up alongside your pancakes one morning."

Frederick let out a chuckle that shook the bed he was lying on. The man had a sense of humor and for that Emma was grateful.

Mr. Kenicky rushed into the room at that moment followed by Jake.

"Thank the Lord you're all right, Corrigan." Mr. Kenicky

folded his arms over his chest and studied Frederick through narrowed eyes. "You know, one of these days your luck is gonna run out."

The doctor maintained that Frederick's wounds were minor. He told him to keep everything clean and change the bandages often.

"Rest assured, Doctor, I'll do that." Emma patted Frederick on the arm and smiled at him. It would be her pleasure to care for this wonderful man. Jake eyed her with suspicion. If he guessed she was now sweet on Frederick, she didn't think he would understand, let alone be happy about the situation. She didn't want either man to think of her as childish, so she straightened herself and acted like a proper lady should.

Later that evening Frederick lay back on the bed and tried not to let on how much pain he was in when Emma brought him his dinner. He pasted on a smile. But Stanley stoked the woodstove and stared daggers at him. Did Stanley admire Emma also? If they both wished to court her and Frederick won out, the boss would probably hear all about it. This was a situation he'd have to gauge carefully, or it could become as dangerous as rounding Widow's Bend without brakes.

"Are you all right?" Emma's sweet voice drew him to the present, and he gazed across the room at her. She stared at him with one eyebrow cocked and her head tilted to one side.

"Um, yes." Frederick cleared his throat. "I'd like to thank you for helping out the doctor."

"You're more than welcome." Emma set a basin of hot water

on an end table along with a fistful of bandages. She then pulled a chair over to where he lay and tenderly pulled the dried bloody bandage from his head. He gritted his teeth against the pain. God forbid he yelped in the presence of a lady. She began to sponge the goose egg on his right temple with a wet cloth. The coolness was soothing against his skin. He sighed then laid his head back against the pillows and closed his eyes.

As good as the nursing felt, he still chided himself for the stupidity of his actions. How much work would he miss due to this injury? He was determined, not more than one day. Even with his new raise, he couldn't afford to miss work.

After a moment, he heard the chair scoot back as Emma rose to her feet. "I must be going now. Mrs. Wilkin needs me to help cook supper tonight."

He smiled. "I'm looking forward to seeing you more. Perhaps this Saturday we could go for a walk and have a picnic."

Emma froze. Her heart skittered along like a pebble on smooth water's surface before sinking into the depths below. Elation that he cared and fear of getting too close wrestled in her heart like two squirrels over the last hickory nut of the season.

"Why, yes, Frederick, I'd love to go."

"Glad to hear you say yes."

"I'm looking forward to it already." Emma prepared to leave the room but couldn't help grinning with excitement.

"Great. We'll leave first thing Saturday morning." Frederick beamed, his blue eyes twinkling.

Saturday morning arrived with a wan mid-fall sun that tried

desperately to warm the frigid air, but didn't quite succeed. Emma took Frederick's arm as they strolled down a path in one of Tumwater's most beautiful parks and watched the waterfalls.

Frederick spread the red-checked tablecloth on a picnic table while Emma pulled a plate of fried chicken from the basket. The aroma made her mouth water.

Throughout their meal, Frederick and Emma discussed everything from their favorite books to the places they'd like to visit.

"Emma, I'd like to take you down to Toledo for a short trip. I spoke with Mr. and Mrs. Wilkin, and they have friends down there they'd like to visit. They would like us to go along. They've offered to cover the cost of the train tickets." Frederick gazed at her with his dreamy blue eyes.

Emma blushed and turned away for a moment to gaze at the water. Again her heart seesawed with emotion, but the desire to get away from the logging camp won out.

"I'd love to, Frederick. When will we go?" She turned back to him and felt goose bumps on her arms, and not from the cold weather.

"We'll take the train next weekend. If I work extra hours this week, I can afford to take off a day, maybe two. You're going to love it."

The November morning was perfect, with one exception. Emma hadn't finished sewing the lace Frederick had gotten her onto her mother's gown. She was resigned to her best Sunday dress of plain blue cotton as she and Frederick boarded the train, followed by Mr. and Mrs. Wilkin.

The whistle blew steam toward the sky with a loud racket. Emma started and clutched Frederick's arm tighter. He laid a tender hand over hers and smiled down at her.

"This is so exciting, Frederick. I don't know how I'll ever thank you." Emma felt heat rise in her cheeks and ducked her head in embarrassment. She was growing quite fond of the wild train engineer and wasn't sure how to handle that fact.

Her thoughts were interrupted when Frederick took her by the hand and held her steady as the locomotive lurched to life and pulled away from the station. A *clackity-clack* sound filled Emma's ears as the wheels rotated in rhythm.

Emma noticed Abigail standing on the station platform with an angry expression marring her features. Jealousy was evident in her furrowed brow and the clenched fists at her sides. Emma cringed, remembering Jake's words. Abigail seemed bent on causing trouble.

Frederick and Emma rode along, chatting about Tumwater and life in the town. They entered into a lively discussion about Shakespeare. Jake had done a good job of keeping Emma educated after the deaths of their parents. Her dark eyes seemed to hold an odd mix of haunted pain and yearning for adventure.

The train slowed to a crawl and came to a stop with a jerk. The Wilkins and Frederick and Emma crowded to the doors to debark. From there the party boarded a stagecoach and rode to Toledo.

"We're about to round the bend and then the town should

come into view." Frederick directed Emma toward a window and pointed past a clump of evergreen trees in the distance.

"The scenery is beautiful, Frederick. Thank you for bringing me here today." Emma looked up at him with longing in her eyes. How he wanted to lean down and kiss her rosy lips. As they rolled into town, Frederick noticed a number of buildings that had sprung up since he had been there last. My, how the place had grown. The stage finally rocked and then lurched to a stop. It felt good to stretch his legs as he stepped down from the cramped confines.

"Allow me." Frederick held his hand out to assist Emma down the stagecoach steps.

"Why don't we get some lunch at the Koontz Hotel?" Mr. Wilkin asked.

"That sounds lovely," Emma replied, her eyes sparkling in the sunshine as she kept her gloved hand in Frederick's strong one.

A stern-wheeler on the river whistled. Emma emitted an unladylike squeal and craned her neck for a better view. She held onto Frederick's waistcoat as if to steady herself.

"Mighty exciting, eh?" he asked, boldly wrapping his arm around her slender waist to keep her from falling as she turned this way and that, looking at everything. The gasp that escaped from her lips caused his heart to beat faster. She looked up at him with dark ebony eyes that brimmed with anticipation and. . . passion?

"Thank you kindly for your assistance." She blinked as if specks of dust had landed in her eyes.

"You're most welcome."

The town of Toledo had turned into a bustling place since

he had last been there. Crewmen loaded and unloaded cargo from the boats lining the riverbanks. They made quite a racket. Frederick was pleased to see the steamboat the town had been named for. The *Toledo* blew its whistle again as several passengers scrambled to board before the boat sailed south again, down the Cowlitz River.

Sidewalks lined a few of the streets while others weren't much more than muddy paths. Ladies strolled along the walkways holding parasols.

Just up and over the hill was Frederick's childhood home, the one his family lived in before they moved to Tumwater to seek better medical care for his mother. The structure could be seen from downtown, and Frederick squirmed with anxiousness to see the old clapboard house once again. Memories came flooding back.

"Right this way, Emma." Frederick guided her along the plank sidewalk that lined the muddy street. Their shoes made a *clompity-clomp* sound as they bustled along. "After lunch, I'd like to show you my childhood home."

"Oh yes." Emma wrinkled her pert little nose and lifted her skirts to avoid getting mud on them from a recent rainstorm. He held out his hand and escorted her across the nasty patch of ground. She looked up at him with that same look in her eyes that made his heart skitter like the clanking of Inferno's wheels across a length of steel rails.

One question popped into Frederick's mind and haunted his thoughts. Would this fragile flower dare to love a rough and reckless man like himself?

Emma glanced this way and that, studying the town. The polite nods of men in suspenders and women carrying baskets of goods made for a cozy atmosphere. Through her gloved hands, she could feel Frederick's muscled arms, making her feel safe. Mr. and Mrs. Wilkin were there, too, of course, following them around like proper chaperones.

"I beg your pardon?" Emma asked as the sound of Frederick's voice drew her from her thoughts.

"I asked if you'd like to have lunch here. It is highly recommended by Mr. and Mrs. Wilkin." Frederick motioned to the hotel they were standing in front of.

He was so handsome. Emma's breath caught in her throat and for a moment she was unable to speak.

The aroma of fresh beef roasting caused her mouth to water. The cold biscuits she had eaten that morning weren't sustaining her. "I think that would be delightful." She gave his arm a squeeze.

After they had eaten their lunch, they walked up the hill leading to Frederick's childhood home. It wasn't much to look at. A medium-sized house with a towering redbricked chimney and a lovely rose garden along one side and a vegetable garden on the other. Frederick chatted about the place as if it were Buckingham Palace. Emma's thoughts drifted as he rattled on about the boyhood pranks he'd pulled.

Emma finally understood Frederick's enthusiasm. It wasn't the clapboards and bricks that made this house so wonderful to Frederick. It was special and cherished because he spent a happy childhood there.

A barb of pain jabbed at Emma's heart. How comforting it must feel to have had been raised in such a home. She vowed if she ever had children of her own, they would not be privy to the horrors she had witnessed as a young girl.

On the way back down the hill, Mr. and Mrs. Wilkin interjected with some rather wonderful news. Their friends in town had offered to take them all out for dinner that night.

"This is such a delightful little town, Frederick. The people are generous in spirit and kind to one another."

"Yes, and Lord willing, it will stay that way."

Excitement flooded Emma's heart, and she fairly burst with gratitude for such wonderful friends as the Wilkins. They had provided this adventure for her, and she knew she would never forget it.

The next afternoon, they boarded the train for the ride home. Emma had enjoyed the trip so much and was glad she had gone. She was thinking of the Lord and His promises while standing next to Frederick on the passenger car's loading platform. Was it really possible for God to heal her deepest hurts and provide her with a husband someday?

The sun was still shining in an iridescent sky, colored with streaks of gold and purple. A cool breeze wafted across the platform as Emma listened to the birds calling to each other. Finally, the whistle blew, signaling their impending departure.

A near frenzy ensued as the locomotive lurched to life and ladies waved handkerchiefs and men hollered good-bye. Conductors busied themselves with ticket collecting and shouts of "All aboard!"

As Emma gazed up into Frederick's tanned face, her heart pounded harder in her chest. The intense gleam in his eyes mirrored a passion that burned in her veins. His strong calloused hands wound their way through her hair and caught on a few strands.

Frederick wasted no time in tilting her head back and placing his lips on hers. For a moment, time seemed to stand still. Emma drank in the warmth of his kiss as her knees went weak. Her heart opened a slight crack and feelings of love for Frederick poured in.

"Oh Emma," he whispered in her ear with a husky voice. "Please forgive me if I've been too forward." He pulled back and stared deep into her eyes as if to search for some flicker of emotion.

"Please forgive *me*, Frederick, if *I've* been too forward." Emma sighed after finding her voice. He simply pulled her closer and held her as the train departed and made its way north to Tumwater.

When the town of Tumwater came into view, Emma excused herself to the powder room to freshen up. She'd cringe and wither away if Abigail saw her in a disheveled state and made fun of her. Especially in front of Frederick.

Chapter 8

Emma held Frederick's hand as they disembarked Inferno later that evening. Her dress would need a good washing, but she didn't care. She'd had a wonderful time, and feelings for Frederick were blooming like fresh apple blossoms under the warmth of a spring sun.

As they walked back to the camp, Emma was about to ask where her brother was when a frantic shout rose above the commotion coming from the bunkhouse.

"Dear Lord, Emma Pearson, there you are," a logger exclaimed as he bolted toward her.

Emma's blood flowed like cold stream water through her veins. Her heart threatened to stop beating but pounded in her chest regardless. Air came in ragged gasps. No, not the last blood relative she had left on this earth.

"Is it Jake?" Emma blurted.

"Yes, he's got a nasty gash on his head, and the doctor thinks his leg is busted."

The man's voice sounded as though he were speaking the words into an empty barrel.

"No!" Emma shrieked as she lifted her skirts and sprinted toward the bunkhouse.

When she burst through the door, she saw Jake lying on a bed with a bloody bandage wrapped around his head. The doctor pulled the bandage away for a moment, and Emma became light-headed at the sight of so much blood. His shirt was stained red and his eyes were closed. He looked dead. If Frederick's strong arms hadn't circled her waist and supported her, she'd have slid to the floor in a faint.

"Oh Jake, you promised you wouldn't leave me all alone in the world." Emma stumbled forward, laid her head on Jake's shoulder, and wept.

"Get this hysterical woman out of here!" the doctor barked. Frederick grasped her by the shoulders and escorted her from the room.

The night crawled on, as if it were passing by on hands and knees. Frederick brought Emma a warm blanket as the chilly night air set in. He held her hand as the minutes ticked past. Without saying a word, his presence radiated strength, and Emma found no shame in leaning into it.

Bacon's warm body lay at her feet, his occasional grunts and snorts telling her he was comfortable. Jake hadn't made a sound.

When the last of the crew members left Jake's side, Frederick reluctantly had to leave Emma alone. She understood the impropriety of his staying in the room all night with her. He left a lamp burning on the table for Emma's convenience. She sat back in her rocker and thanked God for his care and concern.

Orange rays of the sun finally crept over the horizon and soon morning followed. With sore aching muscles, Emma shifted in her chair. Jake had survived the night and for that she was grateful. But how had the accident happened?

A crew member walked in. "Morning, ma'am,"

"Good morning," Emma mumbled, running her hands over her brother's chest, reassuring herself that he still breathed. She looked up at the man. "Do you know how the accident happened?"

"Stanley and Jake were out on a day that we were supposed to have off," the man explained. "According to Stanley, Jake cut down a tree and didn't jump out of the way soon enough. He got caught in the branches."

The details didn't matter to Emma. She was just praying that Jake would wake up. A moan escaped from her brother's bruised lips and drew her attention to the present.

"Jake, it's me, Emma. Please wake up." She grasped his strong calloused hand in her own. Relief flooded through her when he slit his eyes open.

"Emma, what happened?" Jake's hoarse whisper caused her to flinch. He was alive, for now, and that's what mattered.

"There was an accident. You were hurt, but you're going to get better now. I'm here, and I'm going to take care of you." Emma choked back tears as she brushed her fingers through the few wisps of hair not wrapped in bandages. Jake smiled back at her and then, by the time the doctor was summoned, he drifted back to sleep.

The doctor did a thorough examination.

"I think he's going to be fine, but he's not out of the woods yet. He needs some time to recuperate and much rest."

"Thank you." Emma turned back toward her brother, her mouth dry as she wrung her hands with anxiety.

"I'm going to get some coffee and some breakfast. I'll check back in an hour or so. You should get some rest yourself, young lady." The doctor yawned.

Frederick came through the door a few minutes later, and he brought Emma a cup of coffee.

"You look worn out." He plopped down on a straight chair beside her.

"I am." She stifled a yawn and took a sip of the warm, invigorating coffee. The aroma alone was comforting, or was that Frederick's presence?

"You know, if there's anything I can do to help, all you have to do is ask." The sincere look in Frederick's eyes made Emma feel more secure, but the future still held many questions she didn't have answers for.

"Thank you," she replied. "Now if you'll excuse me, I'm heading off to my room to try and get some rest." She finished her coffee and stood to leave. She was exhausted and was unsure if her world would ever be the same.

Every evening when Frederick was finished with his shift, he went to visit Emma. For three days she stayed by Jake's side caring for his every need. Much as he hated to admit it, a part of him longed to be cared for by her with the same concern she showered on her brother. And he desperately wanted to let her know how much she meant to him.

One night on his way to the bunkhouse, he heard voices coming from behind the boss's office. He slowed down and listened, straining to hear their words.

"Stanley's been untruthful and negligent in his work, and he's the one who's responsible for Jake's injury."

"Yeah, but what can we do about it? Who's going to believe

us over the boss's son?"

Jake recognized the voices—they were two of the newer crew members. He didn't want to believe what they said. Was the boss aware of Stanley's guilt? If so, then why wasn't he doing something about it? These questions haunted Frederick, and he debated whether or not to broach the subject with Emma.

What he needed was some solid proof, but that might be hard to come by. Then he could approach the boss, and then the boss could break the news to Emma. But how would Emma react when she knew her brother had almost lost his life and his livelihood because of negligence on someone else's part? It would infuriate her. Frederick sure didn't want to see her get so upset that she did something rash and lost her job. And what would happen if she thought he went behind her back?

"Lord, give me wisdom in knowing how to handle this," Frederick prayed.

If he knew exactly how the accident had happened, he'd have a better idea about how to proceed. The crew boss, Mr. Wilkin, would have the best guess as to what happened out there that day. Without wasting more time, he decided to speak with the man and see if he could find out a thing or two. This teetered on gossip, but the boss needed to know the truth, considering what was at stake—the lives of the crew.

On the fourth night after Jake's accident the full moon cast a romantic light over the quiet and still earth. The stars shimmered in the heavens and the crickets chirped in blissful-sounding harmony. Emma began to believe her brother would live—

probably with a limp in his leg for the rest of his life—but at least he would live. Mrs. Wilkin's sister had come out from town to help for a week or so, and they seemed to be doing fine without Emma's help.

Frederick brought dinner to the bunkhouse for Emma and Jake and asked if she wanted to go for a walk afterwards. She agreed. With a sparkle in his deep blue eyes, he took her by the hand and led her down to the creek.

Emma chuckled at Bacon, who trotted alongside her on their late-night stroll. Frederick talked of his day at work, but Emma, so enthralled at being by his side, her hand clutching his strong arm, hardly noticed what he said.

Frederick paused to run his strong hands through her long dark hair and laid a tender kiss on her eager lips. Emma responded by leaning into the kiss, as if to absorb some of his strength.

"Tomorrow's Saturday and we usually have the afternoon off. Let me take you into town and get you away from this for a while," Frederick said between kisses to her forehead. Emma sighed. She didn't want to leave her brother until he was at least able to get up and about.

"As long as I know Jake will be taken care of." Jake had been through so much, and if she left him and something terrible happened again, she'd never forgive herself.

"I'll ask Mrs. Wilkin to keep an eye on him," Frederick suggested.

Emma saw hope in his eyes, so she conceded.

The next afternoon she rode into town on Inferno with Frederick at her side. He didn't seem to go all that fast, and she wondered why everyone made such a fuss over what a reckless driver he was. Then it occurred to her he was probably being extra cautious with her along.

When they got into town, she held his arm as they strolled in front of the shops. He escorted her down the road that led to his father's house. Much larger than the one in Toledo, it gave off an aura of grand elegance, with a porch swing and tall white columns.

"It really is lovely," Emma said, leaning against his strong shoulder, wishing she could do more for him. For a short minute, she understood how her mother must have felt at times. She was learning to praise God even in the face of imminent hardship.

"I made some extra money selling a share of the land, and along with my savings we made a large payment to the bank. If Pa takes in boarders for about a year, he can pay off the house, and the bank will hand him the deed."

Emma couldn't help but notice how much straighter he stood, obviously proud of himself. "It's not as grand as the Whitworth mansion, but it's Pa's home."

"I heard there's a party at one of the hotels in town right after Thanksgiving to celebrate Elisha Ferry being sworn in as governor," Emma said, to change the subject.

"I'd like very much to escort you to it," Frederick said.

"I'd love to, if it's okay with Jake." Emma's hand rested in the crook of his arm, and he patted her hand with his. The gesture brought comfort to her.

On their way back into town, they stopped in at the post office. There was a letter for Jake and Emma from a man they had lost contact with for more than a year.

"It's from Uncle Irving!" Emma exclaimed, clapping her

hands. She'd assumed the old man had died, and she was delighted to know he still lived. "I can't wait to tell Jake when we get back to camp. He's going to be thrilled."

"I take it Jake and this man were very close." Frederick smiled down at her.

"Oh, they were, and once Jake speaks with Uncle Irving, maybe he'll invite us to live with him in Chicago." Emma dreamed of getting away from the dirty camp. This would be a perfect opportunity.

Frederick's expression indicated he was less than pleased and she understood why. They had begun an earnest courtship, but was she falling in love with him? She didn't know for sure. She couldn't help but wonder what would happen now.

Frederick stormed across the lumberyard the next day, full of gruffness.

"What's wrong?" E.V. asked, his eyebrows raised in question.

"After all this time of guarding my heart, I think I'm falling in love." Frederick scratched his chin with the back of his hand. Knowing E.V. understood, Frederick explained the new developments in Emma's life.

E.V. placed a hand on Frederick's shoulder and gave a reassuring squeeze. "If you really love her, you'll want what's best for her."

"I do," Frederick groaned. "That's why I know I'm going to lose her."

"Just keep praying about it."

"I will," Frederick replied before his friend walked back to the sawmill office.

When the load of lumber was stacked and ready for the saw, Frederick boarded Inferno and steamed back to the landing for another load of timber. The entire time, he talked to the Lord, asking for direction and guidance. Soon he felt God's peace and he began to relax.

That didn't last long however, as he pulled into the loggers's landing to find it in utter chaos. Had someone gotten hurt again or was something else terribly wrong? Was Stanley to blame this time as well?

Chapter 9

Emma bolted from the bunkhouse with anxiety and heartbreak making chase behind her. Their uncle from Chicago had offered Jake a well-paying job, and it didn't matter if he walked with a limp. He'd offered to provide Emma with employment, too.

But Jake wanted to leave her behind. If Jake thought he could run off to Chicago while she stayed behind in this God-forsaken mudhole, he was sadly mistaken! He knew her worst fear was being all alone in the world. After walking off her temper, she returned to the bunkhouse to present her case to him.

At last, after some heated discussion and much pleading on Emma's part, Jake agreed to take her with him as soon as his leg mended enough for him to travel. She blew her breath out in a tired sigh and tramped to the kitchen to help Mrs. Wilkin peel a mountain of potatoes for dinner that night. Now if only she could find a way to tell Frederick she was leaving.

Bacon grunted and lay down in his usual corner.

"Emma, is everything all right?" Frederick asked, mopping his forehead with his customary red bandana.

She hadn't seen him approach.

"Yes, everything is fine," she said. Later she'd ask God to

forgive her for leaving this wonderful man who had done nothing but show her kindness.

"I have something I need to speak with you about." The serious expression clouding his features caused the hair on her skin to tingle. A niggling intuition told her it had something to do with her brother's accident. She knew Frederick wasn't entirely convinced they knew what had happened out in the woods that day.

"I spoke with Mr. Wilkin, the crew boss, the other day. He examined the logging equipment after Jake's accident. He believes it wasn't an accident. He thinks Stanley neglected to set the safety, and that's what caused that tree to roll over your brother."

Emma clenched her teeth to keep from screaming aloud. How could someone be so careless when working with such dangerous equipment? Wasn't it dangerous enough just to be a logger? "I see," she managed to mutter with her jaw set. "Just what do you intend to do with this information?"

"I'm going to the boss first thing tomorrow morning. He needs to send that kid packing before somebody else on this crew gets hurt or killed."

"Do you have any evidence?"

"I've got Mr. Wilkin's opinion. That's as good as any evidence you'll find." Frederick's face flushed deep red as the fire in his eyes burned with obvious indignation.

By Frederick's demeanor, Emma guessed he wanted to tear Stanley limb from limb, and for a brief moment she felt sorry for the young greenhorn. "Well, I do hope you're able to get through to Mr. Kenicky. Please let me know how it goes."

"I'll sure do that." Frederick stuffed his bandana in his back pocket. "Now if you'll excuse me, I'd like to speak with the rest of the crew and get their opinion on how Stanley's holding up out there."

Emma went back to peeling the potatoes. Even though she was numb from the news, she still managed to finish the job. She dumped a bucket of slops onto a plate for Bacon and gathered firewood for the bunkhouse. Frederick's words churned in her head like rushing river water around a sharp and rocky bend.

The boss had to understand what a danger his son posed in the woods. But how would he react once he understood that fact? Worse yet, what if he didn't believe the crew boss? He would more than likely keep his son on the crew. Would Stanley go after Jake again, and with a vengeance?

Remembering how Stanley treated her with such disrespect, Emma shuddered at the prospect. The sooner she and Jake got out of there, the better.

"But sir!" Frederick growled and clenched his fists at his sides. "Have you even heard a word we've been saying?" He wanted to toss his boss down the side of a steep slope at his obvious obtuseness, followed by Stanley, who stood off to the side with a smug expression plastered on his face.

"I said that's enough." Mr. Kenicky slammed his hands on his makeshift desk and rose to his full height from his chair. "Don't you two have things to do? Get out of here and get back to work."

"And wait until the next man gets killed?" Frederick glared at his boss, loathing coating his words.

"Now see here!" Stanley took a menacing step forward.

"Let's go, Fred." Mr. Wilkin grabbed him by the shirt and dragged him out of the office. It was a good thing, or he probably wouldn't have a job by sunset.

"Come, Fred, let's get back to work. We've got a large clearing of trees to cut down and get to the mill today. We need all the hands we've got." Mr. Wilkin turned Frederick around and aimed him toward Inferno.

"That fool needs to wake up and learn how to run a logging business!" Frederick struggled to control his frustration. The last thing he wanted was to bury another crewmate. "And that kid needs to find a job where his negligence won't get somebody hurt, if that's even possible."

"I'll keep an eye on the kid. With any luck he'll learn a few things, and we can avoid another tragedy."

"Thanks." Frederick paced the ground in front of the bunkhouse as the crew was getting ready to head out for the day. The men filed past him, and he couldn't help but wonder if they'd all come back in one piece at dinnertime.

"I'll talk to you tonight." Frederick waved at Mr. Wilkin and headed for Inferno. He had to cool his head, or he'd lose focus and risk his own hide. One thing was certain, he'd be praying for the crew and his friend. But would that be enough?

Emma threw herself into her brother's arms two days later with gratitude seeping from her heart. He had announced to her that he felt they could leave for Chicago very soon. She couldn't wait to get away from the camp and all the drudgery that went with it.

"But it breaks my heart to leave Frederick." Emma bit her lip.

"Bear in mind, sister dear"—Jake interrupted her thoughts—"there are many men in the city who will be vying for your hand."

"Oh no, I'm going to get a job and learn how to care for myself."

"Well, I'm not going to allow you to live by yourself, not in the city," Jake said with enough force to knock over a tall pine tree.

"Of course not, but I can earn my own money, and not be such a burden to you. Maybe get a little something nice to wear—nothing too fancy of course."

"Always pretty things. I can see you haven't learned much during these long hard months," Jake teased.

"Let me go check and see how Mrs. Wilkin is coming along with dinner. I'll be back later to check on you and bring you a plate." Emma stood and hurried from the room before her brother could object.

Even if Frederick was filthy rich and able to provide luxuries, she was still afraid to give her whole life to a man. It was hard enough to give him a piece of her heart.

"Lord, I'm afraid," she prayed as she walked. Guilt wiggled in her middle. She really should tell him that she was leaving soon.

But she wanted to attend the party at the hotel after the governor was sworn in. Who wouldn't want to witness such a historic moment? A part of her didn't want to be put down anymore. She wanted to wear pretty things and silence Abigail's jeering tongue. Was it such a sin to defend oneself against such cruelty? More tangled thoughts wound through Emma's head as she trudged toward the kitchen. Just a few weeks left to cook for the rough men in camp.

She walked into a stifling hot kitchen filled with chaos and in the usual uproar. Mrs. Wilkin stirred some corn and potato chowder with a vengeance, a kettle of water threatened to boil over, and Bacon squealed in the corner, his plate empty. Mrs. Wilkin's sister must have gone back to her own house.

Stifling a groan, Emma pulled the pot of water off the cookstove and dumped a bowl of slops onto Bacon's dish. His hearty grunts communicated gratitude. Rubbing his soft head, Emma thought of Frederick. Bacon had been a gift from Frederick after all.

Granted, he had kissed her and expressed admiration and a desire to court her. So how could she convince herself that he wouldn't care if she left? How could she put off telling him? She knew he'd be angry, and she cringed in terror at the thought of an angry man who might throw things in his rage.

Besides, ladies of better means were best suited for a man like Frederick, and he'd come to realize that, in time. He wouldn't miss her for very long.

Mr. Kenicky glared at Frederick as though he had brought the plagues of Egypt into the camp. Frederick shook his head to clear cobwebs from between his ears. Had he heard the boss correctly?

"Don't you have anything to say on your own behalf?" The man's eyes narrowed into two snakelike slits.

Yep. He had heard the man right. He was being accused of carelessness with the equipment—breaking it and not reporting it, so the next man who used it got hurt. The same equipment that had gone haywire and caused Jake's accident.

A part of him wanted to leap across the desk and shake the man silly, but he knew that wouldn't do any good. How on earth was he going to defend himself against such wild accusations?

"You wouldn't believe it anyway, so no, I guess there isn't anything I can say," Frederick growled. But there was something he could do. Leave Tumwater for good. Just as soon as the loose ends were tied up regarding his father's house. Where he'd go remained a mystery, but parts beyond the horizon looked better by the minute.

"That will be all for now, Corrigan. We'll talk more later." The boss went back to studying the paperwork before him, and Frederick stormed from the office.

He jumped into Inferno and stoked the stove to overflowing with wood. In only a matter of minutes, the engine burned hot and in even less time, Inferno raced down the tracks. He braced his arms so taut around Widow's Bend they actually hurt when he rounded the corner.

Frederick rolled into Tumwater with an aching jaw as well, from clenching his teeth so hard. By God's protective grace he made it without crashing. Instead of moving lumber, E.V. was in his office doing paperwork.

"I'm getting out of Tumwater," Frederick stated the moment he crossed the threshold. "The first chance I get to talk to the bank and make sure Pa's house is okay."

E.V. stared at him and said nothing.

That only made Frederick angrier. "Now that I don't have to worry about Pa losing the house, you bet I'm going. Just as soon as I can find someplace else to go."

The expression on E.V.'s face didn't change, so Frederick continued. "I'm not about to stay in a town where I've got accusations hanging over my head like a two-ton anvil ready to drop. You know how folks talk, especially ladies."

"Whoa, what accusations?" E.V.'s eyebrows rose.

Frederick took a few minutes to explain the situation and then waited not so patiently for E.V. to respond.

"All right." E.V. finally answered.

That stunned Frederick. "All right?"

"I know you wouldn't make a major decision like this without praying." E.V. turned his gaze back to the account book on his desk and resumed writing. "Since you know this is what God wants for you, I won't try talking you out of it."

Frederick flinched. He hadn't prayed, but what was the point?

"I, uh, need to send a telegram to some friends in California about getting a logging job down there." He backed out of E.V.'s office and left before his friend changed his mind and decided to preach to him about being patient and not making rash decisions.

Frederick strode into the post office and eyed the telegram clerk. "I'd like to send a message to Eureka, California."

The clerk quickly took down Frederick's message and agreed to send it that afternoon. Frederick left the office, and when he finished his day's work, he traipsed home. He slept fitfully that night, wondering what it would be like starting fresh in California.

The next afternoon, Frederick stopped in at the post office to make sure the message had been sent. To his surprise, he found a response already awaiting him. The telegram was an offer to come work in the Redwood Forest. Men like him were needed to help clear the mammoth trees that made most pines in the Pacific Northwest look small.

Realizing the opportunity available was not just for him, Frederick flew out of the post office and made a beeline to the construction site where Willum was rebuilding a cracked roof.

"I hear you're leaving us," Will said as he sawed a board down to size.

"E.V. tell you?"

"This morning when I picked up my lumber." Will paused with the handsaw for a moment and studied Frederick. "You don't have to leave Tumwater for work. I'll hire you."

"I'm not a carpenter like you."

Willum stared at him with that same disappointed look that E.V. had yesterday. "Since I know this is what God wants for you, I won't try talking you out of it."

Frederick snapped. "Did E.V. tell you to say that?"

"No." Willum frowned. "You did pray, didn't you?"

"After I take Emma Pearson to the party at the Schmitt mansion," Frederick said to change the subject, "I'm leaving."

With a nod of acceptance, Will returned to sawing, and Frederick walked away. With his stomach rumbling for food, he headed to the tracks and boarded Inferno for the short trip back to the logging camp. As he thought of Emma, dread grew in his heart at how and when he'd tell her he was leaving.

It was the end of November and a chill set in on the afternoon of the party. Emma sat in the parlor of the Wilkins' house and sewed with frantic speed on the dress she hoped to wear that evening. To her delight, the lace Frederick gave her had been long enough to encircle the collar and both sleeves, if barely. Frederick had said he would arrive at five sharp. Emma heard Abigail had been invited and was in no mood to deal with her troublemaking.

Looking forward to one last evening with Frederick, she couldn't bring herself to cancel. She thought she owed it to him to make some beautiful memories on their last night together. The last thing she wanted to do was cause him extra pain, and backing out of the party would surely do that. Why ruin the night for him by skipping the festivities?

Afterward, she and Jake were leaving for Chicago. She didn't want to think about Frederick's reaction. She kept repeating in her head that he was better off without her. Not only was she poor, with no family and no status, but she was broken inside from such a traumatic childhood. He'd probably regret it if they married. Or were these just excuses she used because she was afraid of letting him get too close?

"Oh, this cheap thread!" Emma growled as she snipped the broken ends and rethreaded her needle. How would she ever get the lace sewn when the thread kept breaking?

"Ouch!" she yelped as the needle bit into her fingertip. She stuck the sore finger into her mouth.

"Everything will be fine after tonight." Getting back to her sewing, Emma began singing "Amazing Grace," hoping to sooth her fretful mood.

An hour later, she snipped the ends of the thread and the beautiful garment was complete. Evergreen in color, it matched the name of the new state. And she would celebrate by spending the evening with the local politicians and Mr. Frederick Corrigan.

A stab of pain shot through her heart with as little mercy as was shown to her fingertip only an hour earlier. Just where the feeling had originated she didn't know, but it did nothing to change her plan.

A deafening racket of cheers arose from the street as dozens of loggers celebrated. How grateful she was that Jake had made a full recovery. She was also glad he didn't drink hard alcohol. He would join his friends at the saloon but would return home that evening as sober as a preacher on Sunday morning.

"Emma." Her brother's voice carried into the room.

She rose to greet him. "Yes, Jake?" She hoped he heard her above the whoops and hollers.

"Emma, I'm heading downtown with the men. Fred will be along shortly. You sure about things?" She could hear the concern woven into his tone. He leaned against the door jamb and studied her with seriousness written in his features.

"I'm certain, Jake. Thank you. Now if you'll excuse me, I need to dress before Frederick gets here."

"All right, but be careful now, you hear?"

Jake shook his finger at Emma and made her feel like a child. Well, she wasn't a child any longer. She huffed. Hopefully, once they arrived in Chicago, Jake would be too preoccupied with Uncle Irving to bother with her business.

With a small degree of difficulty she and Mrs. Wilkin managed to get the dress on over her head and keep it from brushing the floor and getting dirty before she ever left the house. Her friend did up the plethora of buttons that lined the back.

"Thank you so much." Emma smiled and then took the time to admire herself in the small mirror. The green yards of flowing material were beautiful. She bit back tears as she thought of the many times her mother had worn the same dress. She hoped that at least Frederick would like it. If only she had the money to get a portrait taken. Something in her heart said it would be a night she would always remember.

Frederick stood before the mirror and tied his necktie for the fourth time. After taking the time to iron it, he was worried it would get wrinkled. With a twist and a turn he managed the small feat.

Now to finish combing his hair, although sometimes he wondered why he bothered. The seemingly endless rain, from mist to downpour, ruffled his locks at every turn.

"Thanks, Willum, for letting me get ready at your place," Frederick declared when he finally finished with his tie. How he hoped Emma wouldn't get upset with him when he told her he was leaving. He said a quick prayer that she would take the news well. He didn't want to break her heart, but he couldn't bear to take her away from the only family she had left either.

Once he had readied himself to satisfaction, he strolled out the door. Sweat beaded on his forehead even though it was cold outside. His nerve endings tingled when he thought about where and when he was going to tell Emma of his departure.

With his friends in Eureka expecting him in three days, and the arrangements already made, what choice did he have but to leave?

Frederick curtailed his thoughts when he knocked on the door. When Emma pulled the door open and stood on the threshold, his heart threatened to stop beating. His breath halted in his throat. Emma stood in a green gown, hair upswept in a neatly coifed bun, her eyes blazing with passion. Frederick wondered if he'd be able to tell her he was leaving, let alone actually follow through with his objective.

"Hello, Frederick. It's wonderful to see you." Emma batted her black eyelashes and aimed a radiant smile at him that endangered his carefully laid plans.

Emma smiled at Frederick and hoped it masked her sudden desire to throw herself into his arms.

"Good evening, Emma." Frederick grasped her gloved hand as she held it out to him, and he lifted it to his lips and laid a tender kiss there. How Emma wanted him to lay another kiss upon her lips, but proper ladies didn't say such things. Good heavens, how was she ever going to make it to Chicago with images of this handsome man tailing her every step of the journey?

"Are you all right?" Frederick looked at her with concern in his eyes.

"Yes, could you help me with my shawl, please?" Emma turned, allowing him to wrap the garment around her shoulders.

"Shall we?" Frederick offered his arm and motioned toward the covered buggy he had borrowed from friends. Even though it wasn't Frederick's, Emma stared at it and felt like a princess in a fairy tale being whisked away to the grand ball. The event was by invitation only, and it was by a stroke of luck that Frederick had obtained tickets from his father. All the more reason for Emma to feel like Cinderella.

Dinner was a delicious combination of roast goose and smoked salmon, along with baby red potatoes, and carrots glazed in sauce. Servants milled about, meeting the guests' every need, including Emma's. Frederick sat to her right, and every so often she noticed him staring at her with a strange expression on his face. Oh dear. She hoped he wouldn't confess to loving her.

There was much discussion regarding Mr. Elisha P. Ferry being sworn in as the new and first governor of Washington State. The orchestra played a collection of hymns, one of which was Emma's favorite. She hummed along with the comforting tune. It was also her mother's favorite. The melody caused memories of her mother to dance in her mind.

The tall woman had been the very picture of elegance, grace, and devotion to the Lord. Someone Emma had admired. Then came the day her father had died and Mama had clung to God with fiercer determination. Emma, who was angry at God for taking her father, didn't understand her mother's commitment to her faith. Things went from bad to worse when her mother hastily married someone she had courted only a short while.

Emma shook the frightening memories from her thoughts. If only she could shake them from her history as easily. Her breath came in gasps, and she couldn't draw enough air into her lungs. The tightly laced corset didn't help matters. This was her body's reaction every time she dared to entertain memories of her mother's final days. Well, she wasn't making the same mistakes, of that she was certain.

The orchestra finished the song. Emma drew courage and sat straighter in her chair as she spoke. "Frederick, I'd like to speak with you in private if I may."

The features on his face flickered with emotion before he replied. "Yes, there's something I need to discuss with you. Allow me."

Frederick rose and once again offered his arm. They strolled along the grounds of the rolling estate and discussed the stars in the heavens. Frederick pointed out the Big Dipper, holding her hand so she wouldn't fall along the path. In the cold night air, his touch lent comfort to the ache in her heart. The moon cast a glow about them.

Emma mustered courage to tell him of her plans to leave Tumwater, but he sat her down on a nearby bench before she had the chance. He sat down beside her with his hands clasped in his lap. For a brief moment she thought he might kiss her, but he acted too strangely for that.

Frederick hesitated for what seemed like an eternity. "I need to tell you something." This time an uncomfortable feeling rolled in Emma's middle. Something about his tone and tense body wasn't right.

Oh dear, please don't say "I love you"!

"Emma," he began, "I can't remain in Washington any longer. I am leaving for California day after next. Please don't be angry."

Emma's breath escaped her in one quick whoosh, and for a moment, she was unable to draw another. Frederick was leaving Washington? She had heard rumors of unrest murmured around camp, and of course, he would take them personally. She wanted to be angry with him, but couldn't, not when she was planning on leaving also.

"So you're not angry?" Frederick raised his eyebrows as if to question.

"No, I'm not angry. Perhaps disappointed." Emma blurted the statement without giving much thought as to what she was saying.

"Disappointed?" Frederick leaned back and aimed a puzzled look at her.

"I never would have expected a man of your caliber to run

away from the face of difficulty." Emma bit her lip at the cruelty of her words. The blaze in his eyes told her she had hurt him and she was immediately sorry. Her soul ached with the sting of her actions. This was her last night with dear Frederick. She never expected her own heart to hurt so much.

"I don't run from anything. But I don't stand around and let folks get away with calling me a liar either. It's a matter of pride."

"Then I guess this is good-bye. I was going to tell you tonight. I'm going to Chicago with Jake." Emma lifted her chin and gave her words a minute to register.

"So you're leaving, too. Just when were you planning on sharing this news with me?" He stood, with his hands on his hips.

"I can't stand living with the camp's drudgeries another day, Frederick. It's so rough and dirty, and besides, I need to stick close to my brother. He's watched out for me for so long, I need to be there for him in return. I owe that to him." Emma paused. "I need him." All this was true, but she didn't have the heart to tell Frederick she was afraid of a man getting too close to her heart.

"Then I guess you're right, this is good-bye." Frederick stood in stony silence, and the words sank to the depths of Emma's heart like a heavy boat anchor.

Without another word, he offered his arm and escorted her back to the carriage. The entire ride back home was made without a word. Like a perfect gentleman, he helped her alight from the carriage and escorted her to her door. He then lifted her hand to his lips and placed a gentle kiss on the back of her gloved hand. She had barely enough time to get inside the door and shut it quietly behind her before the painful sobs tore loose from her heart. Outside, she heard his footsteps echo in the night as he walked away. . .forever.

Two days later, Frederick boarded a train heading south to California. It had been hard saying good-bye to his best friends. Willum had taken the news with understanding, but E.V. had hardly said a word to him since he made the announcement.

Prayer and time with the Lord seemed as dry as a day-old biscuit. Much like it had before he left. This made him question whether or not he was doing the right thing. While studying his devotions at yet another stop along the way, a scripture spearheaded its way into his heart.

"Except the Lord build the house, they labour in vain that build it."

Frederick slammed his Bible shut. The last thing he needed was to second-guess his well-intentioned plans. The next time they stopped he would send a telegram to his three friends in Tumwater to see how they were doing. He missed them already.

The next afternoon, Frederick arrived at his friend's house. A telegram was waiting. Frederick noted the return address—the logging camp. He tore open the message.

Mr. Wilkin said another accident had happened, and it couldn't be blamed on Jake or Frederick this time. Mr. Kenicky and his company were conducting an investigation and getting to the bottom of things. They begged him to come back and testify at the inquiry.

Frederick marched straight to the telegraph office and sent a message that he would be on the next train back to Tumwater.

He had lost the woman he loved, so far as he was concerned, but at least he could clear his good name. Frederick wasted no time in heading back to the train station and back to Washington State.

Chapter 10

Emma stepped off the train in Chicago and searched in vain for the slightest sign of a tree, a bush, or anything that resembled nature. The racket of streetcars buzzing past nearly scared her silly. City life was going to take some getting used to. Jake wouldn't let her bring Bacon along on the train. She had to leave him with the Wilkins, and she feared he would actually become bacon!

Once at her uncle's house, Emma yearned for God's peace. The kind she had at the logging camp, in spite of the conditions. She asked her uncle about churches in town and what services he attended. The man brushed off the question like he would a pesky fly.

Her uncle then showed her where she would be living and where she would be working. Emma was highly disappointed in both. The living quarters were dirty and small. And her place of employment was a loud and smelly factory. It looked dangerous, too. She had thought the conditions at the logging camp were horrid. To make matters worse, the pay wasn't what she thought it would be.

The first night, trying to sleep in the small cot in her tiny room, Emma tossed and turned, thinking of Washington, the towering trees, the cool bubbling stream at the base of camp, of Bacon. . .and Frederick. Perhaps her heart had grown to love more than she thought it had.

Chicago wasn't anything like she expected. She wanted to go home to Washington, but she couldn't bear the thought of being away from Jake. She needed to wash his clothes and make him dinner. She needed to stand by him like he had done with her since their mother died. How could she tell him of her desires after she had begged so hard to come with him?

Working in the factory was nothing like cooking in the wide open spaces of the logging camp. The machines made a racket that hurt her ears and gave her a headache long before noon. Jake, on the other hand, was doing very well working at the newspaper behind his shiny new desk. And he was going to law school at night. He whistled on his way out the door to work and sang when he came home at night. Emma took great delight in seeing him so content.

One night, about three weeks after their arrival, her brother surprised her. "Sis, I know you're not happy here. Why don't you go back to Washington?"

"I can't leave you, Jake. Don't send me back to where I'll be all alone." Emma's mouth went dry as kindling and her eyes pooled with unshed tears.

"Emma, you won't be alone. You'll have the Wilkins and Bacon and Frederick."

"Jake, no." By now, tears streamed down Emma's cheeks like water over Tumwater Falls. "Jake, I'm afraid. I don't want to end up like Mama, hurt by a filthy man who guzzles whiskey from dawn till dusk."

"Mama remarried in haste. She had to do something to put a roof over our heads and clothes on our back. She realized before she passed, she made a mistake in not consulting the Lord. Take a year to stay with the Wilkins and see if you can find Fred, maybe ask his friends if they know where he is. If the Lord leads you to him, take some time to really get to know the man. I've prayed about it, Emma, and I believe this is what God wants. Uncle Irving and I'll come out to visit."

"Uncle Irving. . ." Emma hiccupped and dried her tears.

"He's already agreed to escort you back. You have plenty of time to get there before Christmas and go to Christmas Eve service." Jake smiled down at her. She was pleased that he saw her as a woman who could care for herself if necessary and not some child.

The next morning, Emma and Uncle Irving were on a train headed for Washington. They arrived in Tumwater a few days later, and her uncle checked them into the hotel in town. The Christmas Eve service was that night. Emma wanted to be with people she had grown to care for, namely the Wilkins. For the first time in weeks, her heart was at peace.

When she and Uncle Irving arrived at the church, she saw the back of a tall blond man standing in front of the building. Upon closer inspection, she noted his hand on the stair railing, a hand that looked so familiar. Could Frederick be back from California? It didn't seem possible.

Emma lifted her skirts and stepped closer. She looked up just in time to see the tall blond turn.

Frederick!

The breath went out of her in a wheezy gasp as she advanced

toward him with more speed than what was ladylike.

She fell against his chest and sobbed.

"I'll meet you inside." Uncle Irving planted a kiss on the top of her head then went inside the church.

Frederick held her in his arms and swore to never let her go.

"You, me, and Bacon, we're going to be a family," he teased. He leaned down and kissed her, a kiss she returned without fear and with all her heart. This evergreen night was one she would always remember.

Debby Lee is a happily married author with five children who lives in Centralia, Washington.

All Ye Faithful

Gina Welborn

Dedication

To my Inky Sisters: "Be light. Be love. Believe." isn't merely my calling—it's what I see lived out in you, and for that I am blessed every day. And to Jeremy for listening patiently each time I explained why the backspace key on my laptop was broken (again) and why MS Word is having "issues" (again) and why we need to order pizza for dinner (again).

Where no wood is, there the fire goeth out:
so where there is no talebearer, the strife ceaseth.
Proverbs 26:20 kjv

Chapter 1

Tumwater, Washington
December 1890

I've decided to throw caution to the wind and tell E.V. how I feel," Larkin Whitworth happily announced before plopping down in the wooden chair despite the fullness of her skirts and petticoats. She handed Anna the punch cup she'd refilled for the fifth time since Emma and Frederick's wedding celebration began. Considering how quickly her adorably—and abundantly—pregnant friend downed the apricot-flavored beverage, Larkin also offered the second cup she'd brought for herself while Anna's doting husband, Jeremiah, fetched a second plate of egg salad sandwiches.

"Really?" Anna exchanged the full cup with the empty one. "I can't figure why I'm so parched all day long."

"You're expecting. I think that's expected."

"I suppose." Anna fanned her sweat-glistened forehead. "Are you hot? I'm hot. It's hot."

As the fiddling increased in volume, signaling the beginning of another dance, Larkin took the fan from Anna and attended to cooling her *tillikum*, closest friend. Mama would be proud she was at least *thinking* Chinook jargon.

"I'm fine, but the *Farmer's Almanac* did predict a warm though wet—"

At Anna's raised hand, Larkin fell silent.

"We are both too young and the wrong gender to be discussing weather." Instead of drinking her punch, Anna gave Larkin a slant-eyed look. "Are you really going to tell Mr. Heartless Renier that you love him?"

Larkin glanced at E.V. His smooth face and sun-brightened hair made him easy to find among the many bearded and mustached men in the room. "Yes, and he isn't heartless, and the almanac conveys a wealth of information even women in the bloom of their youth can appreciate."

"Again, you know my rule against almanac talk. Shh. Now what, pray tell, do you call someone who convinces a girl he loves her"—Anna sipped the punch—"and then allows almost two years to pass without proposing? Or at least asking to court her?"

Larkin smiled. "He's—he's—" Her grin faltered somewhat, and she stopped fanning Anna. "Well, he's judicious." She hoped her tone conveyed every ounce of confidence she had in E.V. despite the tinge of doubt that seemed to be growing with each passing day.

"Judicious? Someone has been spending too much time reading." With a disappointed shake of her head that caused her floral-decked straw hat to tilt a fraction, Anna muttered, "I had a different descriptive in mind."

"Like what?"

Anna shrugged. "Oh, I don't know. Maybe something that rhymes with trout." She reclaimed the fan from Larkin and resumed fanning herself.

Larkin looked to the bridal couple doing a Virginia reel in the center of the warm barn with a score of other Tumwater residents, including E.V. and Abigail Leonard. Granted, E.V. didn't seem to be enjoying the dance as much as the other dancers were. Of course, Emma and Frederick Corrigan *were* newly married and thereby unable to *not* enjoy the moment.

Besides, E.V. had never made any overt claims on any woman since arriving in Tumwater two autumns ago, so Larkin had no cause to be jealous or wary or fretful.

Still, this was his third—*third!*—dance with Abigail.

And he had been spending more time than usual with Abigail's father, who was also spending more time than usual at E.V.'s sawmill. In fact, every time Larkin had walked by Renier Lumber Company during the last week—which was only because she passed it on her way to take lunch to her father at the brewery—she'd noticed Mr. Leonard's impressive roan gelding tied to a hitching post. If he was buying lumber, wouldn't he have brought a wagon?

Gripping the empty punch glass and resting her hands on her knees, Larkin's shoulders drooped just a fraction. The corset her mother required her to wear wouldn't allow an unladylike slump under her new yellow-and-ivory-striped gown. The gown her mother had insisted they go to Olympia to buy specifically for the wedding. After all, they needed to have another fitting on her Christmas gown anyway, or so Mama had justified to Papa. Since they were at the modiste's shop, being the kill-two-birds-with-one-stone person she was, Mama also bought a new gown for Larkin to wear to Anna's twentieth birthday party in a month. That brocade dress, unlike this year's burnished-gold Christmas one, was the exact shade of the limes grown in Mama's conservatory.

Lime next to Anna's ivory-with-a-touch-of-coral complexion was beautiful.

Lime next to the copper-toned skin Larkin had inherited from her one-quarter Chinook mother was practically morbid. Not that Larkin would suggest that to Mama, whose 1891 obsession apparently was with the color green. One of these days, though, she would convince her mother that every special event did not require a new gown. Certainly not one in a greenish hue. Or yellow, the color for the year of our Lord 1890. Or purple—Mama's earlier obsession. Or 1887's dreadful Year of the Orange.

She cringed in memory.

Why did Mama have to favor vibrant, look-at-me shades? As if the fanciness of Larkin's gowns weren't attention-demanding enough, Mama had to add rich, bold color. Larkin loved beige, muted browns, and earthy golds that subtly blended in with the surroundings.

Everyone in Tumwater knew Larkin was an heiress. The white Whitworth mansion ostentatiously located on a prominent corner near the center of town was enough of a daily reminder. She didn't need to be dressed like an unapproachable china doll for people to treat her differently.

Still, remembering that others were watching, Larkin sat up like a proper lady, so as to not bring any dishonor on her parents, and refocused on her agenda. The one that had begun after E.V. escorted Abigail to the dance floor for the third—*third!*—time.

She almost felt a tad angry.

All right, she did feel a tad angry. . .in fact, more than a tad angry.

"I think I shall confront E.V. once this dance is over."

"Confront? You?"

"I *can* confront." At Anna's dubious look, she added, "Why do you think I'm incapable of confronting someone?"

"Just where did Tuck go to find those sandwiches?" Anna rested her empty punch glass atop the empty one Larkin held. She rubbed the shifting bump on her almost-nine-month tummy. "This babe is a prized whopper in the making. Larky, you can do better than E.V. Renier. I think—"

"Please don't mention—"

"Willum Tate," Anna continued without skipping a beat, "personifies faithfulness and, according to the grapevine telegraph, those green eyes have stopped many Tumwater ladies in their tracks."

Larkin said nothing because she was used to Anna's weekly Willum Tate exaltation. And, truly, letting Anna have her say was far easier than trying to explain that she had no romantic feelings toward the impeccable-though-surly carpenter. Life had been more pleasant when plucky, fun-loving Anna fished, rummaged through the woods, and swam in the creek with Larkin. Before she ever noticed that members of the opposite gender were, well, quite appealing.

Or at least Jeremiah Tucker was.

Anna leaned closer and spoke low even though they were the only two in this corner of the barn. "Kathleen said when she was in the mercantile this morning she heard Mrs. Bollen tell her daughter-in-law Martha that she heard cranky ol' Mrs. Ellis complimenting Willum Tate at the livery to Mr. and Mrs. Parker, and Mrs. Ellis doesn't compliment *anyone* but you. Ever."

"Why do you think that is?" Larkin asked to distract Anna from praising the splendidly handsome Mr. Tate, who was currently dancing with Anna's sister even while oddly focused on Natalie Bollen, who was dancing with the handsome-but-not-as-quite Mr. John Seymour, who the grapevine telegraph seemed convinced would be Natalie's first official suitor once she turned eighteen next June. Larkin quickly added, "About people saying Mrs. Ellis is cranky. She is quite a dear heart once you get to know her. I don't understand why everyone in town hates her. Poor Mrs. Ellis is truly misunderstood."

Anna didn't answer. Instead she stared at Larkin for what seemed to be a minute or two.

"My friend," she finally said, "you aren't and will never be crafty. There's nice, and then there's you—nicer than nice. You're sweet, sincere, and selfless."

"Thank you, but you're as sweet—"

"Shh. I have never heard either you or Mr. Tate say anything critical about that ornery old woman who almost shot off my left foot when I came within two feet of her back fence because I foolishly—and incorrectly—thought that the skunk chasing me was worse than Mrs. Ellis. You and Willum are clearly suited."

"And E.V. and I aren't?"

"It's been two years, Larky. If he really cared about you, he'd have asked to court you by now. E.V. doesn't deserve you. Willum Tate, though, needs a good woman."

After a sigh at hearing the name of the man Anna had

championed this year as *the ideal husband. . .after mine of course,* Larkin thought back to Anna's descriptive of E.V. rhyming with trout. "There's no fitting word for E.V. that rhymes with—"

"Lout," Anna blurted.

Larkin rolled her eyes. "He isn't a lout."

"Gout."

"That's a disease."

"Indian scout, unbearably stout, German bean sprout."

Larkin fought back her smile. "Now you're being silly."

A smug grin teetered on Anna's lips. Her brown-eyed gaze shifted from Larkin to the dancers, then back to Larkin, and her voice softened with what seemed—no, felt—like sympathy. "Doubt."

Larkin dropped her gaze to the yellow shoes peeking out from the ankle-length ivory-lace hem of her gown. She poked at the straw under her toes. That tingle of doubt she'd been trying to ignore rang like the bells she'd received the last two Christmases from an anonymous admirer. She liked to dream they were from the blond man with an adorable cleft in his chin, the man who gave her such tender attention the first autumn he moved into Tumwater, the man who faithfully attended worship services and always sat in the pew one row back and to the left of her, and who bought her meal baskets at every church auction.

The quiet sawmiller who every Wednesday at a quarter past nine met her at the front steps to the Bollens' parsonage and delivered half a ham while she brought a basket of pies or fruit, and then walked her home. Even on the days it rained, which was most days, after all, because when did it not rain in the Washington Cascades?

A man that faithful, that consistent, had to care, right?

He loved her. She knew he did because he said more in the looks he gave her than in any conversation they'd ever had.

And they'd had myriad conversations in the last two years—enough for her to learn how important overcoming his father's failings was to E.V. and for him to learn she feared embarrassing her parents.

Yet that same man had not spared a glance at the two friends sitting near the entrance of the barn. No, Eric Valentin Renier III hadn't looked her way any more than Willum Tate had. Did he think she'd given up on them having a future together? Or had his feelings merely changed?

They hadn't spoken in over a week. During the last conversation, E.V. had seemed irritated, wouldn't look at her, and jerked back every time she drew close.

"Larkin, you're doing it again."

"What?" she said without looking up.

"That glazed look you get when you're deep in thought. I don't care if it's what those with Chinook blood do. It's creepy."

Oddly not humored by the good-natured ribbing, Larkin turned in her chair to face Anna, whose delicate beauty glowed with love and pregnancy. "Do you think I should tell him how I feel?" she hesitantly asked. "Say yes, and I'll do it, right here in front of everyone."

Anna's winged brows drew together in sadness. "Oh Larkin, when have you ever done anything that would intentionally draw attention to yourself?"

Larkin flinched. Never. But this was 1890, the year she'd vowed would be different, and up to this point, she hadn't done a single thing different or courageous or adventuresome because she never did anything different or courageous or adventuresome unless she was with Anna. And ever since Anna married Jeremiah Tucker, Larkin had even less opportunity to be anything but the dullard she was.

At twenty-one, she was the only female in Tumwater of courting age who had never had a suitor. Either no one had the courage to approach her father or, worse, none wanted a nicer-than-nice wife.

Why not tell E.V. that she loved him? That she wanted to marry him.

She had little to lose and all the world to gain.

A year from now she wanted to be the one sitting in a chair soothing her rounded belly while Anna brought her copious amounts of beverages.

Decision made, she reached over Anna to set the punch cups in Jeremiah's chair. She then deftly removed the pin holding her feathered hat atop her head. The last thing she wanted was to join E.V. in a dance and have her hat slide over her eyes, blocking her view, causing her to trip over his feet, and consequently crash into someone while flipping her skirts up in the air. Not that that had ever happened to her, but it could. One should always prepare for the worst while expecting the best.

She stood and placed her hat in her vacant seat. "Don't let me leave here without it."

Anna gasped. "You're really going to do this, aren't you?" She grabbed Larkin's hand and drew up to standing. Panic blanched her face. "I know I almost lost Tuck by letting him think I loved Garrick when I really loved him, but what will your parents say? Just think about what the grapevine telegraph will say. Don't do it."

As far as the grapevine telegraph went—well, people never gossiped about her, because she never did anything worth gossiping about. She could speak to E.V. here at the wedding reception without anyone listening in because, after all, why would anyone want to overhear what she had to say? She was the last person anyone would *ever* suspect of doing something noteworthy or mysterious.

Considering Papa was at home tending to Mama, they wouldn't know what happened until she told them in the morning. By then she and E.V. would be courting. And Papa would see they were in love and would agree to the marriage.

Being an heiress, being someone everyone except Abigail Leonard liked, being known as sweet and sincere and selfless—none of it mattered much if she had no one to enjoy life with. Anna had Jeremiah and soon a baby, too. Her parents had their own lives.

She didn't want to grow old alone.

She didn't want to be Mrs. Ellis, warning people away with her shotgun because she believed the pain of another broken heart was worse than being alone.

She wanted to love and be loved because she believed—no, she *knew* to the depths of her soul—she was created to love and be loved. And since her father allowed her to court—she was old enough, after all—then, logically, wouldn't it be acceptable for her to initiate the courting? Even Ruth had to nudge the honorable-yet-stubborn Boaz into action.

Time to be bold and adventuresome.

Hearing the music of the dance dwindling to the end, Larkin kissed Anna's cheek.

"I vow before you have that baby, E.V. and I will be married. No matter what it takes. No matter what I have to throw to the wind." She felt the corners of her mouth draw upward. "Within reason of course.

Chapter 2

He wasn't going to look her way. Wasn't. Not even when his position on the dance floor brought her in direct line of sight. Because once he did, E.V. knew he would be lost in the depths of those eyes. Eyes so greenish-gold they reminded him of mossy tree bark—words not worthy of a Shakespearean sonnet and words he certainly would never share with her. He wasn't a man with much to say. And besides, he knew his girl didn't need or desire besotted praise.

Loving Larkin Whitworth made him more, made him want to share more, made him want to be more.

What he needed though, was time.

And he had spent enough of that on his knees in prayer during almost two years of having his marriage proposals rejected by her father, to know he also needed a miracle in the form of a large lumber supplier. Once he'd built Renier Lumber Company into the most profitable mill in Tumwater—and one more large supplier would do it—he'd prove his work ethic, worthiness, and his ability to provide for Larkin to her wealth-focused father.

Tonight he was two steps closer to that miracle.

Literally.

All he had to do was pay enough attendance on Abigail Leonard for the other bachelors in town to realize she was an available female, even if the Caesar-like nose she'd inherited from her father was too large for her face. To be fair, she was no Larkin, but neither was she the least attractive female in the room. Considering the number of men who had already danced with Miss Leonard at the wedding, E.V. felt confident that his—and her father's—plan was succeeding.

Competition brought out the warrior instincts in every man, especially with a woman involved.

As the musicians allowed the last notes to die, E.V. graciously escorted Miss Leonard back to her father and met three other bachelors waiting, he hoped, to ask the slender blond to dance. Harvey Milton, Reverend Bollen's middle son David—the one E.V. long suspected of harboring feelings for Miss Leonard—and Frederick's new brother-in-law Jake Pearson immediately began complimenting Miss Leonard. She did look nice in her odd-shade-of-red (or maybe pink) gown. Larkin would know the exact color. Men needed wives so they didn't need to know these types of things.

As abruptly as the compliments began, the three men facing Miss Leonard fell silent, their gazes shifting from her confused expression to something E.V. would have to turn around to see. Harvey's mouth gaped a bit. Jake stood taller. David though, seemed to recover himself and looked longingly at Miss Leonard, who stepped closer to her father and, E.V. could've sworn, whispered, "Do something, Daddy."

Before E.V. could turn and look, Mr. Leonard clenched E.V.'s arm. "Renier, we need to talk."

At the harshness of Leonard's tone, E.V. felt a ripple of tension center between his eyebrows. He didn't mind helping Silas Leonard secure a husband for his oldest daughter, but his feet were aching, his mouth parched, and stomach rumbling, and if the barn grew any warmer from the body heat of all the wedding guests, he'd have to shed the black tailored coat he'd used his last bit of savings to purchase two years ago to wear to Larkin's birthday party in hopes of attracting her attention. Still, he needed the contract, and if Leonard wanted to talk, E.V. would listen.

He opened his mouth, intent on uttering his well-practiced "yes sir," when the sweetest voice he'd yearned to hear say, "Yes, I'll marry you," broke the taut silence.

"Mr. Renier, might I have a word?"

E.V. found his breath and turned to Larkin, now standing close enough for him to pull her into his arms for a lengthy kiss. Loose strands of her black hair caressed the sides of her high cheekbones. He ached to pin them back into the neat and tidy bun she always wore underneath a hat she was forever taking off and forgetting. Whenever she smiled—and he prayed she wouldn't at this moment, for his sake—the dimples on the sides of her mouth testified she'd inherited all the beauty of her part-Chinook mother and the whimsy of her Irish-English father.

Everything about her took his breath away.

"Daa—dee," Miss Leonard whispered (more aptly, whined) again.

"Yes, a word, Miss Whitworth," E.V. blurted before Silas Leonard could make another demand. "We could speak over by the punch table." He motioned that direction. "I could use a drink." Remembering the contract he needed, he met Leonard's intense gaze. "We won't be but a moment, sir."

Larkin took a step then stopped. Her sweet-natured gaze settled on Miss Leonard. "Oh Abigail, cerise is certainly your color. You look lovely today." Larkin then nodded at Jake, Harvey, and David to acknowledge their presence but spoke only to Jake. "Please express to the newlyweds my apologies for my parents' absence. Mama. . ." She looked uneasy for a split-second. Then the corners of her mouth curved softly. "The wedding was delightful."

E.V. stepped to Larkin's side, touched the small of her back in the most platonic manner he could possibly manage, and nudged her into walking before drawing his hand away from her. He focused on keeping the distance between them not too close to appear as anything but friends. When she would close the gap, he would ease to the left, keeping propriety in mind.

Since she said nothing, he remained silent also as they wove through the wedding guests joining the line for another dance. Though Larkin was several inches shorter than Miss Leonard, he couldn't—nor did he want to—shake the feeling that Larkin was perfectly made for him. To think their relationship began over a tray of cookies spilled by Miss Leonard's brother.

The words *will you marry me?* languished on the tip of his tongue. Only he couldn't ask until he'd gained her father's approval first. The Whitworth family honor was too important to them for E.V. to bring it any shame.

They stopped at the refreshment table. Larkin filled a glass of punch, handed it to him, then picked up a plate and looked over the food offerings.

Aware of how alone they were, yet at a public event, E.V. found himself admiring the curve of her neck and the finger-length strands of hair escaping from the bun, which seemed even blacker against the yellow and ivory stripes of her silky gown. He clenched the punch glass. He wasn't going to touch her. Wasn't. Not even when the distance between them was less than an arm's length.

Was there anything in life he desired more than her?

"I hope you like egg salad and smoked salmon."

E.V. blinked. "Ahhh. . ."

"They seem to be the norm at weddings here in Tumwater," Larkin continued, "which is why I intend on having something totally different when we—umm, when I marry." Her head tilted to the left as she looked up at him, and her mouth curved enough for him to see hints of her dimples. "Were you paying attention to me?"

To her words, not so much.

To her, absolutely.

And he felt as much irritation as joy in being this close to her.

Understanding exactly how a parched man viewing an oasis felt, E.V. downed his punch. Two years of waiting. Two years of once-a-week marriage requests and immediate rejections. Two years of answering even the most obscure question about his family while enduring reminders of his father's failure from Larkin's father. E.V. had been steadfast, resolute, and patient. By remembering his sinful nature was dead and Christ now lived through him, he could endure as long as needed. The reward was too great to give up now.

The prize—Larkin—was too precious to lose.

"You wished to speak to me?" he asked as the musicians began another tune. Immediately he regretted the exasperated sound of his tone. Since he couldn't explain to her the struggle between his honor and his desires, he simply mumbled, "Sorry. Please, go on."

"Yes." Looking unsure of herself, she took the punch glass and gave him a plate of finger-sized sandwiches. "E.V., I know we—you—well, at least I felt there was something special between—" She broke off, and her gaze shifted as if to see who was watching them.

E.V. glanced to his right and groaned.

Miss Leonard strode purposely toward them, her progress occasionally halted by couples exchanging partners in the brisk dance.

Larkin touched his wrist, drawing his attention. "Do you remember when Reverend Bollen preached about prayer the Sunday before Thanksgiving?" she rushed out.

He nodded.

"He said faith in action is trusting God with our future even when our prayers aren't answered." Her gaze focused on where he'd turned his hand enough to touch the inside of her wrist, yet she didn't draw away. "I am trying to trust. I also need to know that I have reason to hope my future will include—"

"Mr. Renier!" Miss Leonard called out.

Larkin pulled away, leaving E.V.'s skin chilled despite the unseasonable warmth in the barn. She turned from him and smiled at Miss Leonard. "Is there a problem?"

Miss Leonard stopped too close to E.V. for his comfort, but the table on his left blocked him from moving away. "Daddy needs to speak to you."

"About?"

She playfully tapped his arm. "About trees, silly."

E.V. took a leisurely bite of an egg salad sandwich. After a quick grimace, he chewed, swallowed, then muttered, "Miss Whitworth and I are in a conversation," before finishing off the bland sandwich.

"Daddy said *now*."

Annoyed by her demanding tone, E.V. reached behind him to pat the table in search of a punch cup. He wasn't their lackey. "Give me a moment, will you please?"

While Larkin refilled his drink, Miss Leonard's lips pursed, and if he were a gambling man, he'd swear one of her feet was tapping impatiently on the straw-covered barn floor.

"Fine. But do know if Daddy feels you aren't serious about working with him, he has an increased offer from a more established and experienced mill that he'd be a fool not to accept. Good day, Mr. Renier." Without even sparing Larkin an *I acknowledge your presence* glance, she swiveled on her heel and began walking away.

E.V. looked across the barn to spy Leonard's ashen-blond, oiled head. The man stood at least half a foot taller than any other man in the room. He was speaking to the other two sawmill owners in town. The shorter, sour-faced one was currently buying Leonard's lumber; the taller, heavily-wrinkled-despite-his-age man was the one E.V. had heard was also courting Leonard's business. His competition.

Panic welled in E.V.'s chest. Earlier this week, Leonard vowed he'd make a decision who to make a new lumber contract with at the wedding reception. So far, he had yet to say a word on the subject to E.V.

Help me, Lord. I need his lumber.

"Wait, Miss Leonard!" Once she halted, E.V. took the drink Larkin offered and lowered his voice so only she could hear. "This is important. I have to— I can't lose—"

"Mr. Renier," Miss Leonard said in that increasingly shrill voice of hers, "Daddy isn't as patient as I am."

E.V. grimaced.

Larkin waved him away. "Go on. What I wanted to say can wait."

"Are you sure?"

With a soft curve to her lips, she nodded.

E.V. downed the apricot-flavored punch as quickly as he could. "Don't leave. We haven't had our dance yet."

Larkin took his plate and empty punch cup and said nothing, which was something E.V. loved about her. Unlike most females, especially the verbose Miss Leonard, Larkin spoke only what needed to be said and not to fill silence.

"You're a gem." After snatching two of the remaining sandwiches off his plate, E.V. leaned forward to place a kiss on Larkin's cheek when he remembered Miss Leonard and no telling how many others watched them. He drew back. Until he secured her father's approval, he wouldn't do anything to slight Larkin's reputation or her family's honor. "I won't be gone long."

She merely nodded again.

E.V. caught up to Miss Leonard and walked with her to her father, who stood talking to the two sawmill owners. Unlike Jake Pearson and Harvey Milton, who seemed to have found other females to dance with, David Bollen stood against the barn wall glaring, it seemed, at E.V.

Mr. Leonard stopped talking and patted E.V.'s shoulder. "Nice to see you again, son. Burr, Odell, and I were discussing how focused you've been in building up your sawmill these last two years. Took Burr four years to achieve the same production level. Took Odell, here, seven."

"Would have taken less than seven," Odell grumbled, "but my wife kept having babies. Women are a distraction."

Burr patted the shorter man's back. "While my success came in half the time, I have a fourth of the children you do. I'd gladly trade years for more sons."

Silas Leonard nodded. "I know what you mean." His gaze settled on E.V. "When a man reaches our age, he realizes how important children and grandchildren are." His eyes narrowed a bit as his gaze shifted to his daughter then back to E.V., who immediately felt a wave of wariness. "Renier, take Abby for a spin about the room. I'll talk to you after I finish with Odell and Burr."

"Sir," E.V. started, while trying not to show his aggravation at having been called *son* by a man he wanted as nothing more than a business associate, "I don't mind discussing the lumber contract right now."

"That's all good and fine," Leonard answered, "but I need to ponder the matter more. Go dance."

"Earlier David Bollen expressed interest in dancing with your daughter. He's right over—"

"David Bollen?" Miss Leonard laughed. "I treasure my toes too much to dance with that clod." Clearly oblivious to how loud her words were, giving audience to the dozen Tumwater residents around them, including Bollen, she tugged on E.V.'s arm. "Hurry, Mr. Renier, the two-step is about to start."

Feeling deceived by the Leonards, E.V. didn't move. If tomorrow he heard folks in Tumwater were wagering on him proposing to Abigail Leonard—

The sudden taste in his mouth was more unappealing than the egg salad sandwiches.

Mr. Leonard's heavy brows rose. "Listen, Renier, I don't have to give ear to what your mill can pay me. I have other options." He nodded to the center of the barn. "Get on. I wouldn't want my daughter's day ruined."

E.V. reluctantly nodded and, with Miss Leonard clinging possessively to his arm, stepped toward the dancers already lining up. Right now he was their lackey. And within reason, he would do what they asked until he secured that five-year, nonnegotiable, fully binding contract to buy lumber from Silas Leonard. The moment he did, he would distance himself from their family.

Minus Garrick Leonard. That man had twice the character the rest of his family members had.

"Before we dance," E.V. said as socially as he could despite his grim mood, "I'd like more punch."

"Why? She's gone." The cheerfulness in her tone was undeniable. Miss Leonard stopped walking in the middle of the barn and pointed to the refreshment table. "See. Larkin left, even though you kindly asked her to stay. Imagine how dishonoring she will be to her future husband when he asks her to do something. She has such a selfish, rebellious spirit. A God-fearing man would be a fool to marry her."

E.V. gritted his teeth to keep from countering her spiteful assessment of Larkin. Confident his girl was merely somewhere else in the barn, he circled slowly, seeking her yellow-and-ivory-striped gown. Once he found Larkin, he'd ensure that she knew he loved her.

Where was she? Probably with Anna and Tuck.

He looked their direction. No, they sat contented and alone near the barn's half-open east door. Tuck laughed at whatever Anna was saying, and beyond them a light rain shower glistened in the afternoon sunshine. On the chair next to Anna was Larkin's feather-decked hat. No Larkin.

"See, I told you she left."

E.V. focused on the rain dripping down the barn door's frame. While wisdom said Larkin was too proper to walk out into the rain, he knew she wouldn't have left unless she had a good reason. "I need to make sure she gets home safely." He took a step, and with both hands, Miss Leonard grabbed his arm, stopping him.

"Oh, no need for the gallantry, Mr. Renier," she said, smiling. "While you were talking to Daddy, I watched Larkin get into the Whitworth carriage. Stop worrying." She tugged on his coat sleeve. "Let's dance. Daddy is watching, and I aim to do all I can to ensure you get that contract you want."

E.V. glanced across the barn to see her father was indeed watching them. Relieved that Larkin wasn't walking home in the rain, he escorted Miss Leonard to the other dancers, minus David Bollen, who also seemed to have disappeared. Tomorrow when Larkin was at worship services, E.V. would find a way to speak to her privately. To encourage her to be patient. To wait.

No one, not Abigail Leonard or Larkin's father, would come between them.

Chapter 3

Who had stuffed her mouth with cotton? Why was the room so hot? Without even opening her eyes, which were too tired anyway, Larkin reached for her chest to remove whatever weight was on it and found several heavy quilts. She felt—

"Awful," she croaked.

"Yes, dear," Mama said softly, "you do look terrible. I imagine you must feel it, too."

Larkin opened her heavy lids to the sunlight brightening her pristine white bedroom, only to shield them from the painful light. She tried to raise her head from the many pillows behind her, but her head, neck, and shoulders ached.

Every time she felt sick, her mother made her stay in bed for a week, not by demanding it but by "medicating" her with the honey-whiskey-herb sleep aid she'd learned from her Chinook mother, who'd learned it from her mother, who learned it from the Scottish fur trader she'd married at Fort Astoria back in 1811. One drink to cure all ills.

And it didn't taste any better with additional honey or spices.

Larkin shuddered.

Mama, sitting in one of the two Queen Anne chairs near the

hearth, put down her embroidery. She lifted a crystal goblet from the circular table between the chairs and brought it to Larkin. Her crimson taffeta skirt rustled as she walked, her slanted brows rising in concern.

"Drink this, dearest." She offered the half-full goblet that Larkin didn't take. She could smell the whiskey on her mother's breath.

"I'm fine," Larkin rushed to say as she kicked off the excessive blankets. Then realizing her head, neck, and shoulders didn't ache as much as they felt stiff from nonuse, she stopped kicking as abruptly as she started. Her bladder was near close to exploding. And everything in her room seemed to spin, which made her nauseous. Remembering the frigid rain she'd walked home through after leaving the wedding, she knew—*knew*—what happened after she'd returned home last night. She closed her eyes and gripped her bed to still the spinning and to think.

Was it last night?

Larkin looked to the clock on the mantel above the fireplace. She blinked until her eyes could focus. Six minutes until eleven o'clock.

She met her mother's gaze. "What day is it?"

"Thursday."

"Thursday?" She immediately regretted yelling because it only made her head ache more. Her day had just started and was turning into one of regrets. She rolled her eyes because that seemed to be the only movement that didn't make her regretful. "You medicated me again. For four and a half days. Mama! Why?"

Tears glistened in Mama's dark eyes. "To ward off *sick tumtum.*"

Sickness of the body.

Larkin never had the courage to remind her mother that the actual translation of sick tumtum was sickness of the heart.

While Maire-Dove Larkin Whitworth dressed with the elegance of any society grand dame, in moments like this, Mama looked more like the superstitious native Papa had tried for years to cure her of being. He'd even had her black hair lightened to almost a blond and required she stay out of the sun so her skin would stay more cream than copper, which caused most in Tumwater to forget she was a *Metis*, mixed-blood. Then again, a good number of Washingtonians could claim a degree of Indian blood. Even Anna boasted being Dutch-Scots so she could be included in the American crucible of races.

"I'm not—I wasn't sick," Larkin clarified.

"Your gown was soaked when you arrived. Your teeth were chattering and your nose was red." Mama paused. "I heard you cough."

"But that didn't mean you needed to medicate me."

"Darling, you're feverish."

"Not from any sickness." Although, she did feel a bit dizzy from the medication—not that she'd tell her mother—and her head felt utterly heavy. Larkin removed the last blanket and unbuttoned the neckline of the ridiculously ornate nightgown she always found herself in after waking up with sick tumtum, real or imaginary. "Mama, you're smothering me again."

"I don't wish. . ." With a broken sob, Mama sat on the edge of the bed. "I am, aren't I? My heart can't bear losing you, too."

Although she figured the pain of losing a sibling couldn't be as deep as that of losing a child, Larkin understood why Mama behaved as she did. Though it had been almost five years since her brother died, the intensity of missing him hurt more than any physical pain she'd ever suffered. Some nights she'd wake thinking Sean had once again stolen into her room and invited her to join him in another adventure that would earn them a paddling, lecture, or usually both. Unlike her, nothing about Sean had been dull. Life without him still didn't feel right.

Her heart and frustration softening with compassion, she eased forward on the bed until she could rest her head on her mother's shoulder. She wrapped her arms around Mama and prayed for patience with—and peace for—her mother. . .and for herself.

Oh Lord God, I know I shouldn't have walked home in the rain, considering Mama's fears, but I couldn't bear seeing Abigail cling to E.V. as if he were hers. Either take away my love for E.V. or show me why I should continue waiting for him.

"Loving and losing someone hurts," she whispered, "but it'll be all right, Mama. I'll be all right. You're going to be all right." Someday. She kissed Mama's shoulder. "God has us in His hands. *Naika ticky maika.*"

Mama patted Larkin's hands. "I love you, too."

Larkin closed her eyes, lids still heavy from the last dose of Mama's feeling-sick drink. While she wouldn't mind sleeping off the aftereffects of the medication, she needed to deliver pies, or something else if the pies weren't baked, to the Bollen parsonage. Bringing the family food every Wednesday was the least she could do for the service and ministry they provided Tumwater.

Considering it was Thursday, not Wednesday, she doubted E.V. would be waiting to walk with her to the Bollens'.

She glanced across the room to the mirror atop her vanity

table. Her hair appeared clean yet tangled from having been washed and dried as she slept; her eyes had violet bags underneath. Overall, not the best she'd looked nor the worst. Yet if she hurried to dress and didn't run into any human obstacles on the way, she could deliver food to the Bollens and still make it to the brewery in time to share a luncheon with Papa.

Yes, a brisk walk would do wonders.

Her stomach rolled. First though, she needed to empty her stomach and bladder.

Knowing something else needed to go down the commode as well, Larkin took the cordial from her mother. "We've both had enough."

Chapter 4

"Still content to pine for your ladylove? I'd have thought with Mrs. Ellis's praise, the 'impeccable Mr. Tate' would have earned the right to court any lady in Tumwater." E.V. shoved the tail ends of the freshly cut pine boards into the filled wagon then smacked his gloves together to rid them of wood shavings. With a crooked grin, he patted Willum's shoulder as Willum leaned over the side of the wagon, staring absently at the wooden planks in the bed. "Well, you know what they say."

"No, what do they say?" Willum grumbled.

"If at first you don't succeed," E.V. said, resting his elbows on the wagon's side, "try and try again. That's my motto."

The "impeccable" Mr. Tate did little more than glare in response. Any frown was hidden by his bristly winter beard, yet despite his lumberjack appearance, Willum was still the grapevine telegraph's favorite bachelor. Apparently, women liked his green eyes, shoulder-length hair, and ability to construct anything from outhouses to rabbit houses to tree houses to homes almost as large as the Whitworth mansion.

Considering how much attention Willum received from women, he should've been the first between Jeremiah, Frederick,

E.V., and him to marry. Would have been if things had worked out differently.

E.V. looked to the buildings opposite the mill. At the right end of the street was the whitewashed church. At the other end of Main Street was the Whitworth Brewery, one of the many businesses in town Larkin's father owned, or partially owned. E.V. didn't want to think about the companies the man owned throughout the Pacific Northwest region.

Everything Whitworth touched turned into a financial success.

After all the thirty-minute Wednesday morning visits they'd shared since E.V. began asking for Larkin's hand in marriage one-hundred-and-two-weeks ago, E.V. knew that for every financial loss, Patrick Whitworth had a dozen successes. The man would have to face losses as catastrophic as Job had to be considered a failure. Unlike E.V.'s father, who had an uncanny ability to lose the family fortune and manage two banks and a railroad into bankruptcy over the course of ten years. For all their differences, his father and Mr. Whitworth shared one commonality: faith in money to solve all woes and none in God.

As E.V. and Willum stood in silence, their breath puffed in misty clouds into the cool December air. Not quite freezing but getting there. To think almost a week ago the afternoon temperature was twenty degrees warmer.

So much for the *Farmer's Almanac*'s prediction of a warm though wet December.

"How much of a prediction," E.V. said breaking the silence, "is it for the almanac to say it'll be wet this time of year when it's always wet this time of year?" He looked into the increasing clouds in the bright yet gray sky. "We have two hours at most before the next shower."

Willum sighed loudly. "I don't see how Whitworth can reject you when you and his daughter are the most weather-obsessed people in town." He withdrew something from his heavy yet tattered woolen coat and stared wistfully at it.

Best E.V. could tell, it was a palm-sized carving of some type of animal. If Willum ever stopped building and repairing houses, he could make a living with his intricate wood carving skill alone.

Content to let their conversation die, E.V. hummed "Joy to the World" as he watched the occasional jingle-bell-decked wagon or buggy roll past. He hoped to see the mail wagon. Any day now, the sterling Gorham bell he'd ordered for Larkin for Christmas would arrive. This year he planned on making it an engagement gift instead of a gift from an anonymous admirer.

"Eric, are you ever going to stop asking to marry Larkin?"

At that moment, E.V. realized Willum was in a more surly mood than usual, because those were the only times Willum ever called him by his given name.

From the corner of his eye, E.V. glanced at Willum. He looked wounded. Broken. Love never seemed to treat Willum well.

"No," he honestly answered. "Is there something else bothering you?"

Willum's grip tightened around the carving. "What if Whitworth never agrees?"

"He will."

"Your confidence borders on foolishness. Sometimes you need to cut your losses." Willum turned to face E.V. "You should sell the mill and start a business where you don't have to be at Silas

Leonard's beck and call."

"Can't," E.V. answered. "My investment partner will lose money, and I won't go back on my word. Besides, with the mammoth amount of wood you're regularly buying from me, I need another lumber supplier to keep up with the demand."

Willum shook his head in obvious disappointment—or maybe disbelief—that E.V. would choose faithfulness over the easy solution. The latter was more likely considering Willum's past. His gaze turned from E.V. and refocused on the carving he held.

E.V. breathed in the cool air. He loved Tumwater more than any other place he'd lived. "Willum, stop worrying on my behalf. The contract I'm offering Leonard makes us equals."

"He's doing his best to ensure his daughter is part of the contract."

"I realize that." *Now.* E.V. shuddered. In all his twenty-five years, he'd never felt as much a fool as he had during the last half of Frederick and Emma's wedding reception. Silas Leonard never had any intention of discussing the contract that day. No, he'd merely wanted it to look like E.V. was courting his daughter.

Willum repocketed the carving. "I need to get back to work, and you need to stop being so optimistic about life and intervene."

"Intervene in what?"

"In *that.*" He motioned to the paved sidewalk on the other side of the street.

At the intersection of Main and the street leading to the Whitworth Mansion, stood Larkin, wearing a mustard-colored cape and clutching a basket with both hands. Miss Leonard, clad in a reddish-pink cape, stood near the rear of the small buckboard she often drove around town. To say the two were having a conversation would be an overstatement because only Miss Leonard was talking, and whatever she was saying made Larkin's normally straight posture slump.

Without another word to Willum, E.V. took off running.

"The perfect Larkin Whitworth is pickled. I never thought I'd see the day." Abigail covered her mouth as if to hide her laughter, but Larkin still heard it, felt it, smelled every greasy bit of it. *Smelled it?*

Larkin breathed deep and grimaced. Since the linen-covered basket she carried only contained fruit from Mama's conservatory, the rancid odor had to be emanating from the white wicker picnic basket on the back of the Leonard buckboard.

"Abigail, stop. I'm not—"

Hearing footsteps crossing the bricked street, Larkin looked to her left and her vision momentarily blurred. How was it possible she felt worse after eating a soft-boiled egg and a bowl of bouillon? Now that she'd stopped walking, she felt so sleepy. She blinked until her eyesight cleared, although the movement—odd but true—sounded as loud as hammers against wood.

E.V. ran toward them, wearing denims and a woolen vest over a flannel shirt. How could he not be cold? Just looking at him made her shiver.

"I think the almanac got this December wrong," she mused aloud. "It doesn't feel warm at all."

Abigail leaned toward Larkin until their noses almost touched. "I know what a drunkard looks like and how one talks," she whispered, and her eyes seemed sad. But the familiar spiteful glee took its place so quickly Larkin knew she had imagined any sadness. The corners of Abigail's mouth indented into a smug grin. "E.V.'s finally going to see you aren't the good Christian girl you've convinced everyone you are. I win. You lose."

Larkin blinked at the surprising and eerily cheerful admission. She'd never felt they were enemies, even though Abigail had never been receptive to her overtures of friendship.

"When did we begin a competi—?"

"Mornin', ladies," E.V. said as he stopped at the back of the buckboard, approximately equal distance between them, Larkin noted. His warm breath showed in the chilly air, the tip of his nose a little red.

Thrilled to end the confusing conversation with Abigail, Larkin tilted her head, which wasn't any less heavy since she woke up an hour ago, and studied him. Something was different. His short yellow hair was still sun-bleached to almost white at the tips because he never wore a hat. His eyes were still a lovely shade—medium brown with golden rays in the iris and possibly some orange. Rather similar in color to the vile honey-whiskey cordial she had dumped out despite Mama's protest.

He wasn't as stunningly attractive as Mr. Tate, but Larkin liked E.V.'s square-jawed, dimpled-chinned, less-than-shining handsomeness. Still, what was different about him?

"Your face is bristly," she muttered.

E.V. nodded. "I didn't shave this morning."

"Why not?" she blurted.

"I hate shaving so I only do it on Sundays, Wednesdays, and special occasions like my friends' weddings. My skin is sensitive."

He looked at her oddly. "Are you all right?"

Larkin smiled and nodded and hoped that was enough of an answer—only she nodded too much. The pounding in her head increased, causing the food Cook had claimed would lessen the aftereffects of the cordial to roll in her stomach.

This was the worst Mama had ever medicated her. She needed to leave before she lost her breakfast, yet propelled by curiosity, she asked, "Then why do you shave at all?"

"Larkin Whitworth!" Abigail sniped in her irritatingly shrill voice. "I can't believe you asked Mr. Renier something so personal." She stepped closer to E.V. and touched his sleeve. "Mr. Renier, let me apologize for my dear friend. I hate to say this, but she's been imbibing."

"I haven't," and "She has?" came out in unison.

E.V. stepped around Abigail to face Larkin. "You don't look well."

"I'm fine," she muttered then realized that was a lie, because she didn't feel the least bit fine. Abigail was correct in that she was pickled—or at least suffering the after effects—but it wasn't intentional, and to clarify everything would mean sharing Mama's problem. Larkin would never bring shame to her mother. Never. Not even to protect her own reputation. "I'm sorry, I must go." She pointed to the parsonage. "The Bollens need fruit, and I don't feel. . ."

Leaving her words to hang in the air, Larkin walked away slowly. She kept her pace steady despite the unevenness of the sidewalk, the churning of her stomach, and the perspiration on her forehead.

For as cold as December was, somehow it had grown as warm as July.

"Larkin's so pickled she doesn't make sense." Miss Leonard wrapped her red-gloved hand around E.V.'s arm. "It's a shame, you know, for her to behave like this, but it's best to know the truth." She gasped and covered her mouth. "Imagine marrying her and then learning about her preference for strong drink."

E.V. stayed focused on Larkin. She'd faintly smelled of whiskey. Because of his past before his salvation, he knew the scent well. Yet something was wrong. His girl wasn't a drunkard or even an occasional imbiber. During the fish fry Anna and Tuck held to celebrate their one-year anniversary, Larkin had shared with him her frustration and embarrassment over her father's ownership of the brewery and had asked E.V. to join her in praying he would sell the business.

E.V. took a breath. He felt ill trying to sort it all out.

"Mr. Renier, you are looking a bit pale. Would you like something to eat?" The concern on Miss Leonard's face wasn't the least bit believable.

"Something is wrong with Larkin."

Miss Leonard's blue eyes widened, mouth gaped open. She looked practically peeved he'd make such an obvious statement. "Good gracious, she's a drunkard. What else would explain her absence about town the past four days?" She gave a dispassionate shrug. "I hate to be the one to share this with you, but this isn't the first time Larkin's breath has smelled of whiskey. However, it is the first time I've seen her inebriated."

Still unconvinced, E.V.'s gaze slid back to Larkin. Her stride faltered. Stopping at the lamppost in front of the milliner's shop, she rested her basket on the ground and wiped her brow.

Someone stopped by on horseback, but she waved him off. Likely with a *no, thank you, I'm fine* response.

When he said nothing, Miss Leonard continued, "Hearing news of this is going to shatter her parents' hearts. For the sake of Larkin's reputation, they'll have to move, which will grieve me greatly because I value"—her voice cracked—"no, *treasure,* our friendship."

E.V. shook his head slowly in hopes of ridding it of his confusion. This wasn't his Larkin. Through his friendship with Tuck, Frederick, and Willum, E.V. had learned a true friend—a man of God—trusts what he knows of another's character. That's what they had done for E.V., even when the gossips at the university claimed the worst about him. While the evidence appeared to paint Larkin disfavorably, E.V. knew the good and right thing to do was trust the character Larkin had demonstrated prior to this moment.

"Mr. Renier, I see how disturbing this must be. I'm meeting Daddy and Garrick for lunch. Usually I drive alone"—she looked to the sky—"but with this weather, I know Daddy would prefer I have an escort."

E.V. blinked. She was always driving the buckboard around town alone.

She looked hopeful. "I've packed enough lunch for four."

"Something's wrong with Larkin," he repeated, removing Miss Leonard's grasp of him. "She needs help." He took one step before she snatched at his arm again.

"But—I—well, this morning I overheard Daddy telling Garrick he was ready to make a decision on the contract."

E.V. glanced from Miss Leonard to Larkin, still leaning against the garland-and-ribbon-decorated lamppost, now using her hat to fan her face. Miss Leonard could be speaking the truth about what she overheard, but after her—and her father's—performance at the wedding reception, he'd grown more wary of believing anything that came out of their mouths.

Willing to risk that Miss Leonard was bluffing, E.V. jerked free of her hold. "Pickled or not, Larkin needs help." *My help,* he wanted to add, but doing so would mean wasting another moment talking to a woman he had no interest in talking to.

For the second time that day, E.V. took off running.

Chapter 5

"I feel poisoned." The words had barely left her mouth when Larkin felt her feet separate from the ground. She dropped her hat and reached for the lamppost. The tips of her fingers brushed the velvet ribbon encircling the metal post, but she couldn't grab hold.

"Relax, Miss Whitworth," E.V. said as two widow ladies new to town stopped next to them. He settled her in his arms. "I've got you."

"Why?"

"You're unwell so I'm taking you home." As he said it, one widow nudged the other with her elbow and grinned.

Home? She couldn't go home yet. She had to fulfill her duty, and she was not about to disappoint the Bollens. "I must deliver the fruit. I always—"

"Miss Whitworth."

At the sound of her name, she stopped squirming and turned to see who'd spoken.

"I'll see the good reverend gets the basket," the milliner, Mr. Dudley, offered as he stood in the opened doorway to his shop. He nodded at E.V. "Y'got her?"

E.V. adjusted her in his arms. "Yes sir."

One of the widows picked up Larkin's hat. "We'll take this to your father, dear, since we're headed that way to get his investment advice." And they hurried off, oblivious to Larkin's, "No, that's all right, I can carry it" response.

She sighed.

E.V. started walking. "It's only a hat."

"I know, but I seem to have a habit of losing my hats. No one returns them to me, so my theory is Papa pays a finder's fee."

"Then I ought to turn in the two in my office."

"You should, and then let me know how well he pays."

Content in the arms of the one who held her, Larkin rested her head against E.V.'s chest as he walked up the shaded alley between the milliner's shop and the barber's. She'd often dreamed of being held by him, but, somehow, she'd never imagined this scenario.

"E.V., how did Mr. Dudley know who I was taking the fruit to?"

"Sweetheart, you always deliver food to the Bollens on Wednesday."

"But this is Thursday."

"So it is."

"I also take food to Mrs. Ellis and to, umm, to other people in town," she finished. Really, her head hurt too much for her to think straight. Only—she felt like she was thinking straighter than she ever had before. And hearing better, too. To hear his calm, gentle, well-educated voice say *sweetheart* again, she asked, "What did you call me?"

Thunder rolled overhead, yet Larkin could have sworn this

time he said *mine*.

And the pounding of her pulse seemed to beat all too perfectly. For a moment everything became nothing but them.

"E.V., I—"

"Shhh, rest," he said softly. His brown eyes held such kindness and love that she'd be a fool to doubt his devotion.

Larkin, again resting her head against his rough work vest, closed her eyes and listened to his steady heartbeat. Someday she'd tell him exactly how she felt. When the time was right. Magical. Lovely. When he didn't so much smell like sawdust. When she wasn't medicated. And then he would say he loved her, too, and would kiss her for the first time, and it would be spectacular. It would be the kiss to end all kisses. No! Even better.

Imagining the moment, Larkin felt her lips curve.

It would be the kiss to *begin* all kisses. Which was completely absurd of her to think as *the kiss to end all kisses,* but she was too deliriously happy to care about being logical.

E.V.'s pace increased, and Larkin opened her eyes in time to see him turn the corner to the back alley that led to the tree-lined street leading to her parents' house.

"I'll get you home as quickly as I can," he said between breaths. He glanced around as if he were looking for someone. "Not many people out right now, I'm guessing, because it's about to rain. Smell the breeze."

She breathed deep. "Sawdust."

"Interesting. I smell whiskey." His intense gaze met hers. "Larkin, what's going on?"

"I want to explain, I truly do, but I need you to trust me."

"I do," he said without hesitation.

And she believed him. Feeling warm and cozy and content despite the queasiness of her stomach, Larkin focused on his bristled jaw. It'd probably scratch when she kissed him.

"Why do you shave on Sundays and Wednesdays since it bothers your skin?" she asked as casually as she could. The pounding of her pulse was nothing like she'd ever felt before. While the beautiful overcast sky was brimming with the promise of rain, the world around them was bright. Magical.

Lovely.

His grin was small but there, and his eyes glinted as when one had a secret too amazing to keep hidden. "I have important meetings those days with two very important people in my life."

"You see me on Sundays."

"And Wednesdays."

"Who else do you meet with on Sunday?"

"The Body of Christ."

"Oh." Dreading he would say Abigail, yet ready to hear the worst, she asked, "Who else do you meet with every Wednesday?"

"I—" He paused and his grin and amusement ended. "I can't share. I want to, but I need you to trust me, too."

Larkin nipped on her bottom lip. Did she trust him? She wanted to. She had for two years, but if he loved her, why hadn't he asked to court her?

I'm impatient, Lord. That's what it comes down to.

"I do trust you." Saying the words sealed them in her heart, chasing away the doubt she'd struggled with. She *did* trust him.

He nodded. "Then be patient."

As E.V. turned the corner from the back alley to the street, Larkin noticed her house in her peripheral view. They'd be home before she could sing the first stanza of—of—well, of any song that she could remember if she could think of anything besides how sick she still felt from her toes to her eyelashes. Yet she also felt wonderful. . .and free to be honest with him.

Time to be a Ruth and motivate her Boaz into action.

She reached forward and touched—poked, really—his bristly cheek. "I. Love. You." While she meant it to sound a bit more melodically romantic, she was happy to finally say the words. She wiped the increased perspiration from her forehead with her sleeve. "Would you like to know something else?"

Smiling broadly, E.V. stepped onto the bricked path dividing the front lawn. As he walked, the sound of his boots on the pavement grew in volume. "I'm not sure how you can top that, but I'll listen."

"I think—" she started, but then he stumbled on an uneven brick.

She bobbled.

He adjusted his hold of her.

That's when she offered an apologetic grin. "I think I'm going to be sick."

And she was.

Chapter 6

Fiddling with the middle button on the black waistcoat he wore over a white shirt, E.V. sat in the chair across from Mrs. Whitworth as they waited for Larkin to join them in the formal parlor decorated in holly, ivy, myriad red candles, and bundles of fragrant cinnamon sticks. The union suit he wore kept his chest modestly covered, so he wasn't sure why Mrs. Whitworth had given him the waistcoat. The dress shirt with his denims and work boots was absurd enough. If he'd buttoned the upturned collar, the contrast would have been even worse.

He was thankful Mrs. Whitworth omitted giving him a tie.

E.V. looked around the oversized parlor that was really more of an elaborate Victorian salon, with its five distinct sitting areas and Steinway square grand piano in the far corner. Two years ago at Larkin's birthday party, he'd gazed about the empty room, from the handcrafted fireplace mantel to the crystal chandelier hanging from the middle of the fourteen-foot ceiling, and debated if talking to Larkin—whom he'd only known as *the pretty Whitworth girl* at the time—was worth enduring an evening of dancing in a home that reminded him so much in appearance to the mansion he'd spent his childhood in.

Each home after that one had grown significantly smaller. Now he lived in a one-room apartment next to his office.

Having gone from riches to rags and having learned to enjoy freedom from the trappings of wealth, he hadn't been too sure he wanted to follow the attraction he felt for a young woman used to a life of luxury. Her beauty drew him in, but her passion for Jesus and for graciously serving others had caught him hook, line, and sinker.

Two years later, he'd turned his sawmill into the most profitable one in Tumwater. Beyond marrying Larkin, E.V. had no grander ambitions.

He didn't want to own businesses and companies throughout the Pacific Northwest that consumed his every waking hour. He merely wanted to prove himself to Larkin's wealth-focused father so he could begin a life with the woman he loved. After an honest day's work, he wanted to spend his evenings and weekends with his wife and children. Not in his office mulling over stock reports.

Yet here he was, sitting in Patrick Whitworth's chair, in Patrick Whitworth's grand parlor, wearing Patrick Whitworth's shirt and waistcoat, while waiting to share tea and crumpets with the man's beloved wife and daughter, while his own scrubbed-clean shirt and vest hung next to Larkin's cape to dry beside the kitchen stove.

It wasn't that he disliked Whitworth.

He merely didn't want to become him.

The ornate grandfather clock in the front foyer bonged once.

Mrs. Whitworth glanced over the shoulder of her red taffeta gown to the two doors on the east wall—one led to the library and the other to a water closet, but which was which E.V. couldn't remember. Truth be told, since moving to Tumwater, he couldn't remember exchanging more than a dozen words with Larkin's mother.

"I suppose we can begin without Larkin." Mrs. Whitworth's hands shook as she filled E.V.'s teacup. "Why is it I find conversation easier in a crowd than with one person?"

Empathizing, E.V. admitted, "I'd say it's because with one person there is an invitation to intimacy which is often intimidating. In a crowd, there's freedom for obscurity. I'll admit I've sought the safety of anonymity." He knew Larkin did as well.

Mrs. Whitworth's head tilted in a manner much like Larkin's. Whereas her face was leaner and more rectangular than Larkin's oval face, E.V. could imagine the children he and Larkin might eventually have looking like her. Only their blond hair could be natural, unlike Mrs. Whitworth's chemically altered color.

"Are you in love with my daughter?" she finally asked.

He leaned forward in his chair to claim his teacup and saucer off the marble-topped coffee table. "You already know the answer to that, don't you?"

The edges of her wide mouth curved. "Patrick has told me of your conversations. Two years is a long time to remain faithful despite the rejections. My husband is less inclined to view your behavior as romantic." With a sad smile, she motioned to the crumpets. "Eat."

While he did, she told him stories of Larkin's childhood. She asked him if he knew who'd contracted the construction of the large house Willum Tate was building, and E.V. answered vaguely. From there, they spoke of politics, the due date of the Tuckers' baby, the approaching anniversary of his parents' deaths, the Pearson-Corrigan wedding she missed attending, church socials and the quilt auction she was organizing in the spring, the growing popularity of baseball (and how much both despised the sport), and finally the family's upcoming Christmas soiree, which E.V. did not have an invitation to. If he had, he'd have to shave and, well, that was that.

She had laughed easily.

He had laughed as much as he did when he was with Larkin.

Then she vowed to call him Eric.

He grimaced. "I prefer E.V."

"I realize sharing your father's name is something you wish to forget." All amusement left her tone. "Your heritage made you who you are but doesn't have to define who you will be. Besides, I like Eric better." She gave him a look that said it was pointless to argue.

That's when E.V. realized this was likely a test to win her approval. More importantly, he realized from their conversation how passionately Mrs. Whitworth loved her husband and daughter. . .and how much she still grieved the loss of the son whose name she never mentioned.

"I won't take Larkin from Tumwater," he promised. "I won't take her away from you."

Her eyes filled with tears.

Since Larkin still hadn't returned to the room, E.V. lowered his voice and whispered conspiratorially, "How about a pact? You call me Eric until your first grandson is born, then I go back to being E.V. That way I can honor my heritage by giving the world an Eric Valentin Renier IV, and still honor you."

She raised a hand to cover her mouth, and though she said nothing, he knew her answer.

"What's this?" barked a voice E.V. knew all too well.

As Mrs. Whitworth wiped the tears off her cheeks, E.V. looked to his right.

With the extravagant angel-and-golden-feather-decorated Christmas tree in the foyer behind him, Patrick Whitworth stood in the parlor's arched entrance beneath the mistletoe. He clenched his black Bowler hat in one hand and his greatcoat in the other, rain from both items dripping on the wood floor. His red tie was the lone bit of color on his lean frame. Contrary to their meeting yesterday morning, the few strands of brown hair that remained on the top of his head were not neatly combed to the side.

He tossed his wet items to a silent, hovering manservant who quickly scurried away.

Clearly Whitworth had gotten word about E.V. carrying Larkin home. And though his cheeks were rosy, he looked not a bit jolly over the news.

Chapter 7

Hearing Papa's voice, Larkin woke with a jolt. She'd fallen asleep against the library door as she'd waited for Mama and E.V. to stop talking. She scrambled to her feet then smoothed the navy fringe on the bodice and three-quarters-length sleeves of her pale yellow gown. Thankfully her stomach had settled, her eyes no longer burned, and the vertigo was gone. However, the mortification she felt over what had happened—

Only a man blindly in love would still wish to court a woman who'd spewed eggs and broth on his chest.

"I cannot believe I did that," she groaned.

Knowing the embarrassment she felt added needed color to her cheeks, Larkin gently opened the door leading to the parlor.

Papa, E.V., and Mama immediately looked her way from where they sat in the west end of the room.

Only E.V. stood.

With a slight grin strained by the tension she felt in every nerve, she tried to think of a logical excuse for having left Mama and E.V. alone for the last—she glanced at the clock—*oh dear*—hour and twelve minutes.

Sometimes the best explanation was no explanation.

She hoped.

As slowly as she could traverse the large rectangular room without making it look like she was stalling, Larkin moved toward the sitting area nearest the double-door entrance to the front foyer.

With one leg crossed over the other, Papa sat in the second chair opposite Mama's place on the settee. The angle at which he sat gave him a clear view of E.V.—whose chair was a good three feet from Papa's—without having to turn to look at him. While the elbow of Papa's left arm rested on the curved armrest, two of his fingers on his right hand tapped his chin. His thinking position.

His *you're about to get a lecture on decorum* position.

Because of the heavy brown mustache covering his upper lip, Larkin couldn't tell if Papa's handsome face held a frown or a grin. Not that she expected a grin.

While E.V. wasn't smiling either, he didn't seem intimidated by Papa's presence, but neither was he as at ease as he'd been talking to Mama.

"Oh, how nice, tea and crumpets." Larkin sat on the empty side of the settee, smoothing the fringe on her skirt while E.V. resumed his seat.

Mama filled a teacup and handed it to her. "How was your nap, darling?"

Not at all surprised by her mother's forthrightness, Larkin casually took a sip of her tea while raising her eyebrows as if to say—*nap?*

"Your cheek has the imprint of the carvings on the library door." Mama lifted a plate off the tea tray. "Crumpet?"

Larkin shook her head. She shuddered at the thought of

putting anything into her stomach for the next twenty-four hours.

Mama put the tray down. "They're here if you change your mind. Eric enjoyed them."

At Mama's use of E.V.'s given name, Larkin looked at E.V. He hated being called by his father's name. E.V. shrugged as if the usage was of no import.

Papa cleared his throat.

Dreading the lecture but knowing Papa would wait until they were alone because he would never—*never*—air their conflicts in public, Larkin met his gaze and smiled softly. She said nothing. This was the moment where E.V. would show himself to be the true hero he was and ask Papa for her hand in marriage. Right here. In the parlor. In the very room where she and E.V. had met over a tray of spilled cookies.

Papa would then agree to the marriage because he loved her, and he wanted her to be happy. Mama would cry yet be happy. And Larkin would cry, too, because she was finally going to marry the man she loved.

All was about to be well with the world.

Papa stopped tapping his chin. "Larkin, are you in love with this man?"

Realizing her hand trembled with nervous anticipation, she rested her teacup and saucer on the tea tray. "Yes sir."

"Have you been cavorting with him?"

"No sir."

"Would you elope with him if I refused to allow you to marry?"

Confused by his line of questioning, Larkin looked to E.V., who leaned forward in his chair, his fingers steepled together, his eyes intent on her face. What did he want her to say? Yes? No? Maybe? It depends? Give me time to pray over it?

Panic welling within, she looked to Mama.

Her mother's dark eyes pleaded with her to say no.

Could she?

Help me, Lord. How do I choose between love for my parents and love for E.V.?

"Stop." E.V.'s voice was so soft, Larkin wasn't sure she'd heard him. "Stop," he repeated, rising to his feet. "I won't let you force her to choose. I'll carry the burden."

Papa's jaw shifted yet he said nothing. He didn't have to. The narrowing of his eyes conveyed his dislike of E.V., which confused Larkin all the more. How could Papa despise someone he barely knew? Someone he'd barely had half a dozen conversations with?

E.V. inclined his head to Mama. "Mrs. Whitworth, thank you for the hospitality." His gaze settled on Larkin. "Miss Whitworth, I pray all will go well with you in your future endeavors. Merry Christmas to you all."

With that, he strolled from the parlor and out the front door, allowing a chill to steal into the room.

Larkin stood. "Papa. Why?"

"Renier only cares about your inheritance."

"He loves me. Me!"

"Has he ever told you?"

She opened her mouth but didn't answer. He had never said the words, but—

"You're money to men like him," he said coolly. "He'll forget you soon enough."

She shook her head. "No. E.V. is faithful and kind and patient and. . .I will never stop believing God will work out things for us to be together."

Papa's fingers tapped his chin again. "So you choose him?"

"I—"

Mama grabbed Larkin's hand, silencing her. "Patrick, please. Don't do this to our family. I can't bear losing another child—I can't. Please make this right."

Papa stood and, without another word, followed E.V.'s path out the front door.

Willum was right. He should cut his losses. Rain soaked through every layer of clothing as he walked away from the Whitworth mansion.

Hearing a door slam somewhere behind him, E.V. stopped in the middle of the street, turned around, and rolled his eyes. Wind gusts were the only thing he could think of that would make the moment worse. Or an audience. Actually *that* would be worse.

Whitworth approached with the fervor of a man on a mission. "Stop proposing!"

"What?"

"You heard me." Whitworth halted before E.V. and looked him directly in the eye—an easy task since they were nearly the same height. "I will never give my permission," he growled.

"Why not?" E.V. growled right back, having simply had enough of being patient with the man he'd thought would be his father-in-law someday.

"You don't have the character to be faithful to her in the tough times."

"I don't—" E.V. bit back his angry retort.

Knowing yelling wasn't the way to bring peace between them, he drew in a breath. *Jesus living through me, Jesus living through me.*

Focused and calm, he said, "After all the conversations we've had, how is it you *still* don't know my character? I know yours. I know that Patrick Whitworth has one of the most astute financial minds in the country. He is loyal, fair, judicious, yet will take educated risks and selflessly help his business associates prosper, too. You love your family, routinely ignore advances from other women, give generously to the community and charities throughout the Pacific Northwest, carry guilt over your son's death, work too much, and are too self-possessed and arrogant to humble yourself before God."

Whitworth's mouth clamped into a thin line. In anger? Shame? Resentment that E.V. knew all that about him?

E.V. wasn't sure and, to be frank, at that moment he couldn't have cared less. "What do I have to do to prove myself to you?"

"You are your father's son." Whitworth gave him a slit-eyed look. "You can't change that."

E.V. flinched. How many times had he accused himself? Were it not for his friends' intervention and determination to pray him to salvation, he would still be following his father's path of debauchery and greed. Yet, as the rain poured down on them, he suddenly saw his past more clearly. Mrs. Whitworth was right.

"Sir, my heritage made me who I am today, good and bad," E.V. said with a peace that could only be God-supplied, "but Jesus living in and through me, not my heritage, defines who I am and who I will be. My sawmill has grown. I'm on the verge of securing a large supplier, and I don't need Larkin's inheritance. I can provide for all her needs."

Whitworth stared in silence. Then he slowly shook his head. "This isn't about money."

E.V. gaped at the man. Whitworth lived and breathed money. "For two years, I worked day and night to build my mill and prove my work ethic to you. For two years, I've allowed you to harass me with questions about my past, and I've respected your demands and honored your rule of not telling Larkin exactly how I feel. If money is not the issue, then what's this about?"

"God may have changed you," Whitworth answered furiously, "but He can't—won't—*hasn't* changed my wife. And now, like her brother, Larkin is showing the same weakness for—" His shoulders slumped, his voice lost its intensity. "I don't hate you. I love my daughter and wife too much to risk trusting you to protect our family honor when your reputation is on the line. They're mine to protect."

"Give me a chance to prove—"

"No, Renier. This is my burden to carry alone."

Unsure of how to respond—how could he when he had no idea what weakness Whitworth was alluding to—E.V. wiped his brow, which did little good because the rain continued to run down his face.

"I don't hate you," Whitworth repeated. "Saying no to you is easier for me." With that, he turned and walked back to his house.

E.V. turned as well. Each step back to his mill took him farther away from Larkin.

Cut his losses. That's what he should do.

Chapter 8

You and a guest are cordially invited to. . .

In the solitude of his office, E.V. stared at the gold letters on the embossed invitation to the Whitworth's annual Christmas soiree on Saturday, December 20. Three days away. Music. Dancing. Food.

Larkin.

Not everyone in Tumwater attended, because not everyone was invited, and the list varied each year. To receive an invitation put one on the *People Significant to the Whitworth Family* list that included business associates, local clergy, politicians, law officials, close friends, family. No one under the age of sixteen allowed.

Dress: formal.

His first year in Tumwater, E.V. attended at the personal invitation of Mr. Whitworth to Tuck, Frederick, Willum, and himself as they were leaving Larkin's nineteenth birthday party. By the time the date of the soiree arrived two months later, he'd already asked Whitworth twice for Larkin's hand in marriage. At that time, Whitworth had still been cordial to him.

Last year he never received an invitation.

What was he to make of this year's invitation? Even more

intriguing, who sent it? Larkin? Her mother? Why write *no reply necessary* on the back?

For the third (or eighth) time since the invitation arrived in his office last week, a few days after Whitworth confronted him in the rain, E.V. tossed it in the wooden milk crate he used to collect wastepaper for kindling. This time he wasn't taking it back out. And he wasn't attending. His heart hurt too much.

Instead, he'd help Willum cut and piece the intricate first-floor crown molding demanded by the increasingly particular owner of the house Willum was building. At the rate the owner was making changes to the design, Willum would be an old man before he'd finish building the house. See—now *that* was a situation for cutting one's losses.

E.V. grabbed his pencil off the accounting book and re-examined the month's numbers. If he sold out his shares in the mill, he could take his profits and move to anywhere he desired, do any job he wanted. He'd find a nice girl and settle down and have a bevy of children. And a dog—no, dogs. A bevy of them, too—as many as he had children, so they'd each have their own and no reason to fight over who the dog loved best.

Frustrated with his absurd thoughts, E.V. dropped his pencil. Elbows on his desk, he rested his forehead against his fingertips. *What do I do, Lord? Where should I go?*

Wait. The word whispered again across his soul, as it had each time he'd prayed for guidance.

Could he wait? Could he stay in Tumwater?

More aptly, *how* could he stay now that the grapevine telegraph claimed Whitworth had given Harvey Milton permission to court Larkin? Harvey Milton, Esq., the very lawyer who had yet to win a case. Harvey Milton, who for the last year, had courted and stopped courting—before starting and stopping again—Miss Abigail Leonard. Every shop E.V. entered, even before and after worship services this past Sunday, someone had been talking about the news.

If that wasn't frustrating enough, the number of women who ceased talking when E.V. approached was making him wonder if someone had overheard him and Whitworth in the rain. He didn't remember seeing anyone out on the street watching them.

But in a town this size. . .with a gossip chain this strong. . .

In the two years he'd lived in Tumwater, he'd never heard anyone—except Miss Leonard—say an unkind word about Larkin. Now the descriptions ranged from princess to imposter to hypocrite to drunkard to Jezebel. The latter occurred when he overheard two of his workers repeating that Larkin had been "leading the boss man on with the goal of making Milton jealous."

With Tuck's wife, Anna, on bed rest because of sporadic contractions, only cranky ol' Mrs. Ellis remained to champion Larkin's reputation, which did little good, because Mrs. Ellis was the least-liked person in town. That left him. As Reverend Bollen had advised, telling people they shouldn't gossip silenced the talk but did nothing to restore the damage to Larkin's reputation. How could E.V. come to her defense if doing so would only cause her father to believe he was plotting a nefarious plan to kidnap Larkin and hold her for ransom? Or elope. Either amounted to the same in Whitworth's eyes. Why add fuel to the gossips' fire?

Doomed if he did, doomed if he didn't.

"Ugh," E.V. groaned. He snapped his pencil and tossed it in the trash. Then he sat listening to the saws buzz and his workers yell orders to each other. And sat. And sat.

The door to his office opened. Willum stepped inside, unbuttoning his winter coat. His bright-eyed gaze fell to the trash crate before centering on E.V. "You busy?"

"Yes—no," he corrected. "Something wrong with your order?"

"No. It's all loaded." Willum motioned to the doorway. "Thought I'd warn you, Silas Leonard just arrived with a manila envelope and his daughter." Removing his work gloves, he stepped to the enclosed stove in the corner of the room to warm his hands. "Saw a few snowflakes earlier. Think we'll get any accumulation?"

Uninterested in discussing weather, E.V. leaned back in his chair, gripped the V-edges of his tweed work vest, and stared at the remaining hat of Larkin's he hadn't had delivered to her at home with her father's shirt and waistcoat. He wasn't ready to part with the only tangible object of hers that he could hold. Larkin hadn't looked at him Sunday. Neither had she looked at Milton. Whatever day she was delivering food to the Bollens wasn't Wednesday.

No, today E.V. had delivered his customary half ham alone.

Two years without declaring himself to her.

Two years being a model of propriety.

Two years of stifling his desire to kiss her senseless.

E.V. rested his head against the back of his chair and grimaced. Two years of being a faithful yet utter fool.

Bam!

E.V. flinched and looked at his surroundings. He then glared at Willum. "Why is there a log on my desk?"

Willum shrugged. "I couldn't reach the back of your head to knock sense into you. Go sign the contract with Leonard. Then you'll at least have half of what you think you want in life."

ALL YE FAITHFUL

"You want *what?*" Feeling his brows draw together in stunned disbelief at what had been asked of him, E.V. stopped reading the contract and looked at Silas Leonard, who stood with his back to the door of the mill's main entrance. With the saws running and workers scrambling to load and unload the machines, this waiting area was the quietest part of the building besides his office.

"Son, it'll be one last favor," Leonard explained, grinning and putting his arm around the shoulders of his daughter's some-shade-of-red (or maybe pink) cloak that matched the bonnet she clenched with both hands.

Now that E.V. noticed what she wore, he realized in all the times he'd seen Miss Leonard since Emma and Frederick's wedding, she'd been wearing either red or pink or a shade thereof. Much like the way Larkin wore clothes in one color spectrum for an entire year—something he had never pondered the reason behind. Some of a woman's mysteries needed to stay mysterious. Though he knew this was Larkin's yellow year.

Why would Miss Leonard want to follow the behavior of someone she clearly hated? Did she want to be—

E.V. looked the young woman over and felt his frown deepen. Her blond hair was pinned in a simple bun at the back of her neck while loose strands grazed her cheekbones, similar to Larkin's preferred coiffure. The style actually made Miss Leonard's Caesar-like nose seem less—no, no it didn't. Her nose was still too large for her face.

"Renier!"

At the sound of his name, E.V. refocused on Silas Leonard. "Why?" he couldn't help asking.

"Abby can't get a husband on her own. She lost her chance with Milton now that Whitworth bought him for his daughter."

Miss Leonard's eyes widened in obvious mortification at her father's words. "Daddy, I never favored Mr. Milton. I like—"

"Hush, girl. Stop making everything about you."

E.V. glanced over his shoulder at Willum watching them unabashedly as he leaned against the doorframe. Based on Willum's smug grin, E.V. didn't want to wager on what his friend was thinking. He turned back to Leonard.

"No," he answered with complete assurance in his decision. "I will not escort your daughter to the Whitworth soiree in exchange for a lumber contract. Nor will I marry her in exchange for one."

"I'm only asking you to escort Abby to the party," Leonard countered. "If you want to marry her, that's your own decision. I won't mind though. The contract price is more than fair, especially if you want Abby, too."

"Fair? For who?" E.V. pointed at Miss Leonard. "For her? How do you think your daughter feels about being a bargaining chip in contract negotiations? She's not a commodity you can sell or trade. Show some respect."

Leonard's nostrils flared as he stepped closer to E.V. in an obvious attempt to intimidate with his Goliath size. "You insult me, boy."

While E.V. never considered himself prone to sarcasm, this was one moment he truly wanted to respond with—*you think so?*

Instead, he wisely responded with, "Sir, I would be honored to sign a contract with you, because my mill could use your lumber, but not at the expense of my self-respect or your daughter's." He returned the contract unsigned. "Have a Merry Christmas."

Leonard stormed outside. "Abigail, come!"

Miss Leonard didn't move. She looked at E.V. with such longing in her eyes that he knew, in his attempt to defend her honor, he'd unwittingly earned her devotion.

"I, uh," he stuttered, trying to think of some response.

A smile spread across her face. She wrapped her arms around him and hugged him as if she would never let go, and then she burst into tears.

Unsure of what else to do, E.V. awkwardly patted the top of her head. "There, there, it'll be all right."

"Oh Mr. Renier, no one has ever loved me like you do."

"Me?" Stiffening, E.V. felt the color drain from his face. "Miss Leonard, I, uh, you, uh. . ."

Her father yelled for her again, and she complied this time, darting out the mill's front entrance, saving E.V. from further awkwardness.

Within moments of the door closing, Willum slapped E.V.'s back. "I suppose I'll give you this instead of burning it like I'd planned." He stuffed a crumpled envelope in E.V.'s palm. "I read what she wrote, and I'm not sorry." Willum stepped to the door and gripped the handle then stopped and turned around. "E.V.?"

"Yeah?" he answered, meeting Willum's intense gaze.

"Mrs. Ellis doesn't take kindly to rejections."

Chapter 9

Bury the booty, hide the corpse, bury the booty, hide the corpse, Larkin repeated over and over as she carried the last two rum bottles securely against her chest with one hand while holding her black boots in the other. She wasn't too sure why the childhood chant her brother had made up resurfaced from her memory. After all, she hadn't thought of it in the last five years since Sean had died. Yet whenever he'd invited her on his nightly escapades, she'd repeat the words to calm her nervousness. He, not her, had been the bold, courageous, adventuresome one in the family.

As she twisted the knob on the kitchen door, her heart pounded. *Click.* The sound of the latch echoed throughout the dark room laden with food and serving items for the Christmas soiree. Larkin held her breath and waited for Cook or one of the maids to stagger into the kitchen and demand to know what she was up to at precisely 1:31 on a Saturday morning. *No good* would have been Sean's honest answer.

Hearing nothing, she opened the door enough to ease into the chilly night, and then she slowly pulled it closed behind her.

Seven trips and yet undiscovered. After days of searching the house, she was confident she'd found all the hidden liquor bottles and Mama's sick tumtum medication.

Larkin breathed a sigh of relief, although the action did little to settle her rapid pulse. So she breathed even deeper until her breath was no longer ragged and her chest didn't feel as if it would explode.

Then. . .she went to work.

Within minutes, she had her boots on and black riding cloak tied tight, the hood pulled securely down over her head. She wedged the bottles with the others in the wheelbarrow then covered them with a couple of horse blankets to dampen the sound of any glass clinking against glass. The cloud cover kept the moonlight from exposing her work.

Determined to accomplish her task as quickly as possible, Larkin quietly pushed the wheelbarrow down the path leading to Mrs. Ellis's property at the end of the street. The tip of her nose already felt frozen. *Please, Lord, please,* she prayed, but for what she begged, she didn't know.

Her heart ached. Her soul grieved. She felt so. . .alone.

"Dig a little quicker," Mrs. Ellis ordered, raising the lamp to shine where E.V. was digging. "I'm freezing out here." She leaned on the butt of the shotgun she held in her left hand. "Make the hole deeper, too. Don't want no varmints digging where they shouldn't."

E.V. held back his grumbles and continued to shovel dirt. He wasn't about to point out that any additional varmints on her densely wooded plot were opportunities to add pelts to the multicolored fur coat she wore over a calico gown hemmed short enough to show the tops of her U.S. Army-issued boots. Likely her dead husband's. Husband one or husband two—E.V. wasn't about to ask in case it would incite her wrath.

This was the first time he'd been on her property and not been shot at.

Thankful the night was void of moisture and breeze, E.V. jammed the shovel again into the soft ground. Why dig a hole in the middle of a walking path?

"Care to tell me what the hole is for, ma'am?" he asked, adding another scoop of dirt to the shin-high mound next to him.

"Nope," came the clipped response. "I suggest you stop talking before I start disliking your worthless hide again."

He opened his mouth, intent on reminding her that other than his lone question she had done all of the talking, when the sweetest voice he hadn't heard in the last sixteen days interrupted their conversation.

"E.V.? What are you doing here?"

E.V. swiveled around and almost dropped the shovel. Larkin stood not five yards away, with a wheelbarrow of all things. Even in the shadowy darkness she took his breath away.

"I invited him," Mrs. Ellis answered crisply.

"Oh. Well, thank you, Mrs. Ellis, for having the foresight to get us aid." While her words sounded sincere, Larkin nervously looked to the left and to the right. "Is anyone else here?"

"Just us three and the good Lord." Mrs. Ellis set the lamp on the ground. "At the rate Renier is digging, we're likely to be here till kingdom come." She turned and walked away, muttering, "I knew I should have brought that second shovel. Back in a jiffy. And I mean jiffy."

The sound of her boots crunching the twigs and leaves underfoot died away.

E.V. spoke first. "I trust you."

She lowered her cloak's hood. Her skin looked pale in the lamplight. "You don't know what I'm doing."

He shrugged. "Mrs. Ellis's note said you needed help."

"I could be doing something reprehensible."

E.V. gave her a look to let her know how unlikely he believed her guilty. "Sweetheart, I have full confidence in the integrity of your character."

Her mouth moved yet no sound came forth. The dimples on the sides of her mouth appeared in one of her rare, glorious smiles.

E.V.'s heart skipped a beat. Whatever she had in the covered wheelbarrow, he didn't know, couldn't suspect, and didn't care. The fact that losing-lawyer Harvey Milton was now courting Larkin had no bearing on his thoughts either.

Two years was an awfully long time to wait to kiss the woman he loved.

Feeling no longer bound to any oaths he'd made to her father, he tossed the shovel to the ground. In hindsight, he'd say he didn't remember running over to Larkin, but he had to have because she was still standing beside the wheelbarrow in his embrace when Mrs. Ellis returned.

"Now that you two have gotten that outta the way, can we get this hole dug?"

Larkin broke free and peeked around E.V., whose hands lovingly rested on the back of her head and on her waist. Mrs. Ellis not-so-lovingly held a shovel and a second lantern in one hand and her shotgun in the other. A myriad of responses ran through Larkin's mind. The best of which—*I had a speck in my eye and I needed his help to remove it*—didn't sound remotely believable. Clearly Anna was right. She, Larkin Whitworth, wasn't and never would be crafty. Thus, this seemed to be another one of those *sometimes the best explanation was no explanation* moments. She hoped.

Besides, Mrs. Ellis's eyesight was too sharp for her not to have seen how splendidly E.V. had been kissing her. Larkin touched her lips and smiled and sighed happily and—*oh my*. Her first kiss had been a lovely and magical moment indeed.

E.V. sighed loudly (perhaps it was more of a groan). "Ma'am," he said to Mrs. Ellis, releasing Larkin and turning around, "I suspect anything I say won't endear me to you."

"Nope." Mrs. Ellis's tone likely sounded as harsh as normal to E.V., but having spent enough time with the woman, Larkin had long learned to distinguish between annoyed grumpiness and amused grumpiness.

Larkin tugged on E.V.'s woolen coat sleeve, drawing his attention. She whispered, "She has a hard time expressing love. She really likes you."

His upper lip curled. He grimaced and muttered, "Her love is toxic."

"Kiss her again, Renier," Mrs. Ellis added louder this time, "and I'll have no choice but to shoot yer worthless hide. Nothing personal, mind you, but she is courting that even more worthless Harvey Milton. You ought not be kissing another man's woman."

Stunned at the news, Larkin stared openmouthed at them. "I'm not courting Mr. Milton."

"You're not?" and "Why not?" came in unison.

Larkin glanced back and forth between the two. "Where did you hear that news?"

This time E.V. and Mrs. Ellis glanced back and forth between each other and her.

"Can't say I can recall," Mrs. Ellis answered, frowning.

With a confused frown of his own, E.V. scratched the side of his head. "Tuck told me because Anna told him. I assumed you'd told her."

"No," Larkin said barely loud enough to hear herself.

While she hadn't seen Anna in the last three days because she'd been focusing on finding all of Mama's liquor bottles, the last time they'd talked, they'd not discussed any men in Larkin's life. Or courting. Anna hadn't even given her weekly Willum Tate exaltation. Anna wasn't a gossiper, so Larkin knew her friend wouldn't have shared the information with Jeremiah unless she heard it from a reliable source. Who would make up a rumor she and Mr. Milton were courting? And why?

"With the soiree approaching, I've been distracted, helping Mama prepare." Dreading what she'd hear, she asked, "Has anything else been said about me?"

She stood in stunned silence as E.V. and Mrs. Ellis took turns sharing all they'd heard about her being a drunkard.

E.V. tucked strands of her loosened hair behind her ears. "Sweetheart, I didn't—don't—believe any of it. I've defended you when I could. Reverend Bollen says he's gone privately to those he's heard gossiping and spoken to them."

Mrs. Ellis added, "I told them all it wasn't true. People tend not to listen to what I say." Her voice had softened, reminding Larkin how wounded her heart was. Back to her normal bluster, she added, "If *you* said something publicly—"

Larkin shook her head. She wouldn't say anything that would cast negative aspersions on her mother. She'd rather people believed she was a drunkard than for them to know Mama was. Those who were her true friends would trust what they knew of her character and not believe any rumors.

Remembering her agenda, she asked, "Is the hole deep enough?"

Mrs. Ellis examined it. "A foot deeper than we need."

"You told me to—" E.V. glared at Mrs. Ellis. "Then why did you get another shovel?"

Mrs. Ellis glared right back. "What did I tell you about talking so much? Don't make me shoot you."

"I wasn't—ugh!" E.V. looked to Larkin. "I take it we're burying something?"

"Yes."

When he didn't ask what, she drew in a deep breath to still her apprehension and fear. Shame. She should have told E.V. this well before now.

"Three days after my brother's seventeenth birthday," she said, focusing on him since Mrs. Ellis already knew everything, "he told Mama he had a cough that was bothering him. Papa said he was pretending to be sick and refused to call the physician. Mama believed Sean, so she gave him the honey-whiskey cordial she always gave us when we were ill. The more Sean coughed, the more Mama medicated him."

His brows drew together. "For how long?"

"A week, maybe. He had a seizure and died. After that, we

moved from Olympia to Tumwater." Larkin swallowed to ease her dry throat. "Mama believes sadness of heart also needs medicating. Birthdays, weddings, holidays, all resurface her grief."

"That's why her hands shook when she served me tea."

Larkin nodded. "She doesn't drink regularly, but when you lose someone you love, the pain is so great that you'll do anything to make it go away, to not feel anything."

Instead of giving his opinion of who was to blame or offer token platitudes such as *life is hard,* E.V. looked at her with compassion. With understanding. He brushed a kiss across her cheek, grabbed the handles of the wheelbarrow, and pushed it over to where Mrs. Ellis stood by the hole.

In the quiet of the night, with Mrs. Ellis shining a light down on them, they laid the bottles side by side in the dirt coffin. When E.V. promised he'd be at the soiree in case she needed him, Larkin paused long enough to wipe away the tear that escaped. Over the next day or two, Mama would eventually realize all her liquor was missing. She'd panic. She'd grieve. She'd break. Who knew what she'd do at the soiree if Larkin didn't confess everything first and promise to help Mama face her grief.

Dreading the conversation she would have later with her parents but loving them too much to keep living as they were, Larkin lifted the last bottle from the wheelbarrow. *Naika ticky maika, Mama. Please, Lord, draw my parents to You, and heal my mother's grief.*

After placing Mama's crystal decanter filled with the sick tumtum medicine in the hole, Larkin stood and watched as E.V. shoveled dirt over the bottles. *Bury the booty, hide the corpse.*

Allowing Mama to suffer was the only way Mama was going to face Sean's death. . .and the only way Papa was going to realize Mama needed more help than he could give.

Her heart ached. Her soul grieved. Only this time she wasn't alone.

Chapter 10

As they stood next to the refreshment table, E.V. cheerfully handed Willum a punch glass filled with eggnog. That Larkin's father hadn't grabbed him by the neck and tossed him out made the evening rather. . .well, enjoyable. The candles around the room glowed brightly. The crystal chandelier glinted with every color of the rainbow. The musicians hit each note perfectly, and, thankfully, not a single person he walked past or stood next to smelled overpowering in either the bad or good range of the odor spectrum.

"Now isn't this more fun than measuring crown molding?" he said, grinning.

"No, I should be at the house working," Willum grumbled. "I'm not going to get it done in time." Yet instead of leaving, he sipped his eggnog and continued to watch the center of the Whitworth parlor where a dozen or so couples were dancing, including John Seymour and Natalie Bollen, who looked prettier than usual in her blue (or maybe green) dress.

E.V. figured Willum would know the exact shade. The man had a good eye for color. But instead of asking, since he could feel tension emanating from his friend, he drank the last of his frothy eggnog in silence. No sense asking Willum questions Willum wouldn't—or more aptly, wasn't ready—to answer.

As the music from the stringed quartet flittered through the open library door, E.V. scanned the parlor for Larkin or her parents. The silver Gorham bell E.V. had given Larkin when he and Willum arrived earlier rested on the fireplace mantel with the crystal bells from the two previous Christmases. Whatever feelings Whitworth had toward the gift, he hadn't shown them. Mrs. Whitworth, on the other hand, had kissed E.V.'s cheek and said she liked how he'd matched his burnished-gold brocade vest with a burgundy frock coat.

E.V. had never bothered much with being a dapper dresser. But the romantic in him had hightailed it to Olympia this morning to find something suitable for the soiree. After learning from Anna what Larkin would be wearing, that he'd match her burnished-gold gown had been his intention. That he had to drag Willum with him and force him to buy something new was because if anyone cared less than he about being fashionable, it was Willum, who, E.V. would acknowledge, looked quite debonair in a charcoal frock coat with a black velvet collar.

Sensing someone gazing in their direction, E.V. looked around and met Reverend Bollen's observant eyes. He and his wife rested near the piano that had been pushed to the corner of the parlor. Several other older couples lingered about the parlor's perimeter, including the mayor and his new bride and Silas Leonard and the affluent widow he was courting. Some sat, some stood, most watched the dancers.

E.V. turned his attention to the busy center of the room.

Garrick Leonard, like the man in love he was, danced with

his wife Kathleen, who looked like she was trying to have a good time but, E.V. suspected, was worried about her bedridden sister who, according to Tuck, was confident their baby would be a ten-pounder, at least.

Next to Miss Bollen and Seymour, Martha Bollen danced with her husband, Isaac.

Isaac's younger brother, David, danced with Harvey Milton's younger sister, both of whom managed to step on each other's toes continually. Both, E.V. noted, were watching Abigail Leonard dance with the newest councilman, who kept glancing at Elizabeth Leonard, who'd recently begun courting Sheriff Phillips and was sitting at the piano moving her fingers above the keys as if she were playing in time with the quartet. At Elizabeth's insistence, Sheriff Phillips was dancing for the second time with the councilman's spinster sister, who was probably the most skilled dancer in the room and who, to E.V.'s amusement, occasionally cast admiring glances in Willum's direction.

The triangles of love in the Whitworth parlor could have populated a Shakespearean comedy.

All that mattered to E.V. was that he wasn't included in any love triangle, quadrangle, or hexagon. And with Miss Leonard having given him distance all evening, he held hope she'd transferred her affections from earlier in the week to a more suitable bachelor.

With a *humph*, Willum gave his empty punch cup to a server walking by.

E.V. quickly added his. "Thank you."

The server nodded and continued on.

"Are you going to ask to marry Larkin tonight?" blurted Willum.

From the corner of his eye, E.V. glanced at his friend. Willum looked. . .hopeful? "No," he honestly answered.

"Ever again?"

"No sense to. Whitworth won't ever agree."

"Maybe in time."

E.V. looked at the dancers moving—most of them—effortlessly to the music, the colorful gowns swishing back and forth like Christmas bells. People lived and loved. People died. Heartaches happened to everyone. Life was loss, and life went on. That was the order of things, and he could let reality steal his joy or focus it.

When he didn't answer, Willum said rather sadly, "You've cut your losses."

"No, I haven't. I've. . ." E.V. wasn't sure how to explain. What he couldn't tell Willum was that last night—this morning, actually—when he was burying the liquor bottles, he realized how his actions had been as misplaced as Larkin's parents' were. In order to have Larkin for his wife, he'd been desperately grasping and arranging and worrying over what he needed to do to earn Whitworth's permission to marry her. He loved her so much that he'd made her an idol in his life. Rather like Mrs. Whitworth and her need to medicate away her grief.

All he truly needed was God. All he really desired was God. God had created him to desire Him, but he'd allowed that desire to be sidetracked with something good but something not God.

The walk back to his lonely one-room apartment had brought him to the place where, once he closed the door behind him, he'd fallen on his knees in worship and repentance.

"No," he repeated. "When God is in His rightful place in my life, all my other desires fall into place. If God makes a way for Larkin to be my wife, I'm content. If He doesn't, I'm content."

This time Willum nodded and said nothing.

The dance came to an end, and several couples made their way to the refreshment table.

"I wonder where she went," E.V. heard Kathleen Leonard say.

"She's probably off having a drink," came her sister-in-law's loud reply. "Poor thing can't go a day without imbibing. Anna befriends her out of pity."

The room silenced.

Kathleen nudged her husband, who immediately glared at his sister.

"Abby," Garrick chastised, "you know that's not true. You shouldn't gossip."

Though her face flushed, Miss Leonard glanced at the dozen people around the table. Panic flittered across her features. "How come you can say you saw Larkin at the mercantile and it's not gossip, but if I say I saw her drunk then it is? The truth isn't gossip." As she spoke, more of the soiree guests crowded around. She turned to E.V., pointing in his direction. "Just ask Mr. Renier. He was there. He smelled the whiskey on her breath. He saw her stumbling about."

E.V. nipped at the inside of his cheek, debating his response. When the murmuring quieted, he noticed Larkin across the parlor standing under the mistletoe. Truth was, as he admired how the fitted bodice of her gown with its waterfall of ruffles on the skirt accentuated her lovely figure, he couldn't quite remember why everyone was looking at him for a response.

As the grandfather clock struck nine, Larkin stood in the parlor's entrance with her parents, holding the basket full of ribbon-wrapped gifts for their guests. Since Mama had abruptly stopped and grabbed the sleeve of Papa's black frock coat, halting them, Larkin assumed she wanted to say something before they handed out the gifts. Only Mama didn't talk, allowing them to hear every mortifying word Abigail uttered.

Almost directly across from them, E.V. and Willum Tate stood at the refreshment table, with their other guests forming a half circle.

Not at all fearing what E.V. would answer because she trusted he'd keep her secret, Larkin tilted her head until she could meet his gaze. His attention drifted briefly to something above her. The moment she realized what she was standing under, the corner of his mouth indented into a half smile, which made her give him a look to say—*Don't you dare.* Were it not for Mama favoring Victorian Christmas traditions, Larkin would banish the mistletoe from the house, sparing all from possible embarrassing moments.

Papa muttered under his breath, "Why is he still here?"

"Patrick, don't make a scene," Mama cautioned.

"Did you send him an invitation?" Papa asked her.

"I was wondering when you would ask."

"That's not an answer."

"No, I did not."

To Larkin: "Did you?"

"No sir," Larkin answered honestly, although she had her suspicions who had. She reached forward with the hand not holding the basket, and gripped Papa's fingers. "I love E.V., but I'd never dishonor you by marrying him or any man without your approval. I choose our family." And although she didn't want to resurrect the pain she'd brought her parents after confessing over breakfast what she'd done with Mama's liquor, she reminded him, "That's why I did what I did last night. That's why I will endure any untruths spoken of me. And that's why you will be a gracious host to *all* of our guests. Please, Papa."

His mouth clamped in a thin line.

Larkin watched his chest rise and fall underneath his cherry jacquard vest that matched in fabric and shade Mama's gown. Before the soiree began, the photographer had captured their images—Papa sitting in a chair and Mama standing elegantly behind him with her left hand gracefully resting on his shoulder. Pity the black-and-white image couldn't depict the depth of love they showed when gazing upon each other. Larkin blinked at the moisture in her eyes. Her heart ached with yearning to grow old and in love.

With another deeply drawn-in breath, Papa offered his arm to Mama. He squeezed Larkin's hand, and they walked toward the crowd together.

E.V. simply didn't know what to say. It was an unsettling, unmanning, unfamiliar feeling, really. While he never considered himself a fluent conversationalist—he preferred to be known for being a good listener—when times called for him to say the right, wise, or practical thing, he'd always known what to say.

But now with all eyes on him, he was speechless.

Even Whitworth looked at him as if he expected—feared—E.V. would share everything Larkin had told him last night about her mother and brother. Only Mrs. Whitworth's hold on him seemed to keep him from intervening.

"Mr. Renier," Kathleen Leonard questioned, "do you have something to add?"

E.V. turned from Kathleen to her sister-in-law, who stood there with a smug grin on her face. And everything became clear. "You started the rumors about Larkin being pickled and about Milton courting her. Why? Because I love her instead of you?"

Everyone's attention shifted to Miss Leonard. Her mouth twisted into a scowl. "Good gracious, no!" she spat out. "I only wanted to stop her from getting another thing she wanted. Larkin is a drunkard, an imposter, and a thief."

"A thief?" Larkin pushed through the crowd. "What did I steal?"

"My friend!" The bottom of Miss Leonard's face trembled. She sniffed. "You stole the only friend I ever had. So I don't feel bad for telling everyone the truth about your drinking."

"Oh Abigail." Larkin answered, in tears. "I wanted to be your friend, too, but you pushed me away."

"Because I didn't want to be your friend! You have everything and I only had Anna. Now I have no one." She broke into sobs and ran from the room.

Garrick and Kathleen took off after her with her father and his lady-friend following.

E.V. looked about the room, seeking the right words to say to break the awful silence and knowing he would never share Larkin's secret.

"I've been everything Larkin has been accused of being," he confessed. "And worse. Thanks to Jesus, who I was isn't who I am today. Who Larkin is, is what you know her to be, and that's not anything she's been accused of. Trust what you know of her character and not any rumors you hear, because that's what you would want others to do for you."

"Renier!"

The crowd separated like the parting of the Red Sea.

E.V. swallowed what little moisture he had left in his mouth.

Patrick Whitworth motioned to one of the members of the string quartet standing outside the library entrance. "You, play something lively for my guests to dance to. Larkin, Renier, you two come with us." He swiveled around then grabbed his wife's hand and walked to the empty front foyer.

Feeling uneasy, E.V. stepped to Larkin's side, and taking care not to step on the train of her gown, he touched the small of her back and nudged her forward before dropping his arm to his side. "Does he know about—"

"Yes," Larkin interrupted. "And he knows who my accomplices are."

Somehow E.V. managed to find a little more moisture to ease the tightness in his throat. In this moment, he'd prefer fisticuffs to a lecture.

They stopped in the foyer. Standing at the end of the staircase, Whitworth rested his right foot on the bottom stair and his right elbow on the handrail, the fingers on his right hand tapping his chin.

"You've been cavorting with my daughter," he stated.

E.V. nodded.

Still holding his wife's hand, Whitworth drew her close. Gently he turned their enclosed hands, raising them so he could place a kiss on her knuckles in what seemed to E.V. to be a comforting manner. "Renier, you pegged me accurately that day in the rain. You missed one thing, though. I can admit when I've been wrong."

E.V. stared in silence.

"I've been wrong about you." Whitworth's eyes narrowed, yet the corners of his mouth pinched upward. "In some things. Others I'm still deciding. What you did last night helping Larkin—" He cleared his throat. "Your faithfulness to her then and now is why in about thirty seconds I'm going to give my wife the dance she's been asking for, leaving you two alone here in the foyer. If my daughter so happens to stand under the mistletoe and you so happen to kiss her a little longer than decorum permits and Reverend Bollen happens to see, well, considering you admitted you've been cavorting with Larkin, you'll have to marry her. You understand?"

For a moment E.V. was struck dumb. But then his mind started processing exactly what Whitworth was suggesting—was granting permission for. No wonder Larkin had such a tender spot for cantankerous ol' Mrs. Ellis. The woman was a female version of Patrick Whitworth.

Trying not to smile, E.V. nodded again. "Yes sir."

Whitworth inclined his head. "Merry Christmas, son." Holding his wife close as she blinked away her tears, he stepped toward the parlor, pausing long enough to brush a kiss on Larkin's cheek.

Wordless, Larkin walked with E.V. to the mistletoe. A struggle of emotions graced her face as she stared at the suddenly intimidating red berries and green leaves. He knew exactly how she hated to be the center of attention.

"What are you thinking?" he whispered.

"If I *really* want to throw caution to the wind, now that the opportunity is before me." Her gaze shifted to the guests dancing and lingering about the parlor. She released a ragged breath. "I vowed to Anna that we'd be married before her baby is born. Jeremiah sent word that her labor began a few hours ago."

"Far be it for me to let you to break a vow."

"We'd have to marry tonight."

E.V. nodded in agreement even though she was more focused on her fears than on him. "If we gave proper cause, Reverand Bollen could arrange a wedding. One good kiss should do it."

"Everyone will be watching."

"I love you."

She met his gaze. "What did you say?"

"I love you?" he repeated.

"Are you not certain?"

He grinned and she grinned, and all E.V. saw was her.

"I'm *quite* certain, sweetheart."

The dimples in her cheeks deepened as her smile chased away her fears. In a movement that stunned the breath from his lungs, she drew him close, far closer than decorum allowed, and her lips found his. She kissed him. She kissed him until he forgot everyone was watching. She kissed him until he was sure *she* forgot everyone was watching, because when Reverend Bollen tapped E.V.'s shoulder and E.V. reluctantly drew his lips from Larkin's, the look on her face was exactly how he felt.

Content.

Gina Welborn worked in news radio writing copy until she took up writing romances. As a member of RWA and ACFW, she's an active contest judge and coordinator. This Oklahoma-raised girl now lives in Richmond, Virginia, with her youth-pastor husband, their five Okie-Hokie children, and a Sharpador Retriever who doesn't retrieve much of anything.

A Carpenter Christmas

Mary Davis

Dedication

To my son, Ben, who loves to
build and create with his hands.

Every wise woman buildeth her house:
but the foolish plucketh it down with her hands.
Proverbs 14:1

Chapter 1

June 1891

Natalie Bollen tried to pick out the *solid* areas of mud, if there were such a thing. But everywhere she stepped her boots sank in at least an inch, if not three. She balanced herself with an umbrella in one hand and held her skirt up in the other. Rain tapped on the fabric of the umbrella like a soft symphony. She loved how a shower cleaned the air and made everything smell so fresh.

She stopped in front of the big house under construction. It had been in such a state for a year now. The builder not in a particular hurry to complete it. It wasn't as big and fancy as the Whitworths' mansion, but clearly it would be one of the larger houses in Tumwater. The owners must be people of importance to need such a fine home.

The hammering told her the carpenter was present, and a giddiness rippled through her. The noise came from above. He wasn't foolish enough to be up on the roof in this downpour?

As she tipped her head back to look up, her hat loosened. She dropped her skirt and slapped her hand on her hat. "Mr. Tate?" She would prefer to call him Willum, but Papa forbade it. He said it wasn't proper for a young lady to address a gentleman outside her family by his first name. Most people would think a logging town like Tumwater to be a simple backwoods place where decorum wouldn't matter. To many, it didn't. But to Papa, the town's only religious influence, it did. When decorum went, he said, so did society.

The pounding stopped, and Mr. Tate peered over the edge of the roof, hanging on to a rope tied around his waist. Sandy brown, shoulder-length waves hung in dark, wet tendrils from beneath his worn hat. He shook his head then proceeded to climb down.

Rain poured from his hat brim. He narrowed his pine green eyes, dark on the outside and lighter on the inside, like the varying shades of the forest. "Miss Bollen, you shouldn't be out in this weather."

As proper as Papa. "And *you* shouldn't be climbing around on the roof like a monkey."

He shook his head again. "Come inside where it is drier."

She released her hat and collected up her skirt again. Mr. Tate guided her by her elbow up the three steps and in through the front door. He took her umbrella and set it against the inside wall.

Natalie smoothed her hands down her pink-striped dress. She looked best in pink, and today was a special day. But even after all her best efforts, mud still managed to get past the hem's mudguard around the bottom of her skirt. Papa would say that this was where vanity got a person. She had just wanted to look her best.

Mr. Tate took off his hat and shook the water from it. "Does your father know you're out in this?" He pointed to the window with his still dripping hat.

She tugged at one finger of her glove then the next and next. "Papa is out visiting members of the flock."

Mr. Tate shook his head again. His wet waves swung gently.

She pulled her hand free of her right glove. Wasn't he the least bit pleased to see her?

Across the room, Mr. Tate's orange-colored dog appeared in the kitchen doorway on her three legs and wagging her feathery tail.

Natalie smiled at the dog. "Hi, Sassy."

Mr. Tate held up a hand to the dog. "Stay, girl."

Sassy's body shook with her obedience, and she whined.

Natalie crossed the room to her and scratched the dog's head around her silky ears.

Sassy sat, and her feathery tail brushed the floor. Mr. Tate had Sassy when he arrived in town three years ago, and said he had found Sassy wandering and hungry. He had no idea how the furry orange canine had lost one of her back legs. But she got around fine on three. She'd taken a shine to him and become his faithful companion.

Sassy rolled over, and Natalie rubbed her soft tummy.

"I think she likes you better than me." Less of a criticism and more of a pleased acknowledgement.

Natalie looked back at Mr. Tate. "I doubt that. You're her master."

He scratched the whiskers on his chin. "No. She just knows where her next meal is coming from."

Natalie held her hand out to him, and he pulled her to her feet.

"I've seen the way she gazes up at you." Natalie was afraid she might have that same expression just now and looked away.

She surveyed the room. Water dripped from several places above. She could see right through the trusses of the upper floor to the underside of the roof. With all the rain they'd had lately, it was no wonder he was trying to get the rest of the shingles on. Then the interior could dry out. They were standing in the largest of the dry areas. "You certainly are taking your time with this house. Isn't your employer anxious to move in? I'm sure his wife is."

"He is not yet ready to move in."

"Not with rain pouring in."

And then he did it. His whisker-framed mouth broke into that smile that melted her heart.

"The house will be ready when *my employer* wishes to move in."

"You still are not going to tell me who it is?"

He just stared at her, grinning. "You'll have to wait until they move in, like everyone else."

"Oh bother."

She wandered into the next room. Bone dry. Not a single leak, and the floor above was finished, too. One wall was lined with bookshelves that had delicate carvings across the tops and down the sides. Mr. Tate had to be a patient man to do such fine work and a master at his craft. She ran her hand over the smooth surface.

She wished to compliment him on his workmanship so turned around. Mr. Tate stood directly behind her. Well, now in front of her. She sucked in a breath. Her heart raced like a runaway Shay engine with a full load of timber.

"Why did you come?"

Why had she come? Because today was a special day, in spite of the rain. And she had wanted him to remember it was special, too. He obviously did not. "Oh, I don't know." She sighed. "I thought it a lovely day for a stroll."

His mouth twitched up slightly at the corners. "Then let me escort you home." He moved back to the front door and retrieved her umbrella and waited.

Truly? He wasn't going to comment that a downpour did not constitute a lovely day? And one should remain indoors in such weather? Mr. Tate was as stubborn as a cantankerous mule. She shoved her hand back into her glove and marched for the door. She wanted to tell him that she could find her own way home but didn't want to be disappointed if he honored her request. If she knew he would still insist on walking her home, she would protest. A great and mighty protest. But she would rather hold her tongue and be able to enjoy his company a little longer, than have her heart crushed by his indifference.

He held the umbrella up just outside the door and extended his work-gloved hand to help her down the steps.

She took it, scooped up her skirt with the other hand, and descended the three steps into the mud. When she was a little girl and had first come to Tumwater, she had enjoyed walking barefoot in such mud, feeling it squish between her toes. "For the grandeur of the house, the porch seems a bit understated."

He laughed and tucked her hand in the crook of his elbow, and they began their promenade through the rain.

She liked his laugh. Full and jovial. Lively.

"Those steps are temporary. They are only to get me in and out of the house without killing myself. When the rain lets up and

I have the roof finished, I plan to build a porch that wraps around the entire house. And a balcony off the master suite."

She could picture it. "Oh, that will be lovely."

A puddle she had skirted fairly easily earlier now stretched out before them. She looked left and right to determine the most suitable course. The land gently sloped up on the right, and the puddle ceased sooner in that direction. She stopped at the water's edge.

Before she could suggest their course, as Mr. Tate had not turned either left or right to survey the hazards, he placed the umbrella in her hand and scooped her up. He then slogged through the muddy waters. She presumed, since he was already soaked from head to toe, that a little more water made no difference to him. She stared at his whiskered face and bright eyes the multihued greens of the forest. Even if he didn't remember that today was special, being carried by Mr. Tate was well worth a soaking. She would find some way to remind him. Perhaps on Wednesday when he regularly ate supper with her family.

He set her down on the boardwalk where the stores began. Under the awnings, out of the rain and the mud, at least for the time being.

At her house just beyond the edge of town, he opened the door for her.

She stepped inside and turned. "Would you like to come in and warm up with a cup of coffee?"

He collapsed the umbrella and shook it before handing it to her. "I better not. I'm a bit of a mess." He motioned with his hands down his muddy, wet attire. "I don't want to drip all over your floor." He took off a glove and reached inside his coat pocket.

He handed her a small carved animal. "Happy birthday."

He had remembered. Her heart soared. So he knew the significance of today. Now that she was eighteen, he would ask Papa to court her. But Papa was out on visitations. "Papa's not here."

He nodded. "You told me he was out visiting."

"We'll see you for Wednesday supper?"

"Wouldn't miss it." He tipped his hat. "Good day."

Natalie closed the door, leaned against it, and looked at the wooden kitten. So detailed.

Mama sighed, her blond hair glowed in the firelight. "You best get that dress off. It's half ruined with the mud. I have some pink fabric goods that we can use to put a border around the bottom, add a little fabric to the collar and cuffs. No one will know."

What she meant was that Papa wouldn't know.

Natalie crossed to where Mama sat in a rocking chair by the fire peeling last year's potatoes and kissed her on the cheek. "I love you, Mama."

"I love you, too. Now scoot, so you can help me fix supper."

Natalie went upstairs to her room and set the carved kitten on her bureau with the dozen other animals Willum had carved for her over the past three years.

Willum whistled all the way back to the construction site, kicking at clumps of dirt, causing mud to spray up. Natalie had thought he'd forgotten she turned eighteen today. He'd been surprised she had ventured out on such a dreary day. Pleasantly surprised. He'd known from the start exactly why she had come and had tempted her to admit it, but she didn't. She looked older, more mature, with her dark hair pulled up on top of her head.

He scrubbed his hand across his bristly chin. He, on the other hand, probably looked like a grizzly bear. It was time to shave off his winter beard.

Natalie had set her cap for him long ago. From the moment he'd first met her three years ago, she had intrigued him. But being seven years his junior, he'd not thought of her in a romantic way at first. Now he thought of her all the time.

His intentions were jumbled where Miss Natalie Bollen was concerned, and his heart troubled.

He knew better than to let a young lady ever manipulate him again. But wasn't Natalie too sweet for deception and games? Too sweet to play with a man's heart then casually throw it away and crush it under her pretty little shoe.

Chapter 2

Natalie sat straight as a board in the front pew at church Sunday morning. They always sat in the same order—Mama on the aisle then the children next to her from youngest to oldest. Even her oldest brother Isaac's wife sat with them. As the family of the pastor, they sat in the front pew every Sunday where everyone could see they were present and on time, and that the family wasn't distracted by the rest of the people in church. But Natalie was distracted *because* she couldn't see anyone but Papa. And today more so than other Sundays.

She could feel someone staring at the back of her head. She didn't dare turn around but was dying to know who. Willum? Nothing up front had a reflective surface that she might be able to see and scan the congregation. She tilted her head and slightly turned it in one direction then looked out of the corner of her eye at the first window. Shadowy figures, but she couldn't make anyone out. So she turned and tilted her head the other direction to see if she could see in the windows on the other side any better. Because of the shadows on the outside of the window, it was darker, and she could recognize people. She turned her head a little farther to get a better view.

Mama nudged Natalie. "Pay attention."

She turned her focus back onto Papa.

After service was over, Natalie stood next to Mama, who stood next to Papa just outside the church doors to shake hands with each member and to send them into their week with the Lord's blessing. Mr. Tate had come through the line early and now stood with his friends Mr. Tucker, Mr. Corrigan, and Mr. Renier, and their wives. She hoped he didn't leave. He'd barely stayed long enough on Wednesday to eat and spent no time alone with Papa to discuss courting her. And going through the reception line after service certainly didn't afford him any time.

John Seymour lingered close as the line drew to an end. He smiled at her. To be polite, she smiled back.

The line ended, and she could go to Mr. Tate herself, not to talk about courting but about visiting with her papa.

Mr. Seymour stepped forward and asked to speak to Papa.

Mama put a hand on Natalie's arm. "Please go invite Miss Leonard to Wednesday supper."

"But Mama?" Nobody liked Abigail. "She's the meanest girl in town."

"And she came to church. Now go."

Natalie looked toward Mr. Tate. "But. . ."

"Go."

Natalie slumped her shoulders and walked off. She heard Mama clear her throat. The meaning of that simple sound was unmistakable. *Stand up straight.* So she did and fashioned her face into a pleasant expression.

"Abigail."

The stunning blond turned with a start. "Natalie?"

She needed to make this fast so she could still talk to Mr. Tate. "Mama has invited you to supper on Wednesday night."

Abigail pulled up her lip on one side in a very unattractive manner. "I'm sure it rubs you into a rash to have to invite the most hated person in town. I can tell you don't want to be here with me, and certainly don't want me in your home."

It wasn't so much that she didn't want to be around Abigail as much as she wanted to be with someone else. "You are not the most hated person in town."

"The most hated *girl*."

Why couldn't Abigail just say yes and let Natalie be on her way? Mama would not be happy until she came back with a yes. Truthfully, Natalie didn't want Abigail at Wednesday supper, although any other night of the week would be fine. Wednesday supper was time to spend with Mr. Tate. "I believe Mrs. Ellis is more disliked than you." Mrs. Ellis had left buckshot in the backside of more than one trespasser.

Abigail's mouth turned up. "Well, at least more feared."

"Miss Bledsow?" Natalie could still feel where the schoolmarm had whacked her knuckles, even though it was years ago.

Abigail rubbed her own knuckles. "Maybe I'm number three then." And she gave a small giggle.

"You'll come to supper?"

Abigail nodded.

Natalie left Abigail with the answer Mama wanted, but Mr. Tate and his friends were gone. Maybe he was talking to Papa. She sighed. Mr. Milton stood close to Papa, deep in conversation. So she walked over and looped her arm through Mama's. "Miss Leonard said she'd come to supper."

Willum woke Tuesday morning long before dawn to the school bell ringing a warning. He dressed in a hurry then rushed with Sassy leading the way to the school to see what the ruckus was about. But before he even got there, he saw the glow of the raging fire that consumed several businesses and the church. He smelled the smoke and heard the hungry crackling. Men, women, and children had formed two lines and were passing buckets of water. One line went to the fire's last victim—the building was only half burned. The other line went to the untouched building next to it, hoping to prevent it from catching fire as well.

There had been no rain since a week ago Monday. Everything had dried out then gone on drying, ripe for fire.

Willum shouted over the roaring to the nearest person, "Is there anyone inside?"

The man shook his head. "Those who live above these businesses got out."

That was a blessing.

Willum joined the volunteer firemen in setting up the water wagon and hose. What they could use was a nice downpour.

By noon the fire had been reduced to smoldering debris. People milled around in the streets, surveying the damage. Three destroyed businesses and the church.

A dripping ladle appeared before him. "Water?"

He recognized that voice. He reached for the ladle, making sure to reach high enough on the handle to partially cover his benefactor's hand. Would she move it? Or leave it there? Her hand was cool under his. He wanted to put it to his forehead to cool his face. Holding her hand this way was all he dared in public. Reverend Bollen would never allow a public display of affection.

Once his thirst was quenched and he'd held her hand on the ladle as long as he dared, Willum looked up into Natalie's rich chocolate eyes. But she was sweeter than any chocolate he'd ever tasted. Her face was sweet. Her smile was sweet. Her heart was sweet. He doubted she knew how to deceive or hurt another person. He'd seen her talking to Miss Abigail Leonard on Sunday. There were precious few who would talk to Abigail outside of a business transaction. She'd hurt too many people. Then there she was at church, and sweet Natalie had befriended her. He knew enough to steer clear of girls like Abigail. She would cast her net for a man and pull him in before he was any the wiser.

"You worked hard here today."

Her words brought him back to the vision in front of him. "A lot of people did."

She looked left then right.

Was she anxious about something?

Then she glanced down at his hand, and he did as well. It still covered hers. He released her hand slowly. He evidently hadn't completed the task when he thought about releasing her hand a few moments ago.

"I'll see you Wednesday at supper."

"See you then." He watched her walk away. Even in a drab gray dress, she looked enchanting.

A hand clasped him on the shoulder. "Looks like you will have plenty of work to keep you busy this summer."

He turned to his good friend Tuck. The last thing he needed was more work. He needed to finish the house. "I have plenty of work, thank you."

"Yes, I saw. Have you officially started courting her?"

Willum backhanded Tuck in the stomach. "Not her. Actual work."

"I saw you two. It's about time, buddy. I thought your broken heart would never mend. And Natalie is a right fine young lady."

"She's so young."

"You missed the boat on eligible young ladies your age. You let Frederick, E.V., and me woo them first. And we all thank you. Wouldn't have stood a chance if you were interested in any of 'em."

Willum gazed at Natalie offering water to her brother David.

"So, are you courting yet?"

Willum narrowed his eyes at his longtime friend. "Why do you care so much?"

Caught, Tuck rubbed the back of his neck. "Anna will have my hide if I don't come home with the information. She's been pestering me all week."

"Pestering? Just because others expect it isn't a good reason to start courting any woman."

"Ah ha. That's good. You haven't started courting Natalie yet." He turned to leave then turned back. "Anna will want to know why you haven't asked to court her yet, and when you're going to ask for permission."

Willum shook his head and walked off. But the question was valid. Why hadn't he asked to court Natalie. . .again? He'd asked just over a year ago, when she turned seventeen and he knew she was too young. Now that she was old enough, he couldn't bring himself to ask. Why?

Chapter 3

Willum sat at the Bollens' table as he had done every Wednesday since he arrived in town. He bowed his head as the reverend blessed those around his table and the food. After the "amens" of nine people echoed, Mrs. Bollen stood and dished up the first bowl of thick bean soup and passed it down the table. Willum took the full bowl and passed it on to Matthew sitting next to him, who passed it on down the table.

Willum avoided eye contact with Natalie sitting directly across from him. He knew she expected him to ask her father tonight to court her. The Reverend Bollen probably expected it, too. Willum didn't know if he could tonight or not. For the first time in three years he hadn't wanted to come to Wednesday supper because of his indecision.

But fortunately, he had other business with the reverend. "I checked the church's rock foundation. It seems solid enough to rebuild on."

The reverend nodded. "Good. We'll need to raise money before any construction can start."

"I drew up plans for a new church building." Willum passed another bowl along. "They're rough."

"I'll look at them after supper."

"The plans will let us know just how much money we'll need to purchase materials."

Then Natalie spoke up. "Mama and I are planning to organize bake sales to raise money. And we are going to ask the quilting circle to make a quilt for a drawing."

Willum glanced over at Natalie but looked away before she looked at him with that expectant expression.

Abigail set down her glass of milk. "Where will church be held until the new building is completed?"

Why had Natalie invited *her* here? She had nearly ruined two of his friends' chances with their now wives. She had meddled and tried to get between several couples in town. What was innocent Natalie learning from her? To be conniving and manipulative? No. Natalie was sweet and just being nice. Or was Abigail trying to come between him and Natalie?

The reverend took a biscuit and passed the basket on. "Service will be held in the schoolhouse. It will be a little cramped, and I'm afraid people might use that as an excuse to stay home."

David, the Bollen's second son, who was a year younger than Willum said, "Do they know what happened? How the fire started?"

Willum buttered his biscuit. "No one is quite sure."

After supper, the women cleared the table and washed the dishes. Willum sat at the table with the reverend and his three sons, Isaac, David, and Matthew. The paper plans rolled out before them. As they hashed over the details, Willum made notations on the side of the brown paper. He would draw up more accurate plans and bring them back for the reverend's approval.

Natalie stayed in the kitchen while Papa and the men talked about the new church building. She heard the paper crinkle as it was rolled up, then some hearty good evenings.

Who was leaving? Wasn't Mr. Tate going to at least bid her good night? She'd hoped he'd tell her that he'd talked to Papa, and they were now courting.

Isaac called into the kitchen, "Martha, time to go."

Natalie's sister-in-law pushed her cumbersome body out of the chair. "I hope this child decides to arrive soon. I want to hold him in my arms. After losing the first one so early, and the second being stillborn, I want to know this one is healthy."

"Him?" Abigail said.

"Isaac really wants a boy." She waddled out of the kitchen.

Natalie followed her to say good evening to Mr. Tate. But he was gone.

Had he asked Papa to court her?

"David, would you walk Miss Leonard home?"

David looked from Papa to Abigail standing in the kitchen doorway, then back to Papa. He stood. "Of course." David did not look like he wanted to, but it was the family's obligation to see that Abigail arrived home safely. David opened the front door. "Miss Leonard."

Abigail thanked Natalie's mother for supper. She seemed genuine. Almost a different person.

"Papa, where's Mr. Tate?"

Papa looked at her with his sympathetic blue eyes. "He has much work to do."

"Did he say anything about me?"

Matthew, her brother who was only ten months older than her, wrapped his arm around her neck and rubbed his knuckles in her hair. "Why would he talk about you?"

Natalie wiggled. "Let me go. You're messing up my hair."

"Matthew! Let your sister go."

Matthew released her.

Natalie stood up straight and smoothed her hair. "I'm not nine anymore."

"Your sister is a young lady, and you must treat her as one."

"But Papa—"

"Even at home."

Matthew hung his head like a scolded puppy.

"Now go fill the wood bin in the kitchen for your mama."

Matthew crossed the room, and once behind Papa, he turned and made a face at Natalie. She desperately wanted to make a face back, but Papa was turned in her direction. He'd called her a lady, so she supposed she should act like one, even at home.

Then she had a horrifying thought. What if Mr. Tate was so comfortable with their family that he thought of her as his sister?

"Papa?"

Papa looked up from stirring the fire. "Yes, child."

How should she say this? She couldn't very well come right out and ask if Mr. Tate had discussed courting her. Papa would send her to her room for being so forward. "Papa, since I'm eighteen and you told Matthew that I was a young lady, I thought it would be a good time to ask if. . .if any young men have asked to court me."

Papa stood and towered over her, silent. He didn't look upset.

His blue eyes had a bemused twinkle in them.

"Well?"

"Well, you haven't exactly asked a question. Yours was more of a statement."

"Papa."

Papa smiled then and laughed. "Several young men have made such a request. Don't worry, the young men in Tumwater have taken notice of you. A little more than I would like, I'm afraid."

"Who, Papa?" *Mr. Tate?*

The twinkle left Papa's eyes. "Don't you worry about that just now. Run along and finish helping your mama in the kitchen."

She turned and left. She knew when Papa had finished a conversation. No amount of begging would keep him talking. And he'd probably tell her she was being childish. If he thought that, he might suggest she needed to do a bit more growing up before courting, and make her wait until she turned nineteen. Why wouldn't he just tell her who?

Chapter 4

Over a month had gone by since the church and three businesses in town had burned. The baker, barber, and milliner had reopened their "shops" in canvas tents, but were eager to have solid buildings again. Willum had been hired by all three to work on the construction. The owners collaborated to have one structure that they all owned part of, so they could share the expenses of building. Cheaper for everyone. And easier for Willum to work with all three owners at once. With the construction nearly complete, Willum could focus on the church, which would take longer because they did not have the funds yet.

Working from sunup until sundown on construction of the new business building left Willum fatigued. He had overslept this morning and had to creep into the back of the schoolhouse while the first hymn was already in progress. There was usually a seat available in the last pew. But with the schoolhouse being smaller, he had to stand in the back corner. He yawned and leaned his head back against the wall. Before he knew it the service was over. *Lord, forgive me for falling asleep. I guess I'm more exhausted than I realized.*

He let the corner hold him up until most of the people had

filed out of the building. The reverend and his wife stood at the door to send his flock on their way. Natalie and her brothers were nowhere to be seen.

Willum shook the reverend's hand then Mrs. Bollen's.

Mrs. Bollen held onto his hand with her gloved one. "Will you join us for supper this evening?"

Willum swallowed hard. Sunday supper? No one was ever invited to the Bollens' for Sunday supper. It was for family only. Willum was not family. The significance of the offer was not lost on him. He was being included with *the family*. If he said yes, they would have expectations of him. If he said no, then what would become of him and Natalie? "I would be honored."

Mrs. Bollen smiled. "Fine. We'll see you before six." She patted his hand and released it.

Willum clicked open his pocket watch. Five fifty-seven. Snapping it closed, he slipped it back into his vest pocket and straightened his jacket. He'd never dressed up for supper with the Bollens before. He'd never felt as though he needed to.

He'd shaved a second time today and tied his shoulder-length hair at the nape of his neck. Should he have gotten it cut? He wasn't sure if he was ready to be that civilized again just yet. And it was too late to worry about it now. He put his palm out to Sassy to make her stay then took a deep breath and knocked.

When the door opened, Natalie's smiling face greeted him.

And he knew he'd come to the right place.

At the conclusion of supper, the reverend stood. "Willum, would you take a stroll with me?"

"Of course, sir."

Natalie smiled eagerly at him.

Sassy darted around sniffing while Willum walked beside the reverend for five minutes in silence. Raising money for the new church building was going a lot slower than the reverend wanted. He had voiced many times that he hoped to have the building complete by the end of the summer. And here they were a week into August and they barely had half the money they needed. Attendance was dropping off as people made excuses for the small, stuffy space. Or did the reverend want to talk about the actual plans for the building? Was he displeased with them? Willum could certainly get started building some of the framing with the money raised so far. Maybe when people saw it starting to take shape, they would contribute more to the building fund. But it was not his place to initiate the conversation. Reverend Bollen was the one to request his presence. He would suffer in silence.

The older man finally spoke. "About Natalie."

Willum's throat went dry, and he couldn't swallow.

"Over a year ago, you asked my permission to court my daughter, rather boldly I might add. I told you then that I would not allow her to be courted until she turned eighteen. She's been eighteen for two months and quite impatient. Have you lost interest in her?"

"No!" The word flew out of his mouth.

The reverend coughed to cover a chuckle. "May I ask what the delay is?"

Delay? "I've been quite busy with the construction in town and the church building project."

"It only takes a moment to ask. And you have had plenty of

opportunities. Inviting you to Sunday supper was no oversight. Your acceptance or regrets would have told me how important my daughter still is to you. You didn't turn us down. Yet you are reluctant to ask."

Willum rubbed the back of his neck. "I was engaged three and a half years ago."

"I take it that it didn't end well."

"If you mean me standing in front of the church in my finest, waiting and humiliated, then, yes, it didn't end well."

"What happened to her?"

"She ran off with a man who had a larger wallet than I did. Three days before the wedding! Her family kept it a secret because they were too embarrassed to tell people, and so they let me stand there like a fool. Waiting. I guess they thought it was fair for me to be embarrassed, too."

"Your heart is afraid to love again."

Willum shook his head. "I love Natalie."

"But you are afraid to declare it."

"I guess I am."

"It's difficult to trust with such a wound. There are five men to every woman here. You are not the only one who has expressed interest in courting my daughter."

Willum's insides tightened.

The reverend put a hand on his shoulder. "I have thought of you as a son. I would gladly welcome you into the family. But I cannot hold off the other suitors much longer. And Natalie's patience is wearing thin. You need to decide if you are ready to take a risk."

Willum nodded. "I'm ready." He couldn't lose Natalie. "May I court your daughter?" The moment he voiced the question, he felt as though a weight had been lifted from his shoulders.

The reverend's mouth broke out into a wide grin, and he nodded. "It's about time, son. Shall we head back so you can tell her the good news?"

Natalie stood by the window, holding the curtain back. Where had Papa gone with Mr. Tate? It shouldn't take this long to ask one simple question.

Mama sighed. "Honestly, Natalie. It is unfitting for a lady to gape out the window like a miscreant. Come away from there."

Natalie swung around and into a chair. "Do you think he's asking Papa right now?"

"I wouldn't know."

Natalie hopped up and took hold of Mama's arm. "Papa must have told you. Mr. Tate *was* invited for Sunday supper."

"You'll just have to be patient and wait."

Natalie darted back to the window. "I hear voices. They're coming back."

"Get away from there and behave yourself. You'll run poor Mr. Tate off before he has a chance."

Natalie sat in the chair across from Mama by the fireplace and opened a book.

Matthew made a kissing sound.

Mama pointed at him and whispered rushed words, "We'll have none of that from you. Just wait until it is your turn. I don't want to hear a sound from—" Mama turned with a smile to the opening door.

Natalie looked down to pretend to be engrossed in reading when she saw the horrifying truth. The book was upside down. She closed it quickly and set it in her lap.

Papa and Mr. Tate stepped inside. Papa gave Mama a slight nod.

Natalie's stomach danced.

Mr. Tate walked over to her with his hands clasped behind his back. "Miss Bollen, would you do me the honor of accompanying me on a stroll?"

"It would be my pleasure." She held out her hand, and Mr. Tate helped her to her feet.

Matthew made a guttural sound almost as though he were choking.

She would like to choke him.

Mama said, "Take a shawl. The night air has a chill to it."

Natalie took one from a peg beside the door and swung it on. Mr. Tate closed the door behind them then offered his arm to her. She tucked her hand in the crook of his elbow, and he covered her hand with his. Neither of them wore gloves. His hand was warm. Sassy followed along beside them.

"I spoke to your father tonight."

She wanted to jump into his arms, but he hadn't said what he'd spoken to Papa about. She knew though.

"I have gained his permission, now I'd like yours."

"Yes!" she blurted out.

He stopped their progress and smiled down at her. "I haven't even asked yet."

"Well then ask, so I can say yes."

He started walking again.

She stopped, and her hand slipped off his arm before he stopped and turned. She planted her fists on her hips. "If you don't ask me right now, I'll go back home."

He let out a jolly laugh then got serious. "Miss Bollen, may I have the honor of courting you?"

She let her hands slide off her hips. "I'll think about it."

He folded his arms, and a smile tugged at his lips.

She wanted to scream yes a thousand times that he could court her. But instead she decided for the ladylike approach. "I believe that being courted by you would be most pleasurable." She took his arm again.

He chuckled. "Now can we drop all this formality?"

She giggled and leaned into his arm. "I'd like that. Now that we're courting, you can call me Natalie. May I call you Willum?"

He seemed to think about it. "Hmm. I kind of like you calling me Mr. Tate. It makes you sound obedient."

She tried to pull her hand free again, but he held tight and kept her at his side. "You are impossible, *Willum*."

"Well, if you say it like that, I especially don't like it."

In her sweetest, most innocent voice, while batting her eyelashes, she said, "Willum."

"I like the sound of that."

She turned to face him. "Are you going to kiss me?"

He gazed down at her. "I'm not sure your father would approve."

"He gave you permission to court me. I'm sure he expects it."

He caressed her cheek and leaned closer ever so slowly, his breath fanning her mouth a moment before his lips touched hers.

Her first kiss was better than she'd imagined. Her insides

turned to mashed potatoes and her knees to jelly.

Willum wrapped his arms around her, keeping her up.

Finally, Willum was hers.

Willum walked home with a huge smile on his face, a smile he couldn't seem to tame, not that he really wanted to. He passed the charred ground that had been the church. He needed to do something about getting the construction started. He couldn't finish the house and the church all at once. And he knew just how to get the extra money they needed.

Chapter 5

By the beginning of September, all the funds were in place and construction on the new church could begin. Monday, the first load of lumber would be paid for and delivered to the building site.

From the kitchen, Natalie studied Mama who looked worriedly at the mantel clock again and again. Supper was always at six. Papa had never been late. Never. He always arrived home well before six. Should they eat or wait? The question on everyone's mind.

At a quarter past, David swung on his coat. "I'm going out to look for him."

Matthew grabbed his coat, but before he could shove his arms into the sleeves, the door opened. Natalie could see Mama's whole body relax at the sight of Papa.

Papa wasn't smiling. He took off his hat and coat and hung them on a peg by the door. "Mr. Whitworth and I were at the schoolhouse counting the building fund money. A man with a bandana over his face came in with a gun. He took all the money. He tied us up and shoved us in a broom closet."

Tears prickled in Natalie's eyes. Papa had been so excited at the possibility of being in the new church building well before

Thanksgiving. Something to be truly thankful for. Now the dwindling congregation wouldn't have their church back even for Christmas.

Mama went to Papa and wrapped her arms around him. "I'm so glad you're safe."

Papa held Mama for a moment. "I'm going to eat quickly and walk over to Willum's and give him the bad news."

Natalie stepped through the kitchen doorway. "May I go with you, Papa?"

"If you wish."

Natalie smiled. She'd never seen Willum's place, just knew he had a cabin outside of town. She would get to see where she'd live after they married, know what kind of curtains she could start making. And if they'd need a rug in the front room by the fireplace. So many plans to make.

After supper, Natalie left with Papa. She couldn't wait to see Willum even though they brought bad news. She had seen him yesterday, but she wanted to see him every day. Off the path, Papa headed for a small plank cabin. Her feet dragged. Papa got ahead of her. Her stomach knotted. This couldn't be where Willum lived. It was too small. He worked hard and long and made a good wage. He was a carpenter. He could build a cabin as large as he wanted with many rooms. This cabin couldn't be much bigger than her bedroom.

Papa stopped and looked back. "Don't dawdle."

She quickened her step, and the knot in her stomach tightened.

Papa knocked on the door.

Someone else would answer. She was sure of it.

But Willum opened the door and smiled. "Reverend. Natalie.

What brings you out here?"

Her hands began to shake. She fisted them to make them stop then gripped one in the other, but they still shook. She followed Papa through the doorway.

Papa removed his hat. "I'm afraid I have some bad news. The building fund was stolen this afternoon."

Natalie gazed around the even smaller interior. Two narrow sets of bunk beds lined each side wall with clothes and tools on three of the mattresses. A small table with two three-legged stools, a potbelly stove with Sassy curled up next to it, and a small bookshelf crammed with books made up the rest of the furnishings. One window, no curtain.

Willum said, "That's terrible. Who did it? Did they catch him?"

She faintly heard Papa and Willum's voices and tried to draw air into her lungs, but they refused to cooperate.

Papa shook his head. "Mr. Whitworth and I were tied up. We had a terrible time getting free. By the time we did, the man was long gone."

She wiped her moist palms down her skirt. Was the room shrinking? She'd been locked in here before. It hadn't been her fault.

The lights began to dim.

Natalie blinked several times. Papa and Willum looked down on her, their voices muffled. They both looked quite concerned. Suddenly their voices returned.

Papa's eyebrows were knitted together. "Are you all right?"

Willum shook his head. "I think she's confused."

"I'm fine. I'm not confused." But she was. She just didn't want to admit it. What was going on?

Willum pulled on her arm. "Can you sit up?"

Papa lifted her at her shoulder.

She wasn't sitting? Mercy. She was lying down. On Willum's bunk! Double mercy.

Not only did she sit up in haste but got to her feet.

Willum grabbed her arm. "Whoa. You aren't too steady yet."

Papa had hold of her other arm, and she swayed between the two. "Maybe you should sit back down."

"No. I'm fine." The walls moved. Or did they?

Papa tightened his hold on her arm. "You fainted. You are not fine. Sit."

She waved a hand toward the door. "A little fresh air and I'll be fine."

Sucking in the cool night air in several long breaths revived her like a slap and brought her back to her senses. Mostly. She still felt weak-kneed, but she could breathe. She drew in another long breath.

Papa kept hold of her arm. "If I had known you were feeling ill, I wouldn't have brought you."

Yes, ill. That could be what it was. But she knew better. "I'm sorry, Papa."

Willum said, "Should I get a wagon to take her home?"

"I'll be fine." If she said it enough times, maybe she would believe it.

Chapter 6

Natalie pulled her shawl tighter around her against the damp air that promised rain as she walked down the opposite side of the street from the house Willum worked on occasionally. Was he there today? She heard no pounding or sawing. The house would be quite nice if he ever finished it. It sat in a semi-prominent location. It would be nothing to the grandeur of the Whitworth home that held the place of prominence. But it had a grandness in its own right.

No wonder Willum was penniless and lived in a shack. He couldn't even finish a simple house in a timely manner. He'd finished the roof, put in windows, and painted the outside her favorite color, a cheerful butter yellow. But the porch had not been put on yet—the extravagant wraparound one. And she was sure the inside still needed walls and upper floors.

He'd managed to complete a building for three businesses in no time with a crew. Why didn't he hire a crew for this house and be done with it, so the man and his wife could move in? And he could get paid for his work.

She was sounding petty. She had nothing against people of diminished means. She just didn't want to be one again. She tried not to think of those black years in her life. She was grateful for all the Lord had given her and didn't want to lose it. She was selfish and petty.

And ashamed.

She hurried on to the mercantile, hoping not to run into Willum. She'd felt too sick for Sunday supper this week and had stayed in her room. But she knew her nausea was from nerves. Though her stomach was a little unsettled again on Wednesday, she forced herself to the table, grateful for the distraction of Abigail. David, of all people, had invited her. He smiled at her all through supper. Smitten beyond belief. She'd felt that way about Willum. Only just last week. She still did, didn't she?

The bell over the door jingled. She made a quick scan of the interior and breathed easier. Until she sorted out this gnawing in the pit of her stomach, she would rather not see Willum.

She quickly gathered the items Mama needed, paid, and stepped out onto the boardwalk. A light mist caressed her face. She wouldn't be arriving home dry. She had better hurry for many reasons.

A covered buggy stopped in front of the mercantile. John Seymour smiled at her and jumped down. "Let me get those for you." He took her parcel and shopping basket, placing them on the floor of his buggy. He held his hand out to her. "It looks like rain. Let me give you a ride."

It was an innocent enough invitation. And it did look and feel like rain. Almost drizzling already.

She stared at his proffered hand then took it. Immediately, a sinking feeling in the pit of her stomach told her she'd made the wrong choice. A large round raindrop splattered on the back of her glove, then her cheek and her nose. Instinct—and Mr. Seymour—propelled Natalie into the buggy.

Mr. Seymour raced around the buggy and jumped aboard, half soaked. He laughed as he shook off some of the rain. "That was close."

She laughed, too.

Her sinking feeling dissuaded for the moment.

Willum stood in the shadows of the livery, watching Natalie with John Seymour. Laughing. John obviously had no compunction about escorting another man's girl without his permission.

He hadn't thought Natalie flighty. He'd seen her walk into town, stop and gaze at the house, then continue on to the mercantile. He'd watched every graceful step she took, like a hummingbird floating.

He'd seen the look on her face when she visited his pocket-sized, boxy cabin. He'd never thought she would ever have an opportunity to see it. He'd made his place small to discourage visitors, squeezing in bunk beds for his friends when they came to town from the logging camp. When he'd come to Tumwater, he wanted to be left alone and cloistered himself away to heal. It had worked. As time passed he became more and more involved in the town, looked forward to Wednesday supper with the reverend and his family. Looked forward to young Natalie's smile and laugh. Now she was laughing for another man.

He tossed the reins of the surrey he'd rented back to the livery owner. "Here, Ulysses. I won't be needing this." He'd planned to escort Natalie home so she wouldn't get wet.

Ulysses dug in his pocket.

Willum waved a hand at him. "Keep it."

"But you paid for an hour."

Willum turned up the collar on his coat and stepped out into the downpour.

Natalie sat in a rocking chair by the fire, knitting.

Mama sat across from her, also knitting. "You're quiet."

She looked up. "Am I?" She'd been lost in her regrets about accepting a ride from Mr. Seymour. He'd been cordial and behaved like a perfect gentlemen, telling her how lovely she looked and how it was his pleasure to escort her home. It hadn't been a pleasure at all. It had been dishonest.

"Mama? If you do something and later realize it might have been wrong but no one got hurt or even knows about it, do you still have to tell anyone?"

"God knows about it."

God knows.

That pricked her heart. "So confession to God would be enough?"

Mama rested her knitting in her lap and looked straight at her. "If someone else were to find out, would it hurt them?"

But it was an innocent buggy ride to stay out of the rain. How could that hurt anyone?

David burst through the door. He held out a wad of cloth. "Would a girl like this?"

By "a girl" Natalie knew he meant Abigail.

Mama unwrapped the gift. A hair comb. More than modest

but nowhere near extravagant. It had tiny pearls along the front edge. "This is lovely." She looked up at her son. "You haven't been courting her long. Are you sure about this?"

Mama was being nice. David had only asked to court Abigail last week. But he was besotted.

"Is it too soon?"

"I think maybe just a bit."

David smiled. "Then I'll hold onto it. But I'll have it for when the time is right."

Natalie held out her hand. "May I see it?"

David transferred the comb from Mama's hand to hers like he was entrusting her with a delicate flower that would wilt upon a single breath grazing it.

A bit of envy pricked Natalie's heart. David had bought a girl he'd only just started courting a gift. Willum had never bought her anything.

The downpour had settled into a steady, gentle rain. Willum had arrived in town three years ago in the rain. It was only fitting that he left that way.

He'd stopped by the house and collected his tools. He secured a tarp around the top of his open toolbox to keep the rain out. He stuffed the rest of his belongings in his knapsack and tied on his rolled-up blankets and pillow. He glanced around the boxy room, sorry he couldn't take his books. Closing the door behind him, he set out. He turned to Sassy and slapped his thigh. "Come on, girl."

He stopped by Frederick's and knocked.

"Come in out of that rain."

Willum shook his head. "I don't want to make a mess of Emma's floor."

Frederick eyed Willum's knapsack and toolbox. "You're leaving, aren't you?"

He nodded. "It's time."

Frederick lowered his voice. "What about Natalie?"

"She's found someone else."

Frederick's mouth fell open. "Can't be."

"She was riding in his buggy. Quite close and laughing."

Frederick grabbed his coat from the peg near the door and shoved one arm in. "Who is it? Let's have a talk with him."

Willum shook his head. "I only came to tell you that I left my books at the cabin. They are yours. Please take them."

Frederick shook his head. "No. You'll come back. You have to come back."

He'd let his friend believe what he wanted. "Please don't tell anyone."

"Tuck? E.V.?"

"You can tell them but not any of your wives."

Frederick let his coat slide off his arm and onto the floor. "This isn't the way you should be leaving. Where will you go? Back to Seattle?"

"Not Seattle. I'll find someplace. Someplace with no women."

"Where would that be? The North Pole?"

"Sounds intriguing."

Frederick held out his hand. "Let me know when you get settled."

Willum shook it and left.

Chapter 7

Willum tossed his knapsack on the bed of the boardinghouse. He'd managed to gain Sassy a warm place by the kitchen stove by agreeing to do a few repairs for the woman who ran the place. He was more than happy to help out.

Tomorrow, he would get a list from her and start. But for now, he just wanted to rest. Exhausted, he sprawled out on the bed and closed his eyes.

"Build My house."

Willum sat straight up. It was dark outside. He must have fallen asleep. He raked a hand through his hair and fumbled for the matches next to the lamp on the bedside table. He struck one and the room was cast in eerie, wavering shadows. The match began to burn his fingertips, so he blew it out. He lit another then the lamp. What time was it? He pulled out his pocket watch and opened it.

Midnight.

Mr. Seymour stepped onto the boardwalk beside Natalie. "May I offer you a ride?"

She kept walking. "No, thank you. It's not raining."

"But it has recently and the ground is all muddy. You'll ruin your shoes."

"I'll bc fine, thank you." She'd been wrong once, she wouldn't be again. She would walk through a monsoon before accepting a ride she shouldn't from any man.

He gripped her arm, pulling her to a stop, and she backed up against the building. He leaned one hand on the planking next to her head. "Rumor around town is that he left. No good-byes, just left."

Natalie fought sudden tears. "He'll be back." He had to come back. She loved him. He wouldn't just leave her without saying good-bye. He had no reason to leave.

"Most folks say he won't."

She ducked under his arm and hurried off. Crossing the muddy street, she went inside the house Willum was building. He would be back. He had to finish this house for the man who'd hired him.

Natalie gazed around the living room. A thick layer of wood shavings covered the floor. The crown molding around the ceiling had a vine of delicate flowers carved into them. Even the molding at the base of the walls had the carvings. No wonder it was taking Willum so long. The details were incredible. It must have taken him hours and hours to carve each section of the moldings. This wasn't the simple house she'd thought from the outside. She'd been wrong about this house and wrong about Willum not being able to complete a "simple" house. There was nothing simple here. Willum had poured his heart into this house. She could see him in all the details.

She crossed to the middle of the room where a worktable made from two sawhorses and a wooden door stood. On the table lay a piece of the lower molding, the design penciled on, the carving barely started. His tools were gone.

Willum must have had a family emergency to not tell her or Papa or his friends where he was going.

She left the house and walked straight to Willum's cabin. She put her hand on the latch and stopped. *Please don't let the same thing happen as last time.*

What if Willum had returned and was home?

She knocked.

And waited.

And knocked again. "Willum?" She opened the door. The room was dim, cold, and damp. No one had been here in several days at least. A lamp and matches sat on the small table. She lit the lamp and a warm glow filled the room. She waited for the feeling, the dread, the shaking, the difficulty breathing, the weak knees, the nausea, the walls moving. None of that happened this time. She took a deep breath then closed the door and looked around.

On the bare bunk sat a small lump of wood. She picked it up. A partially carved doe curled up with her fawn. She hugged it to her breast. She would rather have one of Willum's carved animals that cost him nothing than a hundred hair combs in the fanciest designs.

Willum, where are you?

She slumped onto the bunk and curled up.

He had to come back.

He just had to.

Natalie woke to Papa shaking her. "Natalie!"

She sat up and could see that it was dark outside.

"We were so worried about you. Are you all right?"

She shook her head. "Where is he?"

"I don't know."

She threw her arms around Papa and cried.

Willum woke and looked at his watch. Midnight. He rubbed the back of his neck. That was three nights in a row. He would sleep hard until midnight, wake suddenly as though someone had shaken him, then wouldn't be able to sleep well the rest of the night. What was going on?

"Build My house."

Willum jerked around. "Who said that?"

Silence.

He lit the lamp and held it high. "Who's there?" The room was empty.

"Build My house."

The voice hadn't come from in the room, but closer. But from where? His head? But it had been so audible. Was he going mad? Or was it. . . ?

"Lord?"

"Build My house."

He sat up. The Lord was speaking to him? "Your house? The church? But the money was stolen."

"Trust Me. Build My house."

Had the Lord seen to it that the thief had been caught? "But that would mean returning to Tumwater."

"Build My house."

The thought of seeing Natalie with another man festered the hurt already inside of him. "I don't want to go back."

"Build My house."

He swung his legs over the edge of the bed. "I can't go back."

"Build My house."

He raked his hands into his hair and grabbed two fistfuls. Could he do it and not see Natalie? No. Everyone would know what he was doing once he started swinging his hammer. They would all come to gawk and laugh. He released his hair and stood. "I *won't* go back."

The voice went silent.

"Lord?"

Willum stood on E.V.'s porch in the cold. Was returning the right decision? Part of him said no. The part that was still in love with a girl who had betrayed him. But the other part, the part that knew better than to try to run from God, knew he was supposed to return. He prayed that the money was returned and he could build quickly. He knocked.

E.V. opened the door and immediately pulled him into a back-slapping hug. "Where have you been? Frederick told us you left. I'm so glad you're back. You're staying, right?"

It was nice to know he was missed. At least by his friends.

"Come in."

Willum welcomed the warmth. He sat down at the table with E.V., Larkin brought them each a cup of coffee. "Thank you."

"Did they find the man who stole the church building fund?"

E.V. shook his head. "He got clean away."

He was afraid of that. *What am I supposed to do now, Lord?*

"The church is planning a bake sale this Saturday to get the building fund going again."

"That will take too long."

E.V. furrowed his brows. "Too long for what?"

Last time, Willum had donated money from his own savings so the building could start. He'd thought it an investment in his own future. He took a deep breath. "I need you to do me a favor tomorrow."

"Anything."

"I need you to make arrangements at the sawmill to have my share of recent profits be converted into lumber and delivered to the church building site."

E.V. frowned. "You're going to supply all the lumber?"

"Apparently." Willum took a sip of his coffee.

"You can go into the mill yourself and do that."

Willum shook his head. He'd been a silent partner in the mill from the beginning to help E.V. get started. No one in town knew he was associated with the mill except as E.V.'s friend. "I don't want anyone to know I'm back yet."

"You mean Natalie."

He didn't want to talk about Natalie.

E.V. curled his hands around his cup. "I can put together a crew. Find a reliable foreman to report to you. You would never have to be at the church while it's being built."

He liked that idea. That could be the solution to his problems.

"No. You *build My house."*

Willum lowered his head into his hands. *Alone, Lord? That*

will take a long time. Even Noah had his sons to help.

"This is not the ark."

This deal was getting worse by the minute. Willum shook his head. "No crew."

"You aren't going to build it all by yourself?"

Willum drew in a deep breath. "Apparently so." He really wanted to be gone by Christmas. Could he get it completed by then, working alone?

"Why?"

Willum raised his head. "Don't think I've lost my mind."

"I won't."

"The Lord told me. I know it sounds crazy. Every night for a week and a half I was awakened at midnight. Exactly midnight." He got up and paced. "I heard this voice. I heard it just like I hear your voice. But no one was in my room."

"What did it say?"

Willum stopped pacing and looked E.V. in the eyes. " 'Build My house.' " It sounded ridiculous. "I said no several times. But I kept hearing, 'Build My house.' When I outright refused, the voice stopped."

"So what changed your mind?" E.V. took a swig of coffee.

"I kept waking up every night at midnight. Like a silent plea. After another week of it, I said yes. That was the first night I slept all through the night. I woke up feeling more rested than I had in a very long time."

"I'll get the lumber ordered and delivered."

"You believe me?"

"Of course. Look at what happened to Jonah when he refused the Lord's calling. I don't want you to end up in the belly of a whale, my friend."

Chapter 8

Natalie stood across the street from the church ruins. Last night at supper, Isaac told Papa about the lumber being delivered to the church. Papa had claimed it was a miracle. Natalie knew Willum must be back. She had wanted to go see, but Papa wouldn't let her wander around after dark.

A horse-drawn wagon full of plank lumber pulled up to the rock foundation. Four men jumped off the wagon, two from the front seat and two from the back atop the lumber.

Where was Willum?

She waited for a buggy to pass, and a horse with a rider then crossed. She stepped around several puddles. "Excuse me."

One of the workmen turned her way. "Yes, miss."

"Where is Mr. Tate?"

"Can't say that I know." He turned to the other men. "Anyone know a Mr. Tate?"

Each man shook his head no.

"Well, didn't he order this lumber?"

The workman hefted the end of a stack of at least six planks. "E.V. gave us the order to deliver the lumber."

"Mr. Renier?" How disappointing. She was sure Willum

would be building the church.

"Yes, miss." He slid out the planks and another man hoisted the other end.

"Is Mr. Renier at the sawmill?"

"Yes." Together the men carried the boards to the pile of planks stacked up beside the foundation.

Natalie hurried to the sawmill and knocked on Mr. Renier's office door.

"Come in."

Natalie opened the door.

Mr. Renier looked up from the papers he had in front of him with his easy smile, but it faded ever so slightly. He stood. "Miss Bollen, what can I do for you?"

"The men at the church said you ordered the lumber being delivered."

"Just filling an order."

"Who ordered it? The church's building fund was stolen."

He stood silent for several moments. "One of the sawmill's investors donated the lumber to rebuild the church."

Of course it had to be an investor. Willum wouldn't be able to just order a building's worth of lumber. "Who's going to build it?"

"That will be up to the investor. If that's all, I have work I really need to complete." He walked around his desk and held the door.

Natalie held her ground. "I'm sorry for taking your time. I'm just worried about Mr. Tate. He left without a word."

Mr. Renier's features softened slightly. "Willum has always been able to take care of himself. I wouldn't worry about him."

"Has he contacted you?"

Mr. Renier just stared down at her.

She wrung her hands together. "If you hear from him, would you tell him I'm anxious to speak with him? Thank you for your time, Mr. Renier." She stepped outside, and Mr. Renier closed the door behind her.

Why would Willum leave town without telling her and possibly return in the same manner? Unless he was preparing a surprise for her. She headed off in the direction of his cabin. Maybe he was there.

Willum watched Natalie return from the direction of the sawmill. When she stopped briefly in front of the house, he took a step back from the upper window. He doubted she could see him, but just in case. She moved on down the street to the church building then headed in the direction of his cabin.

He'd been right not to go back to his cabin. But hiding out in the unfinished house made him feel like an outlaw. A house that would never be finished.

He waited until the supper hour when most folks would either be home eating or at one of the saloons. The fewer people who came out to see the spectacle the better. And in the evenings, he was sure Natalie would never come by. He strapped on his tool belt, took up his toolbox, and grabbed an unlit lantern. He wouldn't light it until he needed it. He didn't have much daylight left. He left the house and headed for the church. If there weren't clouds threatening to rain on him, he could work for some time in the moonlight.

He laid out several more floor beams before he needed to light the lantern. When he turned around, three shadow figures stood outside the foundation. He crossed over to them.

Tuck was the first to shake his head then the other two followed. But it was Frederick who spoke. "You would get done faster if you worked during the daylight."

E.V. said, "And if you'd hire a crew."

Tuck put on an Irish accent. "People be talkin'. Some be jokin' it be elves or leprechauns buildin' in the middle of the night."

E.V. said, "Children think it's ghosts because it's at night, and they don't see them."

"The more spiritual say it's the Holy Ghost," Frederick said.

Willum didn't want to fool anyone into thinking he was some sort of deity, and certainly not God Himself.

Tuck leaned over the foundation wall and put a hand on Willum's shoulder. "What are you afraid of? That she doesn't care for you anymore? Or that you may discover that you don't care for her? Or that you do care and don't want to be without her?"

Leave it to Tuck to get to the heart of the matter. His heart.

E.V. said, "She seemed sincerely concerned about you when she came by the sawmill today."

"You can't avoid her forever," Frederick said.

"I can try."

The following morning, Natalie ate as quickly as she could and started in on the dishes. Matthew was still at the table poking along. She stood behind him, and when he stabbed the last of his fried potatoes, she swiped his plate and turned toward the kitchen.

"Hey!"

"I waited until you were done." Natalie quickly finished the dishes, put on a cardigan sweater, and swung on a crocheted shawl. "Mama, I'm going into town. Do you need me to pick up anything for you?"

"You went to town yesterday."

Matthew made a face at her. "She wants to see if Willum is back."

Mama scowled at him. "That's enough. You better hope that one day when you fall in love, your sister doesn't tease you. Now you have work to do. You best be doing it."

Matthew slumped out.

Mama turned to her. "With the way he acts, you would think he was five years younger than you rather than a year older. He is the most worrisome of all you children." She set a basket of apples onto the table. "So Willum has returned?"

"I think so. He wasn't at his cabin when I went out there yesterday, but I think he might be staying with one of his friends."

"Natalie, you shouldn't be going to a man's cabin unaccompanied. We know Willum well, but it's still not proper."

Oops. She hadn't meant to admit that. "I'm sorry, Mama. I won't do it again." She had been so excited to see Willum that she hadn't thought about propriety. "I'm just going to go to the church and see the progress on the construction. May I go?"

Mama smiled. "If it is Willum, tell him we have all missed him at supper."

"Thank you." She kissed Mama on the cheek and hurried out.

Even before she could see the church, she heard the hammer's pounding echoing through the trees. Hoping it was Willum, she picked up her pace. As she got closer, she could see a lone figure swinging a hammer. Even though his back was to her, she recognized him.

"Willum?"

He swung the hammer three more times before turning her way. He was back.

She smiled. "I've missed you."

"I have a lot of work here."

Did he want her to leave? No, he was probably just tired. She tried to sound perky. "I can see that. Where is your crew? Did they take an early morning break and leave you with all the work?"

"No crew. Just me."

"You're going to build the church all by yourself?"

He pulled a nail from the pouch hanging from his tool belt and held it to the board. "Apparently."

"I'm sure Papa could find some men to volunteer. Men in the church."

"No thank you." He pounded the nail.

She waited until the nail had been driven all the way in. "Where did all the lumber come from?"

"Donated." He pulled out another nail and beat on it.

She waited then said, "I know that. By whom?"

"People are tired of meeting in the schoolhouse. I have work to do." He sounded cross and lifted a beam on one end.

"Are you mad at me?"

He stopped but didn't turn toward her. He just stood holding the board.

"Do you not love me anymore?"

He dropped the board and ducked under the beams from the middle of the foundation area to her on the other side of the wall.

"I saw you with John Seymour."

Natalie's stomach knotted, and she felt the blood drain from her face. Mama's words came back. *God knows. If someone found out, would they be hurt?* "I'm sorry. It didn't mean anything." She reached her hand over the nearly shoulder-high foundation to him.

Willum stepped back and into the first beam. "You gave him your hand. You were laughing. Not exactly fitting behavior for a girl who is being courted."

It had been wrong. She knew it then and knew it more so now. "It was going to rain."

"You love the rain. Probably the only person in town who does. Once upon a time, you came to see me in the pouring rain and four inches of mud."

"I'm sorry. It truly meant nothing."

He narrowed his eyes. "I can guarantee you it meant something to John. A young lady doesn't accept a buggy ride from a man unless she's interested in him."

"I never should have accepted his offer. I'm sorry. Is that not enough for you?"

He stared at her for a long moment with hard creases around his eyes. "Three and a half years ago, before I came to Tumwater, I was engaged to be married to a beautiful lady who I loved with all my heart. She was charming and funny, and I was swept away by her."

Natalie didn't want to hear about his love for another woman. Why would he hurt her like this? Had he gone back to this woman? Is that where he went when he left?

"My friends tried to warn me about her. They didn't trust her. I wouldn't listen to them. I stood in the front of a church for half an hour waiting for her to walk down the aisle to me before her parents told me she'd run off with another man."

"Oh Willum." She wanted to reach out and touch him, comfort him. "That must have been terrible."

"I won't let it happen to me again." His words were cold and bitter. "I saw the horrified look on your face when you came to my cabin with your father. I thought you just weren't feeling well. But when the next day I saw you with John, I knew better."

"Willum, you have to understand."

He folded his arms. "Understand what?"

"I was scared. I panicked. I was a little girl again, hungry, cold, and scared. All by myself."

"By yourself? You have a good family who loves you."

She had to make him understand. "I never knew my father. My mother and I begged for food. She died when I was six. I was put in a horrible orphanage. The older children would lock me in a dark closet. When I was seven, I was put on an orphan train. I was sick with a cough and no one wanted me. Until the Bollens."

His features softened. "You're adopted?"

"You couldn't tell? I don't look like anyone in my family."

"I thought you got your dark hair and eyes from a grandparent."

"When I saw your cabin, I became that hungry, scared child locked in a dark closet. I didn't want to go hungry again."

"I understand. I'm sure John can provide well for you."

"I don't love John. I love you."

He remained impassive. "You best find yourself a man that you know can provide for you in the way you want."

"I don't want someone else. I want you."

"I'm sorry. How can I trust you not to leave if things get really tough? If we do go hungry?"

"We won't. I'm sure of it." Papa and Mama would always bring them food if it came to that.

"And if we did, you'd become that frightened little girl and run off. I can't risk that. I had one woman I loved leave me. I won't go through that again. I can't. Go home." He turned and ducked back under board after board.

Tears welled up in Natalie's eyes. He couldn't mean that. He was just scared like she was. She ran home, wishing she could change the past. Wishing she hadn't reacted to his cabin. Wishing she hadn't accepted a ride from John. Wishing.

Chapter 9

Three days later, Willum had finally finished placing all the floor beams. Several good men had stopped and offered help. He thanked them but declined. The Lord had been clear that he was the only man to build the church. Then there were the onlookers who whispered about him. Some called him touched in the head and nicknamed him Noah. He'd heard rumors of others who supported his work as long as they weren't called upon to help or contribute any money for the cause. He didn't care what people called him, so long as they left him alone to do the work the Lord had unfortunately called him to do. Alone. In a town he wished not to be in.

And Natalie hadn't been around either. He'd evidently gotten through to her. He hated to hurt her, but he couldn't trust her. And that made him saddest of all. He hadn't thought her flighty, but he understood. She needed a man she could trust fully, and he evidently wasn't that man.

He reached down and lifted one end of a floorboard. He would get the floor down then raise the walls and roof. He raised his end up above the foundation to the floor level. He would have to walk along the board, keeping the first end on the foundation wall. When he felt the other end of the board lift, he looked down the length of it. Natalie smiled back at him.

He dropped his end. He hadn't meant to, but it pulled the other end out of Natalie's hands. "What are you doing here?"

"I came to help."

"I don't need your help."

"Yes you do. You don't want the church to take as long as the house has for you to build alone."

That stung. Was she goading him? "I should have the church completed in a few weeks, by Thanksgiving. Working by myself."

"I don't see how. Why won't you let me help you?"

"The Lord told me that I was the only man to work on the church."

Her smile broadened. "I'm not a man, so I can help."

"Ladies don't work in construction."

She picked up a basket by the pile of lumber. "I brought lunch. Your favorite." She pulled back a red-checkered cloth and lifted out a bowl. "Fried chicken."

"I have work to do." His stomach betrayed him with a loud growl. He didn't want Natalie doing nice things for him. "Go home." He needed her to go away and leave him alone, so he could build this church and forget about her.

Natalie would not be dissuaded. She had made a terrible mistake in a moment of weakness. She would prove to Willum that she was faithful to him. She would be at his side every day while he worked on the church. He would see he could trust her.

She planted her hands on her slim hips. "I'm not going away, so you might as well give in and let me help you."

Willum glared at her.

She could be just as stubborn as he.

He finally looked away then pointed to the pile of lumber. "You can sit there. And don't move."

So he was letting her stay but wasn't going to let her help. Fine. She would sit for now but would keep a watchful eye for an opportunity to help.

Willum stared at the skeleton of the church building, at the framework for the walls and half the roof trusses. Work on the church had gone slowly. Rain had made it impossible to build. Clear drying nights, and drenching days. If he could get the exterior completed, then it wouldn't matter if it was raining, he could still work on the inside. The gray sky felt heavy. The damp air sent chills clear through to his bones. He hoped the rain held off. It could rain all night every night if the days would just stay dry. It would be impossible to finish in two weeks for Thanksgiving. Even finishing before the Christmas Eve service was in jeopardy now. One drop hit his nose, another his cheek.

Lord, I could use a little help here.

"Hello, Willum."

He spun to see Natalie holding the daily lunch basket. *Not that kind of help. Less rain and a work crew.*

Natalie glanced up, blinking at the sprinkles hitting her face. "Are you going to be able to work today?"

"I'm going to have to if I'm going to have any hope of getting this finished by Christmas Eve."

"But it's starting to rain."

She wore the same worn work skirt she wore every day when she came to help, not that he'd let her. "Go home, Miss Bollen. Get out of the rain."

She made that little pinched face she made when he'd started calling her Miss Bollen again. "I brought you something."

"You don't have to bring me lunch every day. I'm capable of feeding myself."

"It's about the only thing you'll let me do around here."

And he didn't exactly *let* her bring lunch. It was more like she forced it on him. She would literally stand between his hammer and the nail until he ate.

The rain came as only a drop now and then.

She set the basket down and pulled a blue bundle from inside her coat. She shook out a sweater. "I hope I got the size right. I used David to fit it on."

She knit him a sweater?

"It's wool and should keep you warm even if it gets wet."

"I don't need a sweater."

"You've been working in the rain. You'll get sick." She held it out. "Put it on."

The set of her jaw told him she would not take no for an answer. He took the sweater and pulled it over his head. It was almost like having her arms around him. It warmed him inside as well as out. "Happy?"

She gave him a triumphant smile. "I was thinking, if you removed both sets of bunk beds, and moved the table and chairs to one wall, there would be room for a bigger bed." Her cheeks pinked. "Your bookshelf could go at the foot of the bed. A small rocking chair could go in the corner next to the potbelly stove."

She was rearranging his cabin? That was kind of cute, but she was trying too hard to *prove* his small place was fine with her, when they both knew it wasn't. He folded his arms. "Why would I want to go to all that trouble?" He didn't plan on staying around.

"Well, I just thought when. . ." She tilted her head and looked up at him with a coy smile and her big brown coltish eyes.

"When what?"

"You know after. . ."

Yeah, he knew. "After what?"

"After we get married, we'll need a larger bed, and one won't fit in that corner." Her cheeks went from their soft shade of pink to a deep red. "Maybe you could add on a bedroom."

"I never proposed." He didn't want her to think she had a legitimate hold on him.

"Well, we're courting, aren't we?" Her tone held a note of concern.

"I never asked for your hand."

"You asked Papa to court me."

"It's not the same thing."

"Well, you want to marry me, don't you?" The doubt was there in her voice and her eyes.

He did, but he knew he shouldn't.

She seemed nervous with him just staring down at her. She raised her hands and brushed them across his shoulders. "I think it fits rather well."

He grabbed her wrists. He didn't want her touching him. He didn't want to be touching her either but couldn't seem to let go. He didn't want to let go. He wanted to keep her always but didn't know how.

Natalie's heart raced at Willum's touch, even if he did look a little mad. She would take whatever he would give her, so long as he didn't ignore her. She still had hope. His grip was so gentle that she could have easily pulled away. He hadn't said he *didn't* want to marry her.

His grip shifted slightly, but neither tightened nor loosened. "You don't trust me to provide for you."

"I most certainly do."

"How do I know I can trust you not to get scared and run off?"

"I'm here, aren't I?"

He didn't look convinced, but his expression softened. His gaze shifted a shade to the left, and as quick as a whip his features hardened to stone.

To her right she heard a voice. "Natalie, is everything all right here?"

She wished he wouldn't use her first name. She hadn't given him permission. "We're fine, Mr. Seymour."

Willum released her wrists and walked away.

She missed his touch. She wheeled around. "Mr. Seymour, I appreciate your gallant offer, but I'm not in need of it."

"Please, call me John."

She would not encourage his attention. *"Mr. Seymour,* thank you, but good day."

He scooped up her hand. "You deserve better than him."

"You're wrong." She pulled her hand free. "It is he who deserves better than me." She was a weak sentimental girl who thought more of her stomach than the man she loved.

Mr. Seymour tipped his hat. "When you grow tired of him, I'll be waiting. I've always held fond affection for you."

Fond affection? How unromantic. Yet if Willum had said that, she might have swooned into his arms. She guessed that was how love colored words. They sounded better coming from the one a person loved.

"What's made you smile? I hope it's me."

"Mr. Seymour, I am flattered, but I really must go." She dipped her head to him and turned in the direction Willum had gone. To the back side of the church, she thought. She caught a glimpse of movement. Had Willum been watching? She hoped so. Then he'd see there was nothing between her and Mr. Seymour.

Willum crouched near his toolbox, rattling tools. He looked up. "Where's John?"

"I sent Mr. Seymour on his way."

"You could have gotten a ride home."

She smiled. "Are you offering?"

He thinned his lips. "I have work to do. If this rain will hold off, I can make some progress."

"If you'd let me help, it would go faster."

"I'm setting trusses. Too dangerous for a girl."

She could see several A-frames for the roof lying in the grass. "I see you have some built. How do you get them up there?"

"With a rope."

"It's starting to rain again."

He picked up the end of the rope that wasn't attached to his scaffolding and tied it around the top of a truss.

Large raindrops splashed on Natalie's cheek, her glove, hat, shoulder, then everywhere at once, like a full bucket being dumped over her head.

Willum pretended not to notice the rain. He was a stubborn man. He looked so silly with rain running off his hat and him trying to tie a knot in the rope.

A giggle rose up from her tummy and burst out of her mouth.

He shook his head and let his hands drop to his side. Then he slogged through the wet grass and took her by the elbow, leading her toward the street.

She snatched the food basket as he ushered her past it. She hoped the food wasn't ruined. When Willum guided her to the livery, disappointment washed over her.

"I'd like to rent a rig."

She held up the basket. "What about lunch?"

"You're soaked through."

"So are you."

"I'm not cold."

"See, I told you that wool sweater would keep you warm even wet."

He narrowed his eyes. "You're not so lucky."

Mr. Parker hitched a buggy, and Willum helped her up into the seat. He climbed aboard and set the horse into motion, but not fast. A leisurely walk.

This was nice. She wrapped her arm through his and rested her head on his shoulder. She felt his muscles tense under the sweater, and he looked down at her with his eyebrows pinched together in question.

"I'm cold." She was.

He pulled his arm free of hers and her spirits plummeted then rose higher than the sky when he wrapped his arm around her shoulders.

"Is that better?"

She nodded and laid her head back on his shoulder. This was perfect.

Chapter 10

The week leading up to Thanksgiving broke into sunshine. Willum had finished the trusses and shingled the roof. Much to Natalie's dismay. She had been stuck below drawing lines in the dirt with the toe of her shoe. She was cute to watch. . .when she didn't know he was looking. The church looked peculiar with open studwork for walls and a completed roof. But he wanted to get the roof on before more rain. He didn't need walls to work on the interior.

Reverend Bollen's buggy rolled up in front of the church. Natalie wasn't with him. Wasn't she coming today? He would miss her. "Hello, Reverend."

The reverend pulled on the reins then tipped his hat. "Willum."

Willum strode to the side of the buggy. "I hope everything is all right." He hoped Natalie wasn't sick.

"Everything's right as rain. I promised my daughter I'd stop by."

"Is she well?"

"Other than driving her brothers mad with all her fussing, she's fine. She wanted me to tell you that she won't be arriving until lunchtime. Her mama needs her at the house."

So he would see her. "Thank you."

"She'll be right along if she gets her work completed sooner. The way she was going at it, I'd say it will be sooner."

A smile crept across Willum's lips.

The reverend chuckled. "I see you've worked things out with my daughter."

He wouldn't say they'd worked things out, but Willum was softening to her. "We're getting there."

The reverend nodded and snapped the reins, putting the buggy into motion.

If Willum could only figure out how to trust Natalie. How long would it take to trust her again? Years? Would he need a big fat bank account to keep her? He never thought money would have mattered to Natalie—that was one of the things that drew him to her. But if money was what it was going to take for her to trust that he could take care of her, and in return get him to trust her not to get scared off, how much would be enough?

Throughout the morning, as he worked to finish the porch, these questions went through his mind. He anticipated Natalie's arrival with both longing and dread. It wasn't right to let her keep coming if in the end he wasn't going to be able to commit to a life with her. She could let John Seymour or any number of other men court her. But the idea of Natalie with any other man rankled him. Isn't that how this whole affair started?

"What's got you fretting?"

Natalie's lilting voice immediately soothed him like a cool balm. And her smile set his heart to pumping at a healthy rate. He felt a smile tugging at his lips but forced them into a frown. He shouldn't encourage her. He should let her go.

But he didn't want to.

She held up her lunch basket. "Are you hungry?"

He smelled beef stew and biscuits. His stomach gave a silent growl of approval. "You really shouldn't be coming here every day."

"Lunch is the least we can provide with you doing all this work to rebuild the church."

So would she rather not be here? Was this just serving her duty to the church? "You don't have to come."

Her smile turned to that special one that he imagined was only for him. "But I want to. If I had to choose between being here with you—rain or shine—or shopping at the biggest department store in the biggest city"—she sat down on a pile of lumber—"I'd stay right here. Do you know why?"

He couldn't imagine anyone wanting to sit in the cold with the threat of rain day after day when they could be inside a dry building in front of a warm fire. And what woman would ever turn down the chance to go shopping?

"Because I'm happy being near the man I love."

His heart flipped over and over. Was love enough for her?

"Shall we eat?"

"It smells like stew and biscuits." He sat next to her on the stack.

"It's still hot."

After his stomach was satisfied, he knew he *should* get back to work and rose to a stand.

"Pie?"

"Pie?" He hadn't smelled any pie. He sat back down. "What kind?"

"Apple."

After his mouth was satisfied with the sweet taste of cinnamony fruit and flakey crust, Willum stood again, pulling on his work gloves. "I really need to get back to work."

"What are you working on today?"

"I finished the porch entrance and now I'm going to put on the siding while I wait for the hay to be delivered."

Natalie inclined her head. "I remember you putting hay in between the outer and inner walls on the house you're still building. Does it really keep a building warmer?"

He nodded. Even if he filled every crack from top to bottom, a building could still be difficult to heat from corner to corner. But with a layer of hay between the walls, the cold didn't seep in as much.

He set up a sawhorse in the middle by the side wall. He took a siding board and rested one end of it on the sawhorse and walked down the length to the other end and lifted it to where it needed to be on the wall. The other end slipped off the sawhorse. Usually, he would have had another man hold up the opposite end, but working alone didn't afford him that luxury. He'd had to get creative several times to do portions by himself he normally had help for. He replaced the board onto the sawhorse and tried again. It fell. But the third time he tried this system the board stayed and then some. It raised level with where he was trying to nail it on the side of the building.

He looked down the length of the board. Natalie stood at the other end, smiling back at him. He wanted to tell her to put it down and go back and sit, but truthfully, he could use her help, and the Lord hadn't impressed upon him that she was not allowed to help. Quite the opposite. He would be a fool to keep refusing her assistance. "Hold it right there." He reached into his tool belt and pulled out his hammer, quickly pounding in a nail then rushed to her end, raised the board even, and pounded in another nail. "You can sit now. That will hold while I hammer in the other nails."

She gave him a curtsy and sat back on the pile.

When Willum turned back to the side of the church to hammer in the rest of the nails along the first board, Natalie let her feet dance up and down. He'd let her help. Maybe he was finally forgiving her. She hoped so.

She helped him with the next board and the next. When she couldn't reach high enough any longer, he set up an A-frame ladder for her.

He held out his gloved hand to her. "You be careful up there."

She put her pink-mittened hand in his. The contrast between ruffled mitten and worn leather work glove almost made her laugh. "I will." She didn't dare allow herself to be careless or get hurt, or he would banish her from ever returning.

He leaned one end of a board up against the ladder. "Don't touch that yet."

She nodded.

He positioned a couple of boards between two sawhorses and jumped up on it then lifted his end of the board. "Okay, grab that end."

She did and lifted it into place.

"I'm going to slide it your way a bit."

She held it secure.

As Willum pounded the nail, the board shook loose from her hands. She tried to hold on tighter but the board fell out of her hands and slivers jammed through her mittens into the flesh of her palms. "Ow!"

Willum jumped down and ran over to her. "What happened?" The board hung on to the wall at Willum's end.

"I'm sorry it slipped." She held her slivered hand to her stomach. The wood pieces hurt, but she couldn't let him know that.

He snagged her wrist and helped her down off the ladder. "Slivers?"

Dare she admit it?

He pulled gently on her mitten.

She sucked in air through her teeth. "Ow, ow, ow. It's catching on the slivers."

He took a slow breath. "Can you get it off?"

She put the tip of her other mitten between her teeth, but when she began to pull, she could feel a sliver in that hand, too, being embedded deeper. "Ow."

He took her other wrist as well. "Here. Let me. Which one is worse?"

She raised one a little.

He squeezed the other. "Where on this hand is the sliver?"

"I only feel one on the heel of my palm."

He slipped his index finger under the edge of her mitten to free the fibers from the sliver.

Shivers coursed up her arm at his touch.

He worked the mitten off. "That's not too bad. I see a couple of smaller ones as well. Can you get the other off?"

She worked her free fingers inside the other mitten. There were more splinter ends to catch. Once she had her fingers covering her palm and the slivers, she said, "You can pull it off now."

He pulled slowly.

"Ow. There's one in my middle finger."

He pulled the yarn away from the finger and moved it around until the fibers became free of the wood, and then he pulled the mitten off. He shook his head.

She had to have a dozen slivers in that hand.

He walked her over to the lumber pile and made her sit. Then he placed her most injured hand in his. "A few of these I can just pull out, but they might hurt."

She nodded.

He pulled out five easily with just his fingernails. Then he removed his pocketknife and opened it.

"What are you doing?"

"I'm going to use the edge of my knife to get under the end of the slivers to pull them out."

She nodded.

He pulled out three more before he ran into a difficult one. "Look away."

Her stomach flipped. "Why?"

"Trust me."

"I do, but please tell me what you're about to do."

"This one broke off inside the wound. I need to cut the skin to reach it."

"Is your knife sharp?"

He nodded. "And clean."

"Then go ahead." She didn't take her eyes off her palm.

"Don't you want to look away?" Tenderness etched in his voice.

No, she would show him she was strong. "I'm fine."

When he pressed the point of his knife on her palm, she shifted her gaze to his face and willed herself not to jerk her hand when the pain came. She would study his face. He had grown out his winter beard. Pain stabbed at her hand. She sucked in a breath through clenched teeth but did not jerk her hand away.

His worried gaze met hers. "Are you all right?"

She nodded.

"I'm sorry I hurt you."

"It has to be done or it will fester." She was glad he had the nerves to do what needed to be done. When she was younger, she had hidden a sliver once until it festered into painful red sores that were worse than the small piece of wood that lay beneath. To distract herself, she focused on wanting to touch his wavy brown locks.

He went back to his task, finishing with the worst hand and making quick work of the other. He brushed his thumbs back and forth across both her palms, searching for unseen slivers.

The caressing sent tingles up her arm and through her body. Her heart sped up like she'd just been the victor in a three-legged race. She shivered.

He stopped. "Are you all right?"

Fine. Wonderful. There was nowhere else she wanted to be.

He stood. "Stay here. I'll be right back." He disappeared down the street.

He had let her help, and then he tended to her injury. Though it was a small gesture, he showed tenderness toward her pain. She had hope.

Willum returned with a small jar of salve and cloth bandage rolls. He dabbed salve on the palm he'd had to cut the slivers out of then wrapped it. "You shouldn't have any trouble with that."

"Thank you for taking care of me."

His gaze darted between her eyes and her mouth and back.

She licked her lips. Would he kiss her? She hoped so. Then she'd know everything was all right between them.

A dog barking down the street caused Sassy to get up from where she'd been lying and bark.

Willum turned to his dog. "Sassy, come." The dog obeyed.

The spell was broken. She wanted to get it back. "I really am sorry for ever accepting a ride from Mr. Seymour."

Willum looked to the ground. "It was never about the ride."

She realized her mistake. She'd made it worse. She shouldn't have brought up Mr. Seymour. "Then what?"

"Doubts. Trust."

"I don't have any doubts. I trust you. Can you ever trust me again?"

"You doubt I can provide. I have doubts about your steadfastness. We both have doubts. Until we settle those, neither of us can fully trust."

But she did trust him and had no doubts. If it wasn't for her doubt in the first place, he wouldn't doubt her. "What can I do to make you trust me again?"

"I don't know. But I do know I have a church to build." He pulled a pair of new leather work gloves from his back pants pocket. "These may be a little big, but they were the smallest I could get. They will protect your hands."

She took them, and they blurred. He was making it easier for her to help him instead of shooing her away because she got hurt. "Thank you."

"I don't want you getting any more splinters." He cleared his throat. "Besides it's a poor use of time. Daylight's short this time of year."

After securing one more board, Willum stopped to receive a wagonload of hay. He and the men transferred the bales from the back of the wagon through the stud wall in the front to the floor inside. She watched him work. He worked so hard. Hard enough to always provide for her.

He was right. Her thoughts always came back to whether or not he could provide. Needing the proof and not trusting. She kept picturing that tiny cabin. How did one banish doubts they didn't want to have? *Lord, take these doubts from me. Help me trust unconditionally.*

Chapter 11

For the next three sunny days, Natalie arrived at the church ahead of Willum. It pleased him to see her eager, smiling face first thing. She helped him finish the exterior siding then they moved inside to the interior walls. The work went much faster with her help, and by the first week of December, the interior walls were all up and stuffed with straw to make the building hold heat in the winter. Then he finished the surface of the interior walls and painted the church inside and out. He painted the outside, while Natalie painted the inside. The church would be done in time for the Christmas Eve service, with a week to spare.

The congregation would be nice and warm when they celebrated the Lord's birth, because he had installed a stove with pipes that ran through the floor, providing heat from front to back. The heat from the stove turned a fan that would push air through the pipes and up through vents in the floor.

The bare tree branches of the nearby oak scraped against a back window. The eerie sound prickled his flesh. He'd walked Natalie home hours ago before the storm became too strong. He had a little bit of interior work to do before moving in the pews and presenting the building to the reverend. This storm's timing was absolutely perfect. A gift from the Lord.

He lit a candle from the lamp and headed toward the closed front door. A blowing storm was just what he needed to check for drafts. He held the candle up to the frame of the door and moved it around the entire frame slowly. The flame never flickered. No leaks. He did the same with the walls and windows down one side. Sassy followed him around the room. His flame stayed steady.

As he reached the rear window, the branch became more insistent in its knocking. He hoped it didn't break the glass. Then, with a flash of light, a crack of thunder, and a huge crash, the branch careened through the window and smashed the wall around it, blowing out the candle and knocking Willum to the floor. Boards came down, and pain shot through his head and arm.

Natalie sat in a rocking chair near the fire, knitting a scarf for Willum. She had decided that the only way to prove to Willum—and herself—that she was trustworthy, was to be around him as much as possible and be trustworthy. This last month of working on the church had been a challenge and made her ache in places she didn't know she had.

A dog barked at the front door. Not just any dog. She recognized that bark. Sassy! That meant Willum was here. She stood.

Papa looked her direction. "Leave it. It's probably just a stray looking for food or a warm fire."

"No, Papa. That's Sassy. I know her bark."

Papa held up a hand to her to keep her at bay and rose. "Let me check." He opened the door a crack, then wider, looking down and then out into the dark. "Where's your master, girl? Do you want to come in?"

Sassy put her front feet over the threshold and barked then hopped back out. Her coat was soaked through.

Natalie came closer. "What are you doing here without Willum?" She looked out into the darkness but didn't see him.

Sassy barked at her and ran into the storm then returned and barked again. She went back and forth several times.

Matthew came up beside her. "I think she wants us to follow her."

Mama joined them at the door. "In this weather?"

Natalie's insides knotted. "I think something must be wrong with Willum. We need to follow her."

Papa took his and Matthew's coats off the pegs by the door and tossed Matthew his. "Let's go hitch up the buggy."

Natalie grabbed her coat. "I want to go, too."

Papa sighed. "I don't suppose I can stop you. Wait here, and we'll bring the buggy around."

Papa and Matthew were fast, and soon the three were speeding in the storm toward the center of town.

Natalie twisted one mittened hand in the other. "Should we go to the church or his cabin?"

Papa wrapped his arm around her shoulders. "Sassy's heading toward the church. He was likely working to finish the inside. We'll try there first."

Matthew urged the horse faster.

As they neared the church, they saw a fire. Then a flash of lightning lit up the scene. Half of the split oak tree had fallen into the side of the church, and the other half glowed with flames.

When Matthew reined in the horse, Papa climbed down.

Natalie didn't wait for Papa to help her but jumped down behind him and ran in through the front door. A lantern glowed brightly in the middle of the room, sending eerie shadows through the spindly tree branches and fallen timber. Willum lay face-down under the wreckage.

She ran to where his arm lay exposed. "Willum!"

He didn't move or make a sound. *Please, Lord, no.*

Papa knelt beside her. "Take the buggy and get Isaac. Bring him back here then fetch your mama and David if he's come home."

"I don't want to leave Willum." She couldn't leave him.

Papa gripped her arms and turned her toward him. "Go. Matthew and I will start clearing the debris from him so your mama can look at him."

The look in Papa's eyes said what he feared but didn't speak. He didn't want her to see if Willum was dead.

Tears filled her eyes and spilled. "Papa, please save him."

Papa's expression became even more despondent. "I'll do my best. Now go, quickly."

She ran out into the rain and climbed aboard the buggy. *Lord, save him. He was building Your house. Save him. Oh please, save him.*

Willum's arm throbbed and his head felt like a knife was digging around in it. He turned his head. The pain increased. He forced his eyes open. The room was strange. Ceiling beams and trusses. He did not build this room. He'd never been here before. Where was he?

He tried to focus on the rest of his body, from his searing head to his throbbing arm and aching leg. He seemed to be in a bed. Not his bunk or bedroll. A real bed.

His arm that wasn't in pain seemed to be paralyzed. He couldn't move it. He tilted his head to look at it.

Natalie lay with her head on his hand and arm, her face turned toward him.

And he knew.

Natalie didn't have to have confidence in his ability to provide. He had enough confidence for both of them. He could provide, and she would come to believe it, too. He didn't have to doubt her. He could just trust. Trust the Lord.

He wished she didn't look so distressed in her sleep, with her eyebrows pinched. He wanted to soothe away her troubles, and so he raised his other arm with that intent, but it was bound in a plaster cast. The movement shot pain through his arm, and he groaned.

Natalie jerked awake and stared at him. "Willum!"

He tried to talk but only let out a croak of sorts through his dry throat.

Sassy put her front paws up on the edge of the bed. He patted her head.

Natalie picked up a glass of water from the floor and held it to his lips.

He drank with some running out the side of his mouth. "Thank you," he whispered.

She stood. "I'll go get Mama."

He gripped her hand. "Don't leave me." He didn't want to let her go.

She smiled at him then turned her head toward the door.

"Mama!"

He squeezed his eyes shut. "Ow."

"I'm sorry. Mama wanted to know when you woke up. I need to get her."

"I'm sure she heard you."

She bit her bottom lip and sat back in the chair.

Two hours later, after Mrs. Bollen had examined him and deemed he would live, Willum dressed and climbed down the stairs with much help and support of the walls, railing, and Natalie.

Natalie shook her head. "Mama, tell him he shouldn't be up."

Mrs. Bollen shook her head as well but had a look of resignation on her face. "You should be in bed resting."

Willum smiled. "I appreciate your concern, but we both know you can't stop me. I need to survey the damage. The Christmas Eve service is five days away."

Mrs. Bollen exchanged a look with Natalie. "It's three days. You were unconscious for a day and half."

How would he ever make the repairs in time for the congregation to use the church Christmas Eve?

Mrs. Bollen pointed to a chair. "You sit while Natalie and I hitch up the buggy."

Now he was the one to shake his head. "That's not for women to be doing."

Natalie put her hands on her hips. "You sit and wait, or I will be stopping you."

Mrs. Bollen smiled. "My daughter can be quite stubborn. You best do as you are told."

He obliged and was soon sitting next to Natalie on the seat of the buggy. He reached for the reins with his good arm.

She pulled them away. "I'm driving. You rest."

"I've never known you to be so bossy."

"When it comes to your well-being, I am." She snapped the reins, and the buggy lurched into motion.

He gripped his arm around her waist to catch his balance then left it there. "I'm sorry I missed going to the Whitworth party with you. Did you have fun?"

She turned to him. "I didn't go without you."

"Why not?"

"I never could have had fun with you lying in a bed half dead." She turned back to the road.

And he realized the depth of her love. "You never left my side, did you?"

"Of course not."

He saw tears rim her eyes.

"I was afraid if I left you, you would—" She blinked several times. "I was willing you to live, begging you. I didn't want you to slip away."

"Thank you." He kissed her cheek.

When Natalie reined in the horse at the church, the four Bollen men and his three best friends were pounding away, repairing the damage.

No! He was commissioned to build the church.

"You fulfilled your call."

He had built the church with Natalie's help. A peace that could only be from the Lord washed over him, letting him know that this was the way it was supposed to be. He'd been set free of the burden of working alone. The repairs belonged to others.

He turned to Natalie in the seat next to him. "Did you do this?"

"I didn't do much. I asked Papa if he could help. Papa asked your friends."

"Thank you." He leaned closer and kissed her. He'd missed her.

Chapter 12

The day of Christmas Eve, the repairs to the church were complete. Natalie stood happily with Willum's arm around her, holding him up. Willum's mother stood on the other side of him. One of Willum's friends had telegraphed his folks in Seattle about his accident, and they had arrived yesterday. Willum's father, along with Papa, her brothers, and Willum's friends unloaded another set of pews from a wagon. Apparently, in the evenings when Willum couldn't work on the church building, he'd been constructing pews and carving designs on the endcaps. Each end showed an event in Christ's life, either from the Christmas or the Easter story. The congregation could all worship together at the Christmas Eve service in the church this evening.

Willum was healing well and feeling much stronger, though he still walked with a limp. Did he really need to lean on her, or was he just using his injuries as an excuse to so boldly put his arm around her in public? She didn't mind. Part of her liked him needing to lean on her, but for that to continue he wouldn't be healing. She wanted him to heal but didn't want to lose his arm around her. He hadn't kissed her again since the day he'd woken up, but seemed content with her at his side, almost happy with her again.

Willum's arm tightened around her shoulder. "Take a walk with me."

"Are you sure you should be walking?" She worried about his bruised leg. "Maybe you should rest. You've already done too much today."

He squeezed her shoulder. "I'll be fine with you next to me." He took limping steps, Sassy following along beside them.

Why would he want to walk in his condition? But as long as he was willing to let her be with him, she wasn't going to question him. As they made their way down the street, she could feel the tension within him, like he had a huge decision to make. What if he was thinking of telling her it would never work between them? That he couldn't get past her doubt? Her stomach knotted.

Please don't let this be good-bye. Tears welled in her eyes. She blinked them away. "Willum?"

"Hmm?"

She seemed to have pulled him out of his thoughts. "Before, you said that you were only staying in town until you rebuilt the church. You aren't going to leave now, are you?"

He was silent for a moment then pointed to some steps. "Can we sit? I'm tired."

She led him over to the steps and realized it was the house he had been building for a year and a half. Did he realize it, too?

He used his good leg to lower himself to the steps. "I need to ask you a question."

She sat and folded her arms for warmth. Was this a good question or bad? "You haven't answered mine."

"Mine first. Don't answer too quickly. Think about it." He turned and looked her in the eyes. "Do you trust me?"

"Yes." The word shot out of her mouth, and she realized she did and deeply so. Her doubt completely banished.

"Do you trust that I can provide for you?"

"I believe that you will work hard and do everything in your power to provide. That's all one person can ask of another person."

He smiled. "Then to answer your question, I'm not leaving."

So there was hope for them. "Do you trust me?"

He tucked his good hand inside his coat pocket. "I have one more question."

"That's not fair. I asked you a question."

He chuckled. "If I didn't trust you, I wouldn't stay."

She leaned into him and tipped her head onto his shoulder. "Okay, you can ask another question."

"Do you mind if I give you your Christmas present tonight instead of tomorrow?"

She sat up straight. "A lot of people exchange gifts on Christmas Eve. But I don't have your present with me. So let's wait."

"I don't know if I can. You can give me mine tomorrow. I don't mind."

"I want to exchange them at the same time."

He let out a heavy sigh and frowned.

She wound both her arms around his good arm. "I love you." She wanted to bring back his good mood.

"I love you, too, and that's why I'm giving you your present right now. I'm sorry. I can't wait." He pulled his arm free of hers and his hand out of his pocket. In his hand sat a small, wooden box with a pair of connected hearts carved on the lid.

She took it and traced the carving, knowing his hands did the delicate work. "Oh, it's beautiful." Better than any fancy hair comb.

"Open it."

She shook the box, and something inside rattled. She tried to lift the lid but it wouldn't come off.

He put his thumb on the top and rotated the lid sideways.

She looked up at him. "How clever."

He raised his eyebrows. "Your gift is in the box."

She stared at the ring lying in the box.

He plucked it out and held it up. Between his thumb and index finger sparkled a diamond ring, two smaller diamonds beside a larger one. "Will you be my wife?"

She squeaked. "Oh yes. Yes, I will. Yes." She yanked off her mitten and held out her hand to him.

"I don't know. You said you didn't want this until tomorrow."

She wiggled her fingers. "No, I want it now."

He slipped it on her ring finger. A perfect fit. She tilted it in the fading afternoon light. "This is the best Christmas present. I'm afraid my gift to you isn't nearly so grand. Just a silly scarf I knitted."

"Your 'yes' is the only present I need." He tipped her chin up and kissed her.

She pulled away. "You asked Papa, didn't you?"

"Of course."

She stood. "I want to go show Mama."

He thumbed to the door behind him. "Can I show you what I've done inside?"

So he did know where they were. She nodded.

He stood and opened the door.

The interior was dark but warm. Maybe Willum kept it warm while he worked nights on it. Soon a glow showed the room. She gasped. "Oh Willum, it's beautiful."

The floor was swept and polished to a deep shine. All the carved moldings were up, the walls painted, and lights glowed on the walls. She turned to him. "Gas lights?"

"All the modern conveniences."

"Indoor plumbing?"

He nodded. "A water closet and hot water upstairs."

"You can't have hot water upstairs. Is there a stove up there or something?"

"The kitchen stove has a tank behind it, and the hot water is pumped upstairs. Let me show you." He toured her through the empty downstairs first—library, sitting room, living room, dining room, kitchen, a large pantry, and a water closet. Upstairs there were six bedrooms and a water closet with a claw-footed tub.

"This is so beautiful." She would love to take a long, hot bath in that.

After showing her the smaller bedrooms, he opened the door to the master bedroom. The only piece of furniture in the entire house, a four-poster bed, stood in the middle of the room, with delicate carvings in the headboard and footboard, and slats where the mattress would eventually go.

She went to it and traced a flower. "Are these. . . ?"

"Rhododendrons? Yes."

Her favorite. "You carved this?"

"I carved it for you."

She jerked her head around to him. "Me? But— What? How?"

He stretched out his good arm. "I built this whole house for you."

"What? How? You live— I don't understand."

"Just because a man lives modestly, doesn't mean he can't provide for the woman he loves."

"But how can you afford this?"

"I'm not a pauper."

"But your cabin."

"Was a place to hide when I first came to town. Then merely a place to lay my head. Then a place to stay while I built our house."

"But you've been building it for a year and a half, and we only just started courting this summer."

"I asked your father to court you when you turned seventeen."

"He let you?" That didn't make sense. He hadn't courted her.

"No, but I knew. I wanted to build you the most special house I could."

She looked around. She couldn't believe this was all hers. Or would be when they married. Then she realized it was just a thing. It held no real security or happiness. "All I need and want is you."

He covered her hand with his. "It's not quite finished. I still have some interior work to do and that wraparound porch, but I've put a lot of work into this house. I plan on living here. With you."

"When will we get married?"

"Whenever you want. Do you need to know everything at once?"

She just had so many questions.

His gaze shifted to her lips, and he leaned closer. His warm breath fanned her mouth, and she breathed it in.

"Mama!" She straightened. "We have so many plans to make."

He cupped his good hand around the back of her head and kissed her soundly then deepened the kiss.

All her questions floated away.

Epilogue

Willum stood at the front of the church dressed in a new suit, his father and Sassy at his side. His gut tightened a little with each passing moment. He could hear his heart thumping against his ribs. The last time he stood at the front of a church waiting for his bride to appear, he'd waited. . .and left alone.

He wished she'd hurry. He pulled out his pocket watch. It was time. Where was she? She hadn't changed her mind, had she? All this was rather sudden. Natalie had wanted to marry that night—Christmas Eve—when they had arrived back at her home and told her family. When she was convinced to wait, she begged for Christmas Day. Finally, she was granted the day after Christmas by her parents and his.

What if she reconsidered? What if she realized this was all too fast? What if someone had talked her out of marrying him? What if. . . ?

No, this was Natalie, not Wanda. Natalie would come. He was sure of it, but he still could not dislodge the rocks in his gut.

Natalie stood outside the sanctuary doors on Papa's arm. She fluffed out the skirt of her pink dress with thin green plaid lines crisscrossing through it. She had begun making it when she was sixteen and had put it in her hope chest. Mama helped her finish it last night. It had small sleeves that didn't do much more than cover her shoulders. She'd always thought she'd get married in June or the summer, and the dress would be perfect. She wanted to marry Willum, and he wanted to marry her. No sense in waiting till summer because of a dress.

"Papa, Willum is at the front of the church, isn't he?"

"Yes, darling." Papa pulled her veil down over her face.

"Did you see him? Not just heard someone else say it, but *you* saw him."

"See for yourself." He opened the door.

Her breath caught.

Willum stood, dignified and straight in his suit, with his hair tied at the nape of his neck, and his arm in a sling.

My, but he was handsome.

His expression was one of pure love and adoration. . .with a little relief mixed in.

She wanted to run down the aisle to Willum but forced her feet into submission then took her first step toward her future and the man she loved.

She was getting her carpenter for Christmas.

Thank You, Lord, for making this little orphan girl's Christmas dreams come true.

Mary Davis is a full-time fiction writer who enjoys going into schools and talking to kids about writing. Mary lives near Colorado's Rocky Mountains with her husband, three children, and six pets.